A Question of Loyalty

Gillian Poucher

Dec. 2022

To Joan,

Best wishes,

Gillian Poucher

Onwards and Upwards Publishers

4 The Old Smithy
London Road
Rockbeare
EX5 2EA
United Kingdom

www.onwardsandupwards.org

First edition, published in the United Kingdom by Onwards and Upwards Publishers Ltd. (2022).

ISBN: 978-1-78815-893-0
Typeface: Sabon LT

WORDJOY is an imprint of Onwards and Upwards Publishers Ltd.

Acknowledgements

I would like to thank Luke Jeffery and Leah-Maarit Jeffery at Onwards and Upwards for their assistance and creativity in bringing this book to print, with conscientious editing and a striking cover design.

Thanks to family and friends whose eager anticipation of this novel has been a great encouragement.

Special thanks to Neil for his patient support and to Alice for her boundless enthusiasm for my writing adventures.

1

Julia didn't need to worry about being recognised. Her ex and his partner were engaged in a furious row. They were oblivious to a middle-aged woman in a navy waterproof crouching over a vintage pram under a sycamore tree.

'We can't afford it!' shrieked Lisa. 'We can't even afford the rent, let alone a holiday! A week in the sun? I wish!'

'I told you, missing the rent was a one off. It's three months ago. I've had work since. Why do you have to keep dragging it up?' Greg might not have been shouting, but Julia remembered that sulky tone only too well.

'Because you're going on about a holiday we can't afford. Without Nathan! My parents won't be able to cope with him for a week. It's too much to ask. It's totally selfish and completely irresponsible!'

Startled by the shouting, Emmeline screwed up her face. Julia bit her lip as she clipped the last press stud of the plastic waterproof cover over the pram. *Not now, Em, please.* She rocked the pram to and fro, hoping she might soothe the baby and avoid attracting the attention of the angry couple. She tugged her hood forward around her face as the first heavy raindrops fell from the lowering October sky.

Now Greg was shouting too. 'You have become so boring since you had Nathan! Other people manage child-free holidays. Why can't we?'

'I don't want to "manage" it!' Lisa yelled back. 'I want to be with my baby! Why is that so hard for you to understand?' She turned furiously towards him.

'Mind the tree!'

But it was too late. Not watching where she was going, Lisa rammed the front of the fashionable red three-wheeled buggy into the tree. Orange and yellow leaves tumbled down as the baby inside began to scream. Emmeline joined in. Julia closed her eyes.

'Now look what you've done! You finally got him off to sleep and now he's screaming his head off again. You're lucky he isn't hurt. Talk about *me* being irresponsible!'

'It wasn't my fault!'

'Don't blame me when you're the one pushing the buggy!'

'You're unbelievable! It wouldn't have happened if you hadn't started on about this crazy holiday. I thought it was odd for you to come out with us. I was stupid enough to think it was so we could have some family time. But oh no, you only joined us to try to persuade me to go on holiday *without* our baby!'

There was a pause. Julia could hear Lisa breathing hard on the other side of the broad sycamore. Then Greg spoke again, his voice more sullen than ever. 'If you want to be on your own, fine.' He stomped off across the sunken Roman forum towards Bailgate, Lincoln's historic shopping quarter.

'That's right, off you go! Leave us here in the rain!' Lisa shouted after him. She began to cry. Greg neither turned nor replied.

Julia took a deep breath. She'd only met Lisa once. Eight months later, the memory of that one disastrous encounter continued to haunt her. She'd attacked Greg in a shopping precinct when he had been baby shopping with Lisa. No matter how often Julia told herself she'd been at the end of her tether at the time, she still couldn't forgive herself for her violent outburst. Most of all, she regretted frightening the heavily pregnant Lisa. Now, looking at the distraught young mother trying to console her little boy, Julia hoped Lisa wouldn't remember her.

Julia pushed the pram around the tree. 'Are you both OK?' she asked, raising her voice above the wailing infants.

'What?' Reversing the buggy from the tree, Lisa noticed Julia for the first time. She pushed a strand of thick chestnut hair out of her eyes, blinking back tears.

'I just wanted to make sure you're both all right.'

'Oh. Yes, thank you. I didn't see the tree, I—' Lisa paused, colour rising in her cheeks. She looked down at her little boy as he thrashed about in the buggy, his face red and contorted with noisy crying.

'I understand,' said Julia.

Lisa reached under the waterproof cover and placed a calming hand on the small body. Telling herself that she was only concerned for the baby's welfare, and not driven by a masochistic impulse to see Greg's son, Julia stole a glance at the other baby. He had Lisa's colouring, but the nose and mouth were undeniably Greg's. He had inherited his father's square jaw too. Julia swallowed.

Lisa withdrew a tissue from a pocket in her caramel wax jacket. 'As I said, we're fine,' she said firmly. She dabbed at her eyes, smudging her black mascara. She frowned, studying Julia's face more closely. 'Wait a minute. Don't I know you?'

‘I’m glad you’re OK.’ Julia moved off, heart pounding. She stopped at the turn into the car park as a van swung in. *A florist’s,* she noticed distractedly, registering the bouquet painted on the side.

‘Hey! Wait!’

Julia glanced over her shoulder. Lisa was following her, Nathan’s cries audible above the thrumming van engine. A gust of wind whipped up a pile of golden leaves left by a road sweeper. The rain was falling more heavily now, pounding the uneven pavement and bouncing off the hood of the baby carriage. Emmeline’s sobs had subsided and her eyes were fixed on the colourful velour butterfly clipped on to the pram roof.

The van driver pulled in to allow a car to exit the car park on to the narrow street, trapping Julia on the pavement. Lisa drew alongside with Nathan, her red-rimmed brown eyes dark with anger.

‘You’re Julia, aren’t you? Greg’s ex? You attacked him when I was pregnant!’

Next to Nathan’s slim-line buggy, Emmeline’s pram looked more outdated than vintage stylish. *A metaphor for Greg leaving me for a younger model,* thought Julia ruefully.

She met Lisa’s accusing gaze. ‘Yes,’ she said. ‘Yes. I’m Julia. I am so sorry if I frightened you that day at the shopping centre. I never meant to.’ She felt suddenly lighter. She’d always wanted to apologise to Lisa and never expected to have the opportunity.

Lisa considered for a moment. ‘I won’t say that makes it OK, but thank you,’ she said coolly. ‘Nathan was born soon after.’ Her face hardened. ‘The doctors thought the shock might have caused him to arrive early.’

Julia dipped her head. ‘Like I said, I’m sorry.’ She glanced over at the little boy who seemed to have worn himself out crying. She attempted a smile. 'He sounds like he's thriving.'

Lisa didn't return the smile. 'He's healthy enough.'

The florist's van finally completed the turn. It was safe to cross, but something held Julia back. 'I couldn't help hearing…' she began.

'What?' Lisa asked sharply.

'By the tree back there.' Julia pointed her right thumb over her shoulder. 'I didn't mean to,' she added hastily, as Lisa raised her plucked eyebrows. 'I was waiting for you to pass – this contraption can be awkward.' She smiled again.

Lisa remained stony-faced. Julia rushed on.

'I thought I should warn you. Greg isn't good with money.'

Julia hesitated, wondering whether to add that he had left her in danger of losing her home after defaulting on the mortgage. But she decided she had said enough as Lisa edged closer, forcing Julia to shift sideways to avoid being clipped by Nathan's buggy.

'Keep out of it,' hissed Lisa. 'I don't need your warnings.' Her eyes narrowed. 'What were you doing by the tree anyway? Were you spying on us?'

'Of course not! I was just taking a walk with Emmeline, trying to get her off for a nap.' Julia gestured towards the little girl, who was now a picture of sleeping contentment with her tiny fists balled up on either side of her head. Fine strawberry blonde hair framed her elfin face.

'And who's Emmeline?' demanded Lisa. 'Not yours, is she? Greg told me you wouldn't give him a baby.' She rocked Nathan's buggy. 'Or perhaps you couldn't,' she added, flicking her eyes over Julia. 'Not at your age.' She tossed her glossy chestnut ponytail over her right shoulder, holding Julia's gaze before turning the buggy. 'Come on, Nathan. Let's see where Daddy's got to.'

For a moment Julia stood rooted to the spot, stunned. Then she called after Lisa's retreating figure, 'Greg always said he didn't want children!' She was aware that her voice would be drowned out by the wind and traffic, but was determined to say something to set the record straight.

The younger woman didn't turn. Julia stared after her, wondering what other lies Greg had told her. For a moment she thought her cheeks were wet with rain. Then she realised that she was crying. She rubbed her face with the back of her hand before resuming the short walk home along the pavement below the curtain wall of the Norman castle. The fact that the terraced cottage lay under the shadow of the castle had lent it romantic appeal when Julia had bought it in 1996. That was six years ago, and Julia had since developed a more ambivalent attitude to living in close proximity to the medieval monument. Glancing up at the wall now, she suppressed a shudder. On a wet blustery autumn afternoon, the castle's gloomy history as a prison loomed large in her mind.

Within sight of home, Julia saw a familiar blue Ford Fiesta parked outside. In the distance the cathedral clock chimed three. Of course. Pete was finishing work early today and had said he would come over. Immersed in looking after Emmeline, she'd forgotten. She hoped he wouldn't notice she had been crying.

Her heart lifted at the sight of him knocking at the door. Eight months into their relationship, he had given her hope that there was life after Greg. Pete might not be well-off, but he was at least solvent and had generously helped to delay the mortgage possession proceedings against her house. She had initially refused his offer, then given in when she saw that what he referred to as her 'sheer bloody-mindedness' might precipitate their first serious argument. He had reluctantly agreed to her insisting that his contribution was a loan and not a gift. The fact that they shared business premises was working well too, with a few of Pete's reflexology clients approaching Julia for counselling and vice versa.

Pete spun round as the wrought iron gate squeaked open. 'Hey. I was wondering if you'd forgotten.' She saw a flicker of anxiety in his face, quickly replaced by his usual wide grin. His blue eyes crinkled beneath his black beanie as he came towards them along the gravel path. 'Guess you've got your hands full with this one, haven't you?' He leant over the pram as Julia scrabbled inside the deep pocket of her waterproof for the key. Emmeline's closed eyelids were flickering. 'I wonder what she's dreaming about?'

'Something simpler than we do, I imagine!' Julia withdrew the key. 'Sorry I'm a bit late,' she added, not wanting to admit that she had forgotten about his visit. 'I walked further than I meant to. It took a while to get Em off to sleep.' She opened the front door and Pete wheeled the pram into the hall behind her.

'No probs.' He unfastened the rain cover deftly from the pram. Julia watched as she unzipped her waterproof and hung it on the coat stand, appreciating his care not to wake Emmeline. She felt a sudden rush of affection for him. Putting the unpleasant encounter with Lisa out of her mind, she stepped forward to kiss his cheek. He dropped the cover on to the doormat and opened his arms to her. They kissed for a long moment before he ran his thumb down her cheek. 'You OK?' he asked. 'You haven't been crying, have you?'

She sighed. 'I saw Greg and Lisa. With the baby.'

'Ah.' He stroked her back and she relaxed against him. After a moment he asked, 'And they saw you?'

'Greg didn't. They were having a row. He stomped off. Unfortunately, she recognised me.' Julia paused. 'I apologised. For that time when... you know... in the shopping centre.' She'd told Pete about how she had struck Greg.

He didn't answer immediately. He slid out of his black leather jacket and shook the rain from his beanie on to the doormat. His back to her, he hung his outdoor items alongside hers. 'That's good, isn't it?' he ventured cautiously. 'I know you felt terrible about it.'

'Well, yes. It's just that from what she said, Greg has fed her some line about me not wanting children.' Julia's voice broke. 'I'm sorry. I thought I was over this.'

Pete enfolded her in a hug. 'Don't be so hard on yourself,' he said gently. 'It's the first time you've seen the baby, isn't it? Bound to be difficult.'

She nodded, calmed by his steady breathing. She shut her eyes, her tension beginning to evaporate. 'You're right. Thank you,' she whispered.

He tucked a strand of her brunette hair behind her right ear. 'I don't suppose she apologised to you, did she?'

'What?' Julia disengaged herself to look into his face. 'Why would she?'

Pete rolled his eyes. 'Because she started an affair with Greg knowing he was with you? Seriously Jules, you're so busy beating yourself up over losing control that one time that you seem to have forgotten the facts! Didn't it occur to you that it suited her to believe whatever he told her?'

'Well... no.'

'Come on, you're meant to be the counsellor! It gives her a reason not to feel guilty about their relationship, doesn't it?'

Julia ran her fingers through her damp hair. 'I suppose so.' She remembered how quickly Lisa had come back at her, claiming that Nathan's early arrival might have been caused by shock at Julia attacking Greg. Her remarks about Julia's failure to give Greg the baby he wanted had been contemptuous, designed to hurt. 'You could be right,' she conceded.

Pete raised his eyebrows in mock despair. 'There's no "could" about it,' he said. 'Now, where were we?' He pulled her towards him again, kissing her deeply. Behind them, Emmeline emitted a snuffling sound from the pram.

Julia pulled away reluctantly. 'It won't be long before she wakes. Grace says she never naps for long.' She smiled. 'That's something I've learnt. It's not easy, looking after a baby!'

Pete grinned back before asking soberly, 'Have you heard from Grace yet?'

Julia shook her head. A shadow passed across her face. 'No. I can't imagine how she must feel, what she's going through.'

Pete grimaced. 'Poor girl. *Woman,* I should say, but she seems so young somehow.'

'I know what you mean.'

Although Grace was thirty-four, she sometimes seemed much younger. Julia remembered their first meeting. The postgraduate student had come to her for counselling at the start of the year after losing her father. Grieving for her own mother at the time and missing Greg, Julia had failed to realise that she was becoming overly involved with the younger woman. The revelation that Grace was her niece, the daughter of a half-sister Julia hadn't known existed, had brought both joy and pain to Julia. She still found herself wrestling with conflicting emotions about her mother carrying the secret of her wartime love affair with a Canadian Air Force pilot, Ray, to the grave.

The shrill ring of the phone recalled her to the present with a start. Emmeline stirred in the buggy, but didn't wake.

'I'll make some tea.' Pete offered, disappearing through the kitchen door as Julia picked up the call.

She knew immediately from the stifled sob. 'Mum's gone, Aunt Julia.' Grace's voice trembled. 'She died at half past two.'

2

Linda's funeral took place on a bright morning ten days later. In accordance with her wishes, it was a private ceremony, held in the medieval church in the Norfolk village where she had lived. After a brief service using the Book of Common Prayer liturgy, the small group of mourners gathered around the freshly dug grave in the churchyard for the burial. Pete reached for Julia's hand as the undertakers lowered the oak coffin into the ground.

'Earth to earth, ashes to ashes, dust to dust,' intoned the vicar, a tall, angular man with thinning grey hair. He pressed the page of the service book down with his thumb as a gust of wind swept through the churchyard.

Ray moved forward to cast some earth on to his daughter's coffin. Julia blinked back tears as she watched him take a handful of soil from the silver tray proffered by the undertaker. When Julia had first met him back in February, his upright carriage had belied his eighty-six years. Now he was stooped and seemed to have shrunk. He had developed a shuffle, but had refused to bring a walking stick to the funeral. The unforgiving sunlight highlighted every line of his face and he looked grey and haggard.

None of this was surprising in the circumstances, Julia reminded herself. Ray had known nothing of his daughter's existence until Linda had written to him last

December. It had been easy enough for her to track him down on the internet, after she had made contact with her mother Emily. Emily had told Linda the full story of the brief love affair which had led to her conception. Emily had met Wing Commander Ray Brooke of the Royal Canadian Air Force in summer 1943 when he was stationed at R.A.F. Scampton in Lincolnshire. They had fallen deeply in love. But they had only a short time together before Ray disappeared on a mission over Dresden, and was presumed dead.

Broken-hearted, Emily hadn't possessed the strength to oppose her mother's plan to avoid bringing disgrace on the family when she discovered that she was carrying Ray's child, and had gone to stay with relations in Norfolk for the duration of her pregnancy. The relations were a childless couple who had agreed to bring up Emily's baby as their own. Back home in Lincolnshire, Emily had married Julia's father after the war ended. She had never spoken of her tragic wartime love affair to Julia, who had been shocked to meet her half-sister Linda after their mother's death.

Watching the old man now as he scattered earth on his daughter's coffin, Julia wondered how it could be that he seemed to harbour no bitterness towards the God he had served faithfully for so long. She herself couldn't shake off a sense of cruel injustice that Ray had known nothing of his daughter's existence for all those years, and that he should then lose her within months of their meeting. Ray had been taken prisoner after surviving the plane crash over Dresden. He had visited Lincolnshire on his release after the war ended, and heard that Emily was married. He returned to Canada and in time entered the seminary before being ordained as a Roman Catholic priest.

Julia had expressed something of her thoughts to him on the phone a few days earlier. 'It seems so sad that Linda was already ill when you met her.'

Ray's response was immediate and unequivocal. 'Ah, but I count it a blessing that we had even that time together. As Job said, "The Lord gives, and the Lord takes away. Blessed be the name of the Lord."'

The agnostic Julia found she had no reply.

Now Ray stepped back from the edge of the grave to make way for his granddaughter. Grace too had only known Linda for a few months. Linda had suffered from post-partum psychosis after Grace's birth. During her illness, she had set fire to the farmhouse when her husband was out. Fortunately, he had returned in time to save her and their baby daughter. Back in 1968, little was known about Linda's condition, and she had been sectioned and taken into psychiatric care. Her husband had taken their baby to Lincolnshire to make a fresh start. He had changed their names, divorced Linda and remarried.

The undertaker offered Grace the silver tray. She gathered some earth and hurled it down on to the coffin. She had wept throughout the church service, and her eyes were puffy in her wan face. Now she began to sob again. Moving forward to take her turn in the ritual, Julia reached out a hand towards the younger woman's arm. But Grace either didn't notice or ignored the gesture, as she walked rapidly back along the mossy path towards the church.

Julia lifted some earth from the tray and gazed down at the oak coffin for a moment before tossing the soil on to it. 'Goodbye, Linda,' she whispered, dashing away a tear. Pete put his arm round her shoulders briefly before throwing his own handful of earth into the grave. He was followed by the elderly couple who had been neighbours of Linda's for many years. The vicar uttered some final prayers and a blessing. After a few words with Ray, Julia and Pete, he withdrew with Linda's neighbours, his cassock billowing in the wind.

Admitting he was tired, Ray declined Julia's invitation for lunch at the pub in nearby Walsingham where she, Pete and Grace had stayed overnight. He also refused a lift back to Linda's farmhouse where he had been living throughout the latter stages of her illness, insisting the walk would do him good. Sensing he wanted to linger alone by his daughter's grave, Julia and Pete retraced their steps to the church where they found Grace sheltering in the porch from the wind.

They were all quiet on the short drive to the pub, in pensive mood after Linda's funeral. Julia had booked a table, knowing from a previous occasion that the pub was likely to be busy at lunchtime with priests and pilgrims visiting the Shrine of our Lady. After giving Pete her order, Grace lapsed into silence. Head bent, she twirled a beer mat between her slender fingers. Pete went over to join the queue at the bar. Julia's heart ached for her niece as she contemplated her across the table. She found herself suddenly blurting out a proposal which had occurred to her during the last few weeks of Linda's life.

'I've been thinking, Grace. Would you and Emmeline like to move in with me for a while? It would save you rent, and you know I've got the space.'

Grace looked up. 'You're sure?' she asked, wide blue eyes scanning Julia's face. 'You really want us to stay with you?'

'What's this?' Pete resumed his seat next to Julia.

Julia barely glanced at him. 'I've invited Grace and Emmeline to move in with me,' she explained, before turning back to Grace. 'Yes, I'm quite sure. It's much better than you going back to your flat on your own. I don't know why I hadn't thought of it before. I can help with childcare when I'm not working, and in the evenings – well, *most* evenings,' Julia amended, aware of a sudden movement from Pete. 'Then you can get on with studying for your PhD whilst I look after Emmeline. I know how tiring that young lady can be!' She smiled, hoping to lighten the mood, and was rewarded by the ghost of a smile playing around Grace's lips.

It was only fleeting. 'I hope Emmeline's OK,' Grace said anxiously.

'She'll be fine,' reassured Julia. 'Your oldest friend, a mother of twins, is certain to be more competent than I was last week!'

Grace tried to smile, but her eyes brimmed over. 'It's so sad Mum didn't have longer with us.' She began to cry. Fishing in her handbag for a tissue, Julia sensed the two women at the next table glancing towards them.

Pete rose tactfully, muttering something about finding the Gents.

Grace took the tissue and wiped her tear-stained cheeks. 'Sorry.'

'No need to apologise,' said Julia gently. 'It's been a difficult day, a terrible few weeks.'

'I just wanted more time with her, with Mum. For her to get to know Emmeline. For me to get to know her better.' She choked on a sob.

'I know.'

'It just seems so unfair. We'd just found one another, and then to have only eight months together...' Grace buried her head in her hands.

Julia reached across the table and placed a hand on Grace's arm. 'It seems very cruel.' She hesitated, not sure about the wisdom of her next remark, uncertain that it would offer the comfort she intended. 'But at least you had *some* time...' Her voice trailed off as Grace jerked her head upright, shaking Julia off. She slammed her hands down on the table. The cutlery jangled on the discarded plates.

'Not enough! She was already so sick when you found her. Then I had Emmeline, and it took me weeks to get over the caesarean.' She started to cry again, racking sobs shaking her slim frame. More heads craned towards them from neighbouring tables.

Julia found tears welling in her own eyes. 'I know. It is desperately sad.' She paused, remembering the last time she had seen Linda in the hospice two weeks ago. Hollow-cheeked and jaundiced, drifting in and out of consciousness, Linda had still managed to smile warmly when Julia leant over her as she was leaving.

'Thank you,' Linda had whispered before closing her eyes. She'd turned her head towards the window. A ray of late autumn sunshine had fallen across her shrunken face. Despite her sadness as she left the dying woman, Julia had been comforted by the sense of peace in the sunlit room.

Julia had wondered since about that 'thank you'. Was Linda thanking her for visiting? Or for something more, maybe for introducing her to her long-lost daughter, Grace? Too late to find out now. She bowed her head. 'I wish I'd had more time with her too, Grace.'

'*You* wish?' Grace's raised voice made Julia jerk back in her chair, knocking her black trench coat to the floor. 'She was my *mother!* What was she to you? Just a half-sister!' She spat the words out, and Julia was reminded briefly of Grace's difficult relationship with her own half-sister, Suzanne. But she had no chance to pursue her line of thought. Grace was leaning towards her across the table, glaring at her so fiercely that Julia shrank back. 'Besides,' Grace continued slowly, making sure her words had maximum impact, 'I don't believe you.' She sat back, a strange gleam in her eyes.

Julia broke the eye contact, reaching for her fallen coat. She turned further in her seat than necessary to replace it over the padded back, avoiding Grace's stare.

'What do you mean?'

'You know exactly what I mean.'

'I don't, Grace. Really.'

Grace lifted her heart-shaped chin, the one feature she shared with her aunt. Her lips curled in a malicious smile which chilled Julia.

'Come on, Aunt Julia. You can't pretend with me. I'm no longer one of your clients.'

Julia recoiled. She had never seen this side of Grace before. She struggled to keep her voice level. 'Grace, I do wish I'd known Linda – your mother – for longer. I've no idea why you would think otherwise.'

'No?' Grace raised her neatly arched blonde eyebrows. 'Well, I've had plenty of time to think recently, when I've been kept awake by Emmeline. You wish my mother had never come into your life, don't you?'

Julia gaped at her as a waitress came over with a laden tray. Distractedly, Julia told the woman where the meals should be set, then turned her attention back to Grace. 'That's not true, Grace. Whatever makes you think that?'

'It's obvious.' Grace bent her head over her plate and cut into her lasagne with furious strokes. 'My mother shattered your picture of your happy family, didn't she? Your father, the injured war hero, dying young, not being your mother's first love.' She looked at Julia defiantly, flicking her strawberry blonde plait over her right shoulder. 'Perhaps not even her true love.'

'You don't know what you're saying.' Julia choked back a mixture of sorrow and anger.

'What's going on here?' Pete's voice was sharper than Julia had ever heard it. He briefly touched her shoulder before sitting down. She exhaled and managed to smile weakly at him.

'I'm sorry, Aunt Julia.' Grace began to cry again. 'That was horrible. I didn't mean it.'

'Didn't mean what?'

'It's all right, Pete.' Julia placed her hand over his on the table. Grace was looking at her pleadingly through her tears, clearly not wanting her to divulge what had passed between them.

A moment passed. 'OK,' said Pete finally.

Julia and Pete ate in silence, whilst Grace toyed with her lasagne and salad. Pete lined up his cutlery when he had finished and glanced over at Grace's plate. 'Aren't you going to try to eat?'

Grace shook her head. 'I'm not hungry.' But she did manage a couple of forkfuls of lasagne before pushing her plate away.

Pete opened his mouth as if about to say something else, then closed it again. Julia looked at him questioningly. 'Was there something you were going to say?'

'Um...' He ran his hand over his head. 'It's just... Look, Grace, I don't want to interfere or anything, but I'm wondering if you might consider involving Emmeline's father now?'

Grace sat bolt upright. 'Absolutely not! I want nothing more to do with him!'

'But what about Emmeline?' persisted Pete. 'He is her father. Wouldn't it be good for her to have him in her life?'

'No! She's better off without him.'

Pete hesitated before asking, 'Is that really for you to say? What about his rights as a father?'

'It's none of your business!' Grace snapped, staring at him defiantly across the table.

'Grace!' protested Julia.

'I'm sorry,' said Grace. 'I don't mean to be rude.' Her face crumpled. 'Can we not talk about this now? I can't cope with it today.'

'Yes, let's leave it,' said Julia quickly, concerned that Grace might succumb to a further bout of weeping. She turned to Pete. 'How about coffee?'

He took the cue. 'I'll get them. Grace?'

Grace nodded her agreement, and Pete made his way to the bar to place the order. Presently, a stout middle-aged waitress brought over a tray carrying three steaming cups of coffee.

They drank in uncomfortable silence. Pete drained his cup first and returned to the bar to pay the bill. Julia glanced around. Most of the lunchtime customers had now left, but a corner table was still occupied by four middle-aged priests in their black clerical shirts and black suits engaged in deep discussion. She had never seen so many priests gathered in one place as she had on her two visits to Walsingham. Her thoughts turned inevitably to Ray. She consulted the delicate gold watch which had belonged to her mother. They had agreed to meet at Linda's house at two o'clock.

'I think we'd better go and see how your grandfather is when you've finished your coffee.' She hesitated. 'I hope you'll eat something later. You hardly had anything when we got here last night, or for breakfast.'

Grace looked down at the table. 'I'm not hungry.'

'I know.' Julia weighed her next words carefully, not sure if Grace was capable of thinking of anyone besides herself at present. Who could blame her after all she had been through during this tumultuous year? Julia tried anyway. 'I appreciate how difficult the last few months have been, but you've got Emmeline and your grandfather to think about too. They need you, you know.'

Grace gazed back at her across the table. Her tear-stained face was pinched and white above her black dress suit. She looked exhausted, and Julia regretted mentioning her responsibilities towards her baby and grandfather. 'I'll help you all I can,' she added.

'I will try. But Aunt Julia, it's just so *difficult*.' Grace's voice rose. 'I'd no idea looking after a baby would be so demanding. I keep picturing Mum in the hospice, so sick and weak. Those last few days were just awful. I worry about Grandpa, how long I'll have with him, how he's going to cope with losing Mum so soon after they found one another. Then I'm anxious about my research, when I'm going to find time to get on with it. When I gave up teaching to do my PhD, I planned to take the minimum time to complete it, so I could get on with an academic career as quickly as possible. I hate to think I'm falling behind. Even when Emmeline goes off to sleep, I've got all this running through my mind. I—'

She broke off as Pete returned to the table.

'Hadn't we better go and see if Ray's OK?'

Grace hauled herself to her feet, holding the table for support like an old woman. Julia bit her lip. *Bad timing.* It was the first time Grace had opened up to her since Linda's death and she sensed that her niece needed to talk. 'Could you give us a minute?' she asked Pete.

'All right,' he said curtly. 'I'll be in the car.' He turned before she had time to thank him and went across to the heavy oak door. A draught of chilly autumn air filtered towards their table as he opened it.

Julia shivered. She hoped he didn't mind, but nothing was more important than for Grace to speak freely and express some of the emotion she had been bottling up recently. Surely Pete could understand that?

Grace had slumped back down on the padded bench, shoulders hunched inside her jacket. She began to toy with the beer mat again.

'You were saying that you're finding things difficult at the moment?' Julia invited. 'That it's hard to switch off?'

Grace spun the grubby coaster a few more times. Then she flung it down on the table. Looking across at Julia, she said coldly, 'You're not my counsellor any more, Aunt Julia. All you need to know is that I can manage. I am coping and I will cope. For Emmeline's sake.'

Julia's heart plummeted. 'All right, Grace,' she said quietly. 'Let's go and see your grandfather.'

3

'Smells good.' Julia sniffed the aroma of fresh coffee appreciatively. Pete had insisted on buying the high quality coffee machine when they moved into the business premises, suggesting that it would create a good impression with their clients.

'There you are.' His smile revealed his uneven white teeth.

Julia smiled back, leaning against the glass door to close it against the strong wind. She was grateful for respite from the warning beep of a reversing lorry which had accompanied her along the street.

'You're in early.' Moving round the reception desk, she gave him a quick peck on the cheek. 'Didn't you say on the phone that your first client isn't due till ten thirty?'

Pete turned back to the machine, pouring the brown liquid into two mugs. 'Thought I might catch you before your ten o'clock.' He held out a mug. 'Welcome you back to the office after your long weekend. I thought you were planning to come in earlier to catch up on paperwork?'

'Thanks.' Julia took the coffee. 'The paperwork will have to wait.' She yawned. 'Emmeline started crying just after one. I took her into my room for a while so Grace could get some rest, but she wouldn't settle. Grace took her back around four. I dozed off after the alarm.'

Pete considered her. 'You look shattered.'

'Thanks. That makes me feel so much better!'

Pete didn't join in Julia's laughter. He wiped some coffee grounds from the work surface with a J-cloth.

'What is it?'

Pete rinsed out the cloth. 'I don't want to interfere or anything,' he said eventually, 'but are you sure you've thought this through?'

Julia paused in the action of raising her mug to her mouth. 'Thought what through?'

'Taking in Grace and Emmeline.'

'How do you mean? It seems quite straightforward to me.'

'It's a lot to take on, isn't it? A woman and baby?'

Julia frowned. 'I don't see it like that. The poor woman has just lost her mother, and she's only recently become a mother herself. She's had a year of emotional upheaval and needs some support. I feel it's the least I can do. She is family, after all.'

'Though you didn't know she existed until a few months ago.' Pete folded the cloth and laid it over the faucet.

'So?'

'Just saying.'

Julia waited. When he didn't volunteer anything further, she changed tack. 'It's not as though I don't have the space, is it?'

'No, but it must still be an adjustment after living on your own.'

Julia shrugged her slim shoulders. 'I've not really noticed so far. Besides, it's only just over a year since Greg moved out. I've not been on my own that long.' Seeing his jaw tighten at the mention of Greg, she added quickly, 'It's like having visitors.'

'They're not normal visitors though, are they? Not when you don't know when they're going to leave.'

Julia's frown deepened. 'Where are you going with this, Pete?'

Pete looked down at his coffee, sloshing it back and forth in his chunky red mug. 'I'm not sure. It seems a big commitment to me.' He sipped his drink, holding her gaze. 'I've not said anything whilst they've been settling in, but I thought you might have talked it through with me before you brought it up at the pub.'

'Oh.' Nonplussed, Julia pushed a stray coil of hair back into her bob. 'It was an impulse. Grace was so distressed after Linda's funeral. I was trying to encourage her.'

'Yeah.' Pete gulped some more coffee, not looking at her. 'It must have crossed your mind before you blurted it out though.'

Julia shifted her weight from one foot to the other. 'It had, but I didn't think that it would affect us. I mean, it's not as if we're living together, is it?'

An unreadable expression flitted across his face. 'No. But we have been together a few months. Long enough for us to talk through decisions.'

'I guess so.' Julia tapped her fingers on the rim of her mug. 'I suppose I've been so caught up with Linda's illness, and then helping Ray and Grace with the funeral arrangements…' She swallowed.

He grimaced in sympathy. 'No worries. I know you've had a lot going on.' He took a slurp of coffee. 'I know you're the counsellor, Jules, but if you need to talk… It's been a hell of a year for you as well as Grace.'

She forced a smile. 'It has. You've been great. My supervisor has been good too.'

He twiddled with the gold stud in his right earlobe. 'I realise that.' His tone was unusually cool. 'That's her job, isn't it? Besides, you only see her once a month.'

'That's how it works. You know that.' She closed her eyes, regretting her sharpness. 'Sorry.' She yawned again. 'Like I said, I'm tired.'

He turned away and put his mug down on the beech unit, running his hand over his shaven head in the way he did when struggling to find the right words. 'I get it,' he said finally. 'I know you have your supervisor. Just don't forget I'm here too. I might not be a counsellor, but I can listen.' He turned back to her, his blue eyes wide and appealing. 'Don't shut me out, Jules, OK?'

'Oh, Pete.' She stepped forward and laid her right hand against his cheek, smooth from his shave. 'Of course I won't. I've never meant to. You're right. It's all been so difficult, turned everything upside down for me.'

He held her gaze for a long moment. 'All right. Do one thing for me. Take care of yourself.'

'How do you mean?' She let her hand fall to her side.

Pete looked down at his trainers. 'You've been good enough to take in Grace and Emmeline. You've offered to help with childcare so she can get on with her research. Within a few days you're exhausted, and you have no idea how long the situation will carry on.'

'It's only temporary,' insisted Julia. 'Just until Grace comes to terms with losing her mother. I want to help her get back on her feet, so that she's able to cope with Emmeline as well as her research.'

Pete raised an eyebrow in which the grey hairs outnumbered the blond. 'Are you saying Grace isn't coping with Emmeline?'

'No, no.' Julia stared unseeingly towards the window, wondering if her rapid reply were true. On three occasions in the four days since Grace and Emmeline had moved in, Julia had arrived home from various errands to find Grace hunched over her laptop and books in the kitchen, with Emmeline screaming inconsolably in their bedroom. When Julia had tentatively asked if Emmeline might be happier downstairs with her mother, Grace had either burst into tears or said that she had read that it was better to let babies cry themselves out without always rushing to pick them up. Taking in the younger woman's white face and the dark shadows beneath her eyes, Julia had bitten back a reply that not all the answers to babies' needs could be found in textbooks.

She turned back to Pete, who was still surveying her sceptically. 'I'm sure all new mothers must struggle to adapt,' she said. 'I expect Grace will feel better once Emmeline settles at home and begins to sleep through.'

'I hope so.' He stepped forward and stroked her cheek with his forefinger. 'You know I care about you, Jules,' he said softly. 'I just don't want to see you taken advantage of.'

'Thank you.' She placed her hand over his forefinger, the last shreds of defensiveness ebbing away in the face of his concern. 'But I need to do this, to support Grace and Emmeline.' She took a deep breath. 'I feel that I owe it to Linda and to Mother. Thinking how they were separated from their daughters, Mother from Linda, then Linda from Grace, for all those years. It's not just that.' Her voice quivered as she continued. 'I feel guilty. Guilty that I grew up with Mother, and Linda didn't.'

'Oh, Jules.' Pete drew her close and she laid her head on his shoulder, the wool of his cream Aran sweater prickly against her face.

After a moment he said carefully, 'Is there anyone else who could look after Emmeline sometimes? I get that it wasn't the right time to ask about her father just after the funeral, but maybe Grace will change her mind. Meantime, what about Grace's stepmother?'

'Huh! I don't think so!' Julia stepped out of his arms and rolled her eyes. 'I mean, I know Grace has been back in touch with Frances since Emmeline was born. Both Ray and Linda wanted her to. I have to say, I didn't understand why, from everything Grace has told me about the woman.' The corner of her mouth twisted. 'They're both more gracious than me – or *were,* in the case of Linda.' She blinked back sudden tears. 'Sorry.' She wiped her eyes with the back of her hand. 'Linda was such a generous spirit, wasn't she?'

Pete smiled sadly. 'She was. Maybe Emmeline might build a bridge between Grace and Frances?'

Julia shook her head, remembering some of the things Grace had told her during their counselling sessions before they had discovered that they were related. 'I doubt that. From what Grace has said, Frances's attitude towards Grace when she met her father was pretty awful. Grace was only a little girl.'

'I understand.' Pete hesitated, searching again for the right words. 'But maybe Ray and Linda thought it would be good for Grace and Emmeline to have some extra support besides you. And you only have Grace's opinion of Frances, her version of events. You haven't met her yourself, have you?'

'Well, no, but—'

Pete pounced immediately. 'There you go. Is it really fair to take Grace's view at face value? You have to admit that her behaviour can be... *erratic* sometimes.'

Julia stared at him. 'That's hardly surprising, is it? A new single mother, reunited with her own mother who she hasn't seen since she was a baby, who then dies within eight months?'

Pete shrugged. 'I know. When you put it like that...' He placed his hands on her shoulders. 'Maybe I'm being overprotective. But you never told me what else happened at the pub last week. I could see Grace had had a go at you. Whatever that was about, however much she's grieving for Linda, I don't think she should be taking it out on you.'

'It was nothing,' said Julia quickly.

'You sure?'

'Sure.'

She circled both hands round her mug, staring down at the wisps of steam. The truth was that Grace's words, about how discovering Linda had disturbed Julia's image of her 'happy family', had tormented her during the nights when she had been woken by Emmeline's crying. She liked and respected Ray. But whenever she read her mother's diary from 1943, Julia couldn't dispel a sense of betrayal on behalf of her father. He had died when Julia was only eight, and she held cherished memories of him. Even though Julia considered that she had long since shaken off romantic ideals, it was impossible to read the diary without believing that Ray had been her mother's true love.

Julia was well-aware that Grace's remarks contained more than a grain of truth, but her complex emotions were still too much for her to unravel. She took a gulp of coffee and met Pete's concerned gaze.

'You've got Ray coming soon as well, haven't you?'

'Yes, a week on Thursday. He said he won't be staying with us for long. He should be able to get some accommodation for retired priests in Lincoln. That reminds me, he's travelling by train and is due in at eleven.

I've got a client then, so I'll need to rearrange their appointment.'

'Eleven next Thursday? My ten o'clock cancelled earlier, and I don't have another client till the afternoon that day. Shall I pick him up?'

'Thanks.' Julia smiled at him, then became serious. 'It sounds like he's coping as well as can be expected since Linda died, though I was concerned about him at the funeral. He's suddenly aged, hasn't he?'

Pete turned away, picked up the cloth again and began to scrub at the sink. 'Bound to happen,' he said. 'Watching someone close to you die of a terminal illness is one of the worst things life throws at us.'

Julia remembered Pete's father had died of cancer ten years ago, before they had known one another. 'Sorry,' she said instantly. 'I know you went through it all with your dad.'

'I didn't mean...' Pete flapped his free hand. 'Doesn't matter,' he muttered, peering into the chrome sink and rubbing hard at some stain which Julia couldn't see. 'You were saying, about Ray?'

'Yes, he seems determined to be around for Grace,' went on Julia. 'It will be lovely to have him nearby.'

'I'm sure he'll help you as much as he can for as long as he can,' said Pete. 'But...'

'But?'

'Ray's well into his eighties, Jules. How long before he needs care himself?'

Julia looked down. She nudged some biscuit crumbs on the blue flecked carpet with the toe of her black ankle boot. 'I want to be there for him at this stage of his life, for Mother's sake. I feel sure it's what she would have wanted.'

Julia's voice cracked and again Pete drew her close. She breathed in his familiar sandalwood scent before she broke away. 'We'd better get on, hadn't we? Thanks for being concerned. It will work out, I'm sure.'

He turned to the sink and ran water into his mug. 'Are you?'

She frowned. 'Yes. Why not?'

'What about us, Jules?' he asked quietly. 'Will we be OK? Like I said, we've been together a while. I understood you needed space after losing your mum, and finding Linda, Grace and Ray. Your life's completely changed. I get that.' He paused, his blue eyes fastening on hers. She saw a vulnerability there which tugged at her heart. 'But when do we get some time? I've missed you these last few days.'

Now it was Julia who broke the eye contact. She set down her empty mug on the draining board. Yawning again, she leant against the black swivel chair by the desk. 'Sorry, Pete,' she said. 'It's been so hectic with Grace and Emmeline moving in. Once things have settled down, there'll be time enough for us, won't there?'

Pete chewed his lower lip without saying anything.

She went on, trying not to sound accusing, 'You said you understand. I've got to help Grace and Emmeline. I have to. You do see that, don't you?'

He hesitated before replying with a sigh. 'I do. You wouldn't be you if you weren't involved with them.' He paused again.

'But…?'

He cleaned his mug with the dish brush before bursting out, 'How well do you know her?'

Julia gaped at him. 'Well enough,' she said stiffly. 'There was the counselling before I found out we were related. You know I was her birth partner, and I've tried to support her as much as possible during Linda's illness.' She gulped back more tears.

Pete's expression softened. He turned off the tap and touched her arm briefly before moving round the desk. 'You've been brilliant with her. I'm sure she wouldn't have coped anywhere near as well without you. Remember though, I'm here for you too. It's not just about you on your own any more.'

She managed a half-smile. 'I know,' she said. 'Thank you.' She glanced at her watch and gathered herself. 'Better get on, my client's due in fifteen minutes.'

'Sure.' Pete turned and lifted his leather jacket off the coat stand. 'I've got to nip out for some stuff. Incense is running low and I know you'll miss it.' He grinned at her and disappeared through the door, promising to be back in ten minutes so that Julia wouldn't be alone when her new client arrived.

Julia shook her head as she headed towards her office. It was impossible to escape the scents and incense which Pete used abundantly in his reflexology in their cramped premises. One of her clients had refused to return after her initial counselling session, claiming that the fragrances aggravated her asthma. Pete had used it as an argument to look for more spacious offices after their initial tenancy expired. Julia had been non-committal. She felt that she had enough changes to adjust to with the discovery of her new family members and the developing relationship with Pete without the added disruption of another office move.

Inside her small office with its freshly painted daffodil yellow walls, she sank down into her cream armchair and massaged her temples. Pete's concern about her indefinite living arrangements with Grace and Emmeline had fed the intermittent misgivings she had had since giving out the impulsive invitation in the Walsingham pub.

Julia tried to shut out the conversation with Pete as she prepared to meet her new client. But one of his questions echoed in her ears as insistently as the warning beep of the reversing lorry on the street earlier: *'How well do you know her?'*

4

Julia continued to mull over the conversation with Pete as she prepared to meet her new client. His misgivings about Grace had surprised her. His question, *'How well do you know her?'* buzzed around her head like an angry wasp as she rummaged through the filing cabinet for her new instruction form.

It was true she'd only known Grace for ten months, first as a client and then personally when she had discovered Linda was Grace's mother, meaning Grace was Julia's niece. Linda's separation from her baby daughter in 1969 following the psychotic episode which led her to set fire to their home was a tragic parallel to Linda's own early life, when she had been parted from Emily.

A harrowing image of the burning house and the screaming infant had lodged in Julia's subconscious and occasionally surfaced in nightmares. It saddened her to think that if Grace had been born a few years later, post-partum psychosis would have been better understood, and Linda would have received the medical help she needed without being separated from her child. The reunion of Linda and the daughter she hadn't seen for thirty-three years had been particularly poignant as Linda was already suffering from the brain tumour which killed her. Julia had hoped Pete would understand that she felt a strong sense of responsibility towards Grace and her baby in the sad circumstances, but their conversation had left her uncertain of his support.

She knew that his comment that she hadn't been treating their relationship as a priority was justified. Nor could she argue with his point that her current living arrangements wouldn't help. There would be no privacy for the two of them with Grace and Emmeline staying indefinitely in the cottage.

Julia was startled from her musings by a cough. She spun round, catching her arm on the open drawer of the cabinet. She had forgotten to lock the door after Pete had gone out. They needed to employ a receptionist, but that was a cost they couldn't afford at present. So far, they had managed by covering for one another as much as possible.

'Ouch!' She rubbed the area below her elbow.

'Sorry. I didn't mean to startle you.' A stocky man of medium height was standing in the doorway. His wavy hair and pencil moustache were almost black, and he wore a black leather jacket over a lumberjack shirt and jeans.

Julia smiled. 'My fault. I'm guessing you didn't see the buzzer on the desk in reception?'

The man shook his head. His dark eyes, small behind black-framed glasses, flicked over her.

Beneath his gaze Julia pulled the fronts of her grey shawl neck cardigan closer together across her small bust. 'You must be Mark Smeaton?'

He nodded.

'I'm Julia Butler. I wasn't expecting you for another few minutes.' She looked pointedly at her watch. It was eight minutes to ten.

'I was hoping you could see me a bit earlier. I've got another appointment at eleven. I thought you might be flexible, since you asked me to rearrange from yesterday. It will be Mondays in future, won't it?'

Julia noted he didn't apologise for his early arrival, and seemed not to have understood this was a taster session. She hesitated. Pete should be back very soon. 'OK. Come in.' She indicated the chair under the window.

The man didn't move from the doorway. 'Do you work here alone?'

'No,' said Julia quickly. 'With a colleague, a reflexologist. He'll be back in just a moment.' To her irritation, she found herself laying slight emphasis on 'he'.

Mark Smeaton stepped forward and rested a hand on the armchair near the door.

'Here, please.' Julia pointed again to the chair by the window, moving quickly to place her clip file on the other seat. The requirement to sit closest to the door in the interests of security had been instilled from the beginning of counselling training.

He raised an eyebrow but sat where she requested.

'If I could begin with your contact details…' Julia took the routine information, her client responding briefly. She learnt that Mark Smeaton was a thirty-five-year-old conservation architect. She had just reinforced the information she had provided on the phone that this was an initial session to see how they felt about working together, when the front door opened. Julia excused herself and went out to reception.

'Sorry. Got held up.' Pete raised two bulging carrier bags with a grin. 'Sale on all aromatherapy products at the market stall.'

'It's fine.' But Julia was surprised to realise how relieved she was that he had returned. She had been alone with clients a few times in the premises without feeling uneasy. What was different about today?

Back in her office, she found herself appraising the man in front of her as she completed the form. She was uncomfortably aware that her assessment was contrary to the non-judgmentalism which she sought to practise, as advocated by the American psychologist Carl Rogers. Telling herself that it was a combination of fatigue and the unsettling conversation with Pete which had unnerved her, she asked Mark Smeaton the standard question about what had led him to contact her.

He leant forward in his chair, steepling his stubby fingers across his mouth. Then, lowering his hands, he said tersely, 'Relationship problems.'

Julia nodded encouragingly.

'Yeah.' He rubbed his moustache. 'My girlfriend broke up with me. I've been finding it very difficult.'

'I see.' Julia let a beat pass. When her client didn't expand, she asked, 'Could you tell me more about how it's been difficult for you?'

He drew his brows into a single line above his nose. 'Don't most people find break-ups difficult?'

'Maybe. But everyone finds them difficult in different ways. Tell me more about your experience, Mark.'

He stared back at her without speaking.

Aware that she would have waited for most clients to take the lead at this point, Julia counted to ten. When he remained silent, she tried again. 'I'm wondering if you'd like to share some of your particular difficulties, tell me more about what's brought you here today.'

He shrugged. 'I've found it hard to accept, I guess.'

'The break-up?'

'Yeah. That's what I said, isn't it?' The verbal challenge was matched by a flash of hostility in his dark eyes behind the specs.

Julia waited a moment, careful to maintain eye contact. 'I'm just clarifying,' she said evenly. 'It's important that I understand exactly what you're saying.'

'Right.' He nodded slowly, glancing down at his hands folded in his lap. Julia noticed black hairs sprouting from the backs of them.

This time Julia waited during the silence which followed.

When she looked over at him again, she was disconcerted to find that he had raised his head and was gazing at her intently. She shifted in her chair to conceal her shiver.

'I thought she was The One,' he said suddenly, as if there had been no gap in their exchange.

'Ah. Could you tell me more about what you mean by "The One", Mark?'

'You know what I mean, surely?'

She made a conscious effort to maintain a neutral expression. 'It would help if you explain.'

A muscle in his cheek twitched. 'I thought it was obvious. She was The One destined for me. The One I should spend my life with.'

Julia let the words hang in the air, framing a careful response. 'So from that perspective, it must be very difficult if the woman you thought of as "The One" sees things differently and initiates the break-up?'

'Exactly!' For the first time he brightened. 'She's got to be wrong, hasn't she?' He leant forward, rubbing his hands up and down the thighs of his jeans.

Julia blinked. 'She's got to be wrong?'

'Yeah.' Smeaton nodded his head several times. 'We're meant to be together. She's made a mistake breaking up with me. You get it, don't you?' He scanned Julia's face eagerly.

'Let me check what you're saying. You believe that your ex-girlfriend was your intended life partner, and that she didn't realise this when she decided to end your relationship. Is that right?'

'That's it!' He sat back in his chair, watching her closely. 'But it's not just my belief. It's one of those things that's meant to be, isn't it, when you meet The One? Written in the stars and all that?'

Julia hesitated.

'You don't believe that?' His face darkened. He chewed his thumbnail, still fixing her with that disconcerting stare.

Julia considered trotting out the usual counsellor spiel that they weren't concerned so much with her beliefs as his. In response to his intensity she decided on a more direct approach. 'No. Personally, I don't believe that.'

He scowled. 'That's going to cause a problem, isn't it? How are you going to be able to help me if you don't hold my beliefs?'

Julia tried to explain that the counselling relationship didn't require counsellor and client to share the same convictions, but that she always endeavoured to understand the frames of reference of her clients. Smeaton remained sceptical.

'So tell me, what benefit am I going to get from counselling?' he demanded.

'That depends on what you would like to achieve.'

'What would you suggest from what I've said?' He folded his arms across his barrel chest. 'I've told you I'm here because of the split from my girlfriend. I'm not happy about it, not at all. It's upsetting me.'

'I understand. Then I wonder, if we decide to work together, whether we might explore how your idea of "The One" is impacting your relationships?'

'Not all my relationships,' he said sulkily. '*This* one.'

'OK.'

'It's not OK though, is it?' He eyeballed her. 'You're not getting what I'm saying, are you?'

Julia steeled herself not to look away. 'I understand that this girlfriend was very special to you,' she said levelly. 'I appreciate that you are very upset about the separation.' She considered for a moment. This was proving a difficult introductory session. She was far from convinced that she wanted to work with Mark Smeaton, whatever he might say when she posed the question in a few minutes. Perhaps the best way she could help the man was to challenge his view more candidly than she would do in her usual person-centred practice. 'It can be very difficult to move on if we believe there is only one person destined for us, as you say you do.'

'I don't want to move on!' He was almost shouting. His knuckles were white as he gripped the beech arms of his chair. Julia shrank back in her matching armchair. 'I want to get back with her! Don't you get that?'

She inhaled. 'I do,' she said quietly. 'I'm afraid—'

'You're afraid she doesn't feel the same,' he interrupted. He paused. His head sank to his chest and he pushed at his spectacles before mumbling, 'If only I'd done things differently.'

Julia had been about to say she was afraid they would be unable to work together in view of his aggression, not to comment on the improbability of a reconciliation with his ex. But seeing that he was calmer, and telling herself that his anger was with his situation rather than with her, she decided to hold off terminating the session.

'You have regrets about how you handled the relationship?' she prompted.

He pressed the fingers of his left hand to his forehead before answering, grimacing as though in pain. 'I shouldn't have been unfaithful to her,' he muttered, not looking up.

'Right.' Julia took a deep breath, not sure if she could pose her next question without sounding ironic. 'So you were involved with someone else at the same time as you were in a relationship with the woman you consider was meant to be your long-term partner?'

He nodded miserably. 'Stupid mistake,' he said. 'I tried to explain when she split up with me, but she didn't want to know. She said it was the end, that she never wanted to see me again.'

'I see.' *Not an unreasonable response.* Evidently her client thought otherwise, and professionalism required her to try to understand his perspective. 'Have you seen your former girlfriend since?'

He shook his head. 'She got involved with someone else briefly when we were struggling. I know that didn't last long. I went round to her flat a few times, but she wasn't there. Last week when I called, a new bloke had moved in. He didn't know where she'd gone.' He jabbed at his glasses again. 'I think she's changed her mobile. She hasn't answered my calls.'

Julia let a moment pass before saying gently, 'I'm wondering if she might not want to be in contact, Mark, if she hasn't let you know her new address or mobile number.'

'She's got it all wrong,' he said. 'I made a mistake and I'm sorry. She has to understand that.' Unexpectedly he began to sob.

Julia silently nudged the tissue box towards him over the small table which lay to the side of their chairs. She registered a coolness towards her client which concerned her. It could impede their counselling relationship if they went ahead after this initial session. She was sufficiently self-aware to know that Mark's admission of infidelity had reopened the wound she carried from her ex-partner's unfaithfulness the previous year.

'Thanks.' He blew his nose noisily and then looked over at her. 'Do you think you can help me?'

Julia weighed the question carefully. She had reservations about working with the man in front of her. But she never liked to give up after one session. 'Picking up on what I asked earlier, could you tell me more now about what you would like to achieve from counselling?'

Another hard stare. 'That's obvious, isn't it? I want you to help me work out how I can persuade her to come back to me.'

She suppressed a shudder. 'I'm sorry, Mark. As a counsellor, I hope I can help you explore your own feelings, maybe work out how to cope in the aftermath of this break-up. I appreciate it has been very difficult for you. Perhaps, if it was something you wanted to explore, we could consider what led you to be unfaithful to a woman who meant so much to you?'

'Yeah.' He nodded vigorously. 'I'm sure that would help.'

'I'm afraid that might not lead to the resumption of your relationship.' Julia paused, uneasy about her client's unwillingness to accept that the break-up with his ex-girlfriend might be permanent. Then she reminded herself how difficult she had found it to accept that her relationship with Greg was over when he moved in with Lisa. Hadn't she reacted in a very similar way to the man in front of her? But there was a big difference, she reminded herself. Greg had been unfaithful to her, and he had initiated the break. He had made it crystal clear that he had moved on. By contrast, Mark Smeaton seemed to regret his infidelity and was desperate to get back with his ex.

She focused on her client, who was pulling on some hairs in the middle of his moustache. 'It is possible it might help me get back with her though, isn't it?'

Julia scrambled to recover the dialogue, annoyed with herself for her distraction. 'There's no guarantee, I'm afraid.'

His mouth set in a hard line beneath the moustache. Once more Julia felt prompted to encourage him to confront the reality of the situation.

'I'm curious about what makes you so certain your ex-girlfriend would be willing to resume your relationship? You've told me that she's moved without letting you know where she's gone, that she's changed her mobile number without contacting you.'

He sidestepped the question. 'We were so good together,' he said. 'I'm sure she'd see that if she gave me another chance.' He turned his head towards the window. 'I told you I'm a conservation architect,' he said. 'Working on ancient buildings like I do, I know the importance of good foundations. And our foundations were solid. Built to last. I know it was.'

'But if you don't have any contact details for her...'

A slow smile spread across his swarthy face. 'I know where to find her.'

Julia's skin prickled. She took a deep breath. 'And if she doesn't want to see you...?'

'She will.' His smile widened into a grin. 'I'll make sure of it. Like I said, we're meant to be together.' He glanced at his watch and sprang to his feet. 'Sorry, got to get the 10.45 bus. Nine o'clock next Monday, isn't it?' He didn't wait for an answer, brushing past her chair on the way to the door.

5

'Another coffee?' Pete poked his shaven head round Julia's office door. Julia started in her armchair. 'Hey, I've not woken you, have I?'

'No.' Julia stretched her arms above her head. She hadn't moved since Mark Smeaton had left so abruptly. 'I was just thinking.'

Pete looked down at his trainers. 'You weren't worrying about what I said earlier, were you? I know it wasn't great timing just before your client was due. I didn't mean to put pressure on you. Sorry.'

'No, it wasn't that. Bit of a difficult session, that's all.'

'That bloke nearly knocked me over on his way out, barely apologised. Is he coming back?'

'He said he'd be back next week.'

Pete picked up on the flatness in her tone. 'You agreed that between you, did you? I know these first sessions are trials for both of you.'

Julia bit her lip, reluctant to divulge any of her misgivings about a client to Pete. 'The session finished very suddenly when he dashed off for his bus.' She rose and gave herself a little shake, exercising the tip she often used from training. Her class had been taught that the physical action dispelled the 'bad vibes' some people left behind. Julia wasn't convinced by the idea, but with his pent up aggression and intensity, Smeaton had certainly left her perturbed.

She smiled at Pete, seeing the concern in his blue eyes. 'You did have a point before,' she said quietly. 'I'm sorry I haven't been giving us enough priority, and that I didn't think of talking to you about Grace and Em moving in before I blurted out the invitation.'

His face softened as she moved towards him. 'That's OK.'

'But I think you're wrong to have misgivings about Grace,' she went on, as he lowered his head a couple of inches to kiss her.

He drew back. 'Grace again.' He retreated to the reception area.

'What do you mean?' Julia followed him out. 'You're the one who brought her up earlier.'

Pete didn't reply immediately, apparently absorbed in lining the coffee filter basket with fresh paper. 'Can we drop it?' He took the coffee container down from the shelf above the machine. 'I do have misgivings about Grace. You don't. We're not going to agree.'

His chest was rising and falling rapidly beneath his cream Aran sweater. Julia realised that despite his calm tone, he was struggling to retain self-control. Unwisely she couldn't leave the topic, struck by a sudden thought.

'You're not jealous, are you? Jealous of Grace and Emmeline?'

Pete shook his head. 'No, I'm not jealous. Can you just leave it!' He plunged the scoop into the container with so much force that coffee scattered across the grey work surface. 'Blast!'

'OK, OK.' Julia took the cloth from the sink and wiped up the spillage. Her heart was beating quickly. They rarely argued.

Pete ran fresh water into the jug and poured it over the coffee grounds. Replacing the jug on the hot plate, he flicked the switch. Julia gave him a sideways glance as she rinsed out the cloth under the tap. He was chewing the inside of his right cheek, his eyes fixed on the percolating drips of fresh coffee.

Finally, he turned to her. 'I'm sorry, Jules,' he said quietly. 'There's something I need to—' He closed his eyes in frustration as the door opened. A lorry thundered past.

'Any coffee going?' asked their visitor, a slight, blond man in his mid-thirties dressed in a navy parka.

'James! I thought you were still on sabbatical!' exclaimed Julia.

'I got back a few days ago.' James unzipped his coat, looking round the office appraisingly. 'Better than your last place, but maybe a bit on the small side?'

Julia was glad to see that Pete's easy-going smile was back in place. James's comment supported Pete's view that the premises were only temporary.

'Thanks, mate. That's what I've been trying to tell your sister. This is just a stop gap until we can afford somewhere bigger.'

James nodded and moved towards the desk. 'I don't think we were properly introduced when we met at our late aunt's birthday lunch.' He glanced at Julia.

'No. I'm sorry. James – Pete. Pete – James.'

A faint whiff of alcohol drifted across the desk as James leant over to shake hands with Pete. His cheeks were faintly flushed. Julia sighed. They'd barely spoken since their row in January. He had turned up in the early hours after his wife Clare had thrown him out when she had discovered he was having an affair with a student.

'Poor old Aunt Ada,' said James. 'She'd probably still be here now if that woman hadn't turned up.'

Julia drew in her breath and counted to ten. 'If you mean Linda, she died three weeks ago. Surely Clare told you?'

James's face clouded. 'I haven't heard from Clare.'

'Ah.' Julia hesitated, but she wouldn't let James criticise Linda, even if he was upset that Clare hadn't been in touch. 'You know Linda wasn't crazy. She was suffering from a brain tumour. I told you that in an e-mail. Not that you replied,' she couldn't help adding.

'I was busy with research,' he replied brusquely.

Pete interposed. 'Coffee's ready.' He turned to James. 'Milk? Sugar?'

'Just milk, thanks.'

They stood in silence as Pete poured the steaming liquid into three mugs. He placed one on the desk for James. 'I'll leave you to it. I know you two have a lot of catching up to do.' He placed a hand briefly on Julia's arm before heading through to his office.

'So how's it going with him?' James asked once Pete had closed the door behind him. 'A bit more than "just good friends" now, is it?'

He was grinning in a way which annoyed Julia. Determined not to get off on a bad footing, she forced a smile.

'It's going pretty well. You said you haven't heard from Clare?'

The smirk left James's face. 'No.' He blew on his coffee. 'I'd hoped…' He broke off and grinned at Julia again. 'What about Mum then? Bit of a dark horse, wasn't she?'

Julia swallowed a sharp response. 'It's a very sad story. I wish she'd been able to tell us about it herself before she died.'

James shot her a quizzical expression. 'Are you sure about that?'

'Absolutely.' She gripped her mug tightly. 'It would have been a shock, but at least she would have been free of the burden of her secret in her last few months. And we'd have got to know poor Linda better too.' Tears pricked the backs of her eyes. She bowed her head.

'You don't think you'd have judged Mum?'

'What? No! What makes you ask such a question?'

James held up his free hand. 'Your high standards.' He paused. 'I mean, you made it clear that you disapproved of my affair last winter, didn't you?'

'That's completely different!' Julia's voice rose. 'You were married, a grown man. Mother was only a girl. She and Ray truly loved one another. You can't compare the two!'

James snorted. 'True love where Mother's involved and you can dress it up as a tragic wartime romance. A grubby affair for me. I get it.' He drained his coffee and slammed the mug down on the desk, leaning towards her. Julia stepped back from the trajectory of his alcohol-laden breath. 'Still the same critical Julia, aren't you?'

'You'll criticise everyone but yourself, won't you, James?' she retorted.

His mouth twisted in the sullen pout she remembered from childhood. 'Here I was thinking you might be more understanding after finding out about Mum's secret. Even hoping that absence might have made the heart grow fonder. Not a chance. Not with you, not with Clare.'

Julia noticed how his shoulders sagged as he mentioned his wife's name. 'Look, I'm glad you dropped in,' she said, striving for a more conciliatory note. 'Honestly. I hated you leaving for France without a goodbye after our row. But Clare – she was very hurt by what happened, finding out about your affair when you were going through IVF. Surely you understand that?'

He chewed his thumbnail without answering, staring down at the desk.

For the second time in an hour, Julia wondered how much her own experience of infidelity with Greg had scarred her, making it difficult for her not to judge unfaithful men like Mark Smeaton and now her brother.

James looked up and met her gaze defiantly. His eyes were bloodshot, with dark shadows beneath. Despite herself, Julia felt another pang of compassion.

'It wouldn't have made any difference, would it?' he asked. He swirled his coffee around in his mug. 'Surely Clare told you it was because of me that we couldn't have a baby?'

'Yes. I know that must have been very painful for you.' She ducked her head. The ache over her own childlessness had dulled since that excruciating moment when she had struck Greg, when he and Lisa were baby-shopping. But it still hurt. She found she couldn't let James off the hook for his infidelity though. 'Don't you understand how much damage you've caused? What about Clare?'

'Professionalism always comes first with you, Jules, doesn't it? What about family loyalty?'

She laughed, her brown eyes widening in disbelief. 'Family loyalty? Who are you to speak about family loyalty? Disappearing off to France, leaving behind the mess you've made here? Not to mention I had to sort out Mother's probate on my own. What about your loyalty to Clare?'

He shook his head. 'You just don't get it, do you? I had to get away. I knew I'd made a mess, as you call it.' He laughed hollowly. 'A bloody catastrophe. Don't think I didn't realise! I needed space to think. Research was a distraction. My sabbatical couldn't have come at a better time.'

He lowered his head, massaging the bridge of his nose. When he looked at her again, the anger in his eyes had been replaced with a despair which plucked her heart strings. 'Have you any idea, Julia, what a total failure I feel for not being able to give Clare the baby she so desperately wants?'

'Oh, James,' Julia reached across the desk and placed a hand on his elbow. 'I am sorry. Truly. It's just... *your affair*. Clare was so devastated, especially after the last IVF cycle failed.'

He shook his head miserably. 'I know. The affair was a distraction from the IVF. I understand that doesn't excuse it.' He pushed at his fringe again. 'I just hope that maybe it's not over for me and Clare, that she'll give me a chance. What do you think?'

Julia withdrew her hand. 'I can't say, James.'

Julia hadn't seen Clare for several weeks. Coincidentally, they were going out for a meal that evening. She had a strong suspicion that Clare had moved on, still hopeful at thirty-six that she might have a longed-for child. But witnessing James's evident despair, rare for such a confident man, and hearing his desire to make up with Clare, Julia couldn't bring herself to puncture his hope. 'You need to talk to Clare, don't you?' she asked gently.

He grimaced. 'If she'll talk to me. She's not picked up my calls or answered my e-mails whilst I've been away.' He toyed with the wedding ring on his finger. 'We'll need to talk about the house and stuff anyway if...' He left the sentence unfinished. 'So that gives me a reason to contact her.'

'Yes.' Julia attempted a reassuring smile. She changed the subject. 'So how did your sabbatical go? Did you get all the research done that you'd planned?'

James spoke for a few minutes about the study he had carried out during his sabbatical and a paper he was drafting for a conference on the life of peasants in late medieval France. Julia only half-listened. She was pleased to hear him sounding so enthusiastic, but it had been a fraught morning. First the friction with Pete over Grace, then the unsettling session with Mark Smeaton, and now conflict with James. Coming after a broken night's sleep courtesy of Emmeline, Julia felt drained. It was a relief when her brother said he needed to leave for a departmental meeting at the university.

'Thank Pete for the coffee.' He grinned, opening the door on to the street, noisy with traffic and pedestrians. 'It'll cover up the hangover.'

Julia's smile was strained. She was pleased that they were back on terms after the recent fracture in their relationship, but found herself wondering whether her brother's hangover was a one off or a more regular occurrence. And if Clare refused to consider a reconciliation, what effect would that have on James's alcohol consumption?

6

Emmeline's screams greeted Julia when she arrived home that evening. In the kitchen she found Grace pacing the floor, Emmeline red-faced on her shoulder. The front of Grace's blue polo neck jumper was stained with regurgitated milk. The baby's sobs subsided when she saw her great-aunt. Julia gave Emmeline a cuddle, then excused herself so that she could go to shower and change. Grace looked as though she might burst into tears herself when Julia mentioned that she was going out. With Pete's reservations about her new living arrangements fresh in her mind, Julia suppressed a twinge of guilt. She had offered Grace and Emmeline a home and would help look after Emmeline when she could, but she had a right to a social life.

It was a battle against the wind going down Lincoln's famous Steep Hill. Lost in her thoughts, Julia barely noticed the leaves and litter scuttering around her black ankle boots. She hadn't had the chance for more than a few snatched words with Pete after James left. They were both busy with clients during the afternoon, and Pete had left at 4 p.m. to take his mother to a hospital appointment. Julia hoped Brenda was OK. She was a friendly, cheerful woman who had greeted Julia warmly when Pete had introduced them at his nephew's baptism in the summer. They had met a couple of times since, and Julia was invited over on Saturday for her birthday lunch. Making a mental note to ask Pete about the appointment tomorrow, she turned up the side street which led to 'Giuseppe's', the Italian restaurant suggested by Clare.

The cathedral clock chimed the half hour above her. Julia's steps slowed as she passed the boarded up shops on the poorly lit street. She smiled sadly. She hadn't been back to 'Giuseppe's' since eating there with Linda in January.

Julia started at a movement in a doorway. 'Any spare change?' a man asked hoarsely.

Julia halted and reached into the pocket of her black trench coat. Linda had given money to a rough sleeper here all those months ago. Julia wondered if it could possibly be the same man. On that occasion Julia had rushed past, though she had been moved by Linda's generosity. She'd made a point of keeping a few coins in her pocket ever since. Now she dropped them into a hat on the cobbles in front of the man.

'Thanks, duck. God bless.'

'And you.'

Julia was surprised how much she wished the man well, even if she doubted the existence of the deity. Unexpectedly, she had a vision of Linda's wide warm smile, and seemed to hear her say, 'I always think, there but for the grace of God, don't you?' Words Linda had used after giving her donation last winter. The sense of Linda's presence was so palpable that Julia had to stop herself turning round to look for her.

Dashing a tear from her cheek, she peered into the shadows of the doorway and dimly discerned a bearded face. The man's features were otherwise indistinct in the darkness.

'Are you often here?' she asked impulsively. 'I mean... I was here once before, with' – she swallowed – 'with my sister, and she gave a man some money. I wondered if it might have been you?'

'Very likely. I often stay hereabouts.'

'Oh. That's good. Not that you stay here,' Julia amended hastily. 'It's good that it was you. My sister – she died.'

'I'm sorry for your loss,' said the man quietly. He coughed wheezily.

'Thank you,' said Julia. 'What's your name?' It suddenly seemed important to know.

There was a long interval before the man replied. Then he said, more gruffly than ever, 'Derek. My name is Derek.'

'I'm Julia. I'll...' She'd been about to say that she would look out for him, but broke off, worried it might be tactless.

High heels clacking along the cobbled street announced Clare's arrival.

'Julia? Is that you? I thought I heard your voice.' Clare stopped alongside and glanced towards the doorway, alerted by the noise of Derek shuffling backwards. 'I'm sorry. Did I interrupt something?'

Julia found herself smiling at the uncertainty in her sister-in-law's tone. 'We were just chatting,' she said. 'I last came to "Giuseppe's" with Linda in January. I think we might have met this gentleman then.'

There was a fractional pause. 'I see.' Clare stepped in front of Julia and moved on briskly. 'We'd better get on, hadn't we? I did book for seven thirty.'

'Of course. Good night, Derek.'

There was no reply, but Julia was glad that she knew the man's name now. Derek was no longer an anonymous rough sleeper. 'Thank you, Linda,' she whispered as she caught up with Clare outside the welcoming lights of 'Giuseppe's'.

'Pardon?' Clare turned, pushing open the door of the restaurant.

'Nothing.'

'Giuseppe's' was exactly as she remembered it: the chef sweating over the brazier, the low ceiling and yellow walls, the terracotta floor tiles, the strong aroma of garlic and cheese. The proprietor was as immaculate as ever in his black evening suit and white shirt. He was pouring a small amount of red wine into the glass of a solitary middle-aged man in a business suit sitting at a table in the far corner. The man nodded his approval of the wine, and Giuseppe filled the glass with a flourish before making his way towards the two women. His eyes narrowed when he saw Julia. She guessed he was trying to place her.

'We have a table for two booked in the name of Sullivan,' said Clare.

Julia registered that Clare had reverted to her maiden name. Glancing at her sister-in-law's ring finger, Julia saw that it was bare. A new cropped haircut emphasised Clare's pointed chin. The signs didn't augur well for a reconciliation between Clare and James. Julia's heart sank. If James was already drinking too much, as she suspected from his morning visit to the office, how would he react when he realised that his marriage was definitely over?

'You dined here with Signora Linda, did you not?' Giuseppe's smile of welcome was wistful as he led them to a table by the window. With a jolt, Julia recognised it was the same table she had shared with Linda on that snowy night in January.

Julia eased herself out of her black trench coat. 'I did.'

Giuseppe took the coat, shaking his head. 'I was so sorry about Signora Linda. She was a wonderful person.' He moved round the table to take Clare's olive green wrap.

'She was.' Julia smiled at him and sat down.

Giuseppe went to hang their outer garments on a mahogany coat stand by the door, returning with maroon leather-bound menus. He advised them of the day's specials before hastening to greet a smart couple in late middle age. Julia frowned. They looked vaguely familiar.

'Everything OK?' asked Clare.

'Yes. It's that couple. I've seen them somewhere.' Julia screwed up her eyes. 'I remember. They were at Linda's exhibition last January.' She recalled the exhibition, which had included Linda's 'Open Door' series of paintings. The series included a picture of their late mother Emily in her rocking-chair. Linda had wanted Julia to have the paintings, but no firm arrangements had been made. Julia wondered fleetingly if they were back at the Norfolk farmhouse. Presumably they would form part of the artist's estate now. Nothing had been said about whether Linda had left a will. Sensing Clare's eyes on her, Julia drew herself back to the present.

'Strange,' she mused. 'I've not been back here since that night in January. We sat at the same table, now they've turned up' – she nodded towards the couple who were settling into a table on the opposite side of the room – 'and Linda gave money to a man I suspect was Derek on the way. It's like Groundhog Day!' She smiled, her heart beating faster at the coincidences.

Clare furrowed blonde plucked eyebrows. 'Derek?'

'The man in the doorway,' said Julia.

Clare's frown deepened. 'How do you know his name?'

'I asked him.' Julia opened her menu, holding Clare's gaze. 'Why do you ask?'

'Well, it's one thing giving them spare change, but isn't it a bit... *familiar* to find out their names?'

Julia shrugged. '"They" are people, Clare,' she said mildly.

'I know, and it's sad to see them.' Clare's indifferent tone gave the lie to her apparent concern. 'You never know how safe they are though, do you? There you were, walking along a dark side street on your own. What if he'd attacked you or something?'

'But he didn't, did he?'

'Well, no.' Clare dropped her gaze to her open menu and forced a smile. 'Maybe I'm just more cynical than you.'

'To be honest, I used to be,' admitted Julia. 'No thanks to Greg, he was such a cynic! Linda's influence changed me. I think it started when she gave money to Derek that night. She was so kind, towards me too. I wouldn't have blamed her if she'd resented me for having all those years with our mother, whilst she never knew her until those last few months.'

'Mm.' Clare ran a manicured thumb down the menu. 'I think I'll have risotto. Shall we share a bottle of Valpolicella?'

Julia nodded, studying her menu in turn as Clare requested the wine. On one level she understood Clare's detachment, especially following her separation from James. There was no real reason why the discovery of Julia's and James's half-sister should interest Clare. But Julia still felt a stab of disappointment on Linda's behalf.

There was something else she sensed in Clare too, she realised, as Giuseppe brought the bottle over for Clare to sample. A new hardness, which Julia suspected was rooted in James's affair and her ongoing childlessness. Julia sighed as she mentally rejected pizza and risotto and considered the pasta options. She suddenly missed Pete, wishing she were eating out with him instead of Clare. Perhaps she would suggest 'Giuseppe's' to him one night...

'Have you decided?' Clare glanced over expectantly as Giuseppe returned, pen poised over his pad.

Julia nodded, ordering a vegetarian pasta dish. Clare selected the seafood risotto.

They chatted about their respective jobs over the wine. Clare was a legal secretary and had recently moved to a larger law firm. Noticing how animated she became when she talked about one of the solicitors, Julia asked the inevitable question. 'Is he married?'

'Yes,' said Clare. 'Unfortunately. Mind you, if I had the chance...' She twirled the stem of her wine glass, smiling suggestively.

'Clare!' Julia failed to keep the disapproval out of her voice. 'You wouldn't!'

Clare's smile disappeared and she grimaced. 'Probably not,' she conceded. 'I would feel terrible if the wife found out, especially after what I went through with James's affair. It's just sometimes I can see the advantage of the father being a married man. Bit of fun for him, I get the child without the hassle of a relationship...'

Julia decided to add a practical point to the moral argument. 'It's not easy, being a single mum. Grace looks permanently exhausted! That's why I'm so tired.'

'Who's Grace?'

Julia set down her wine glass. 'Linda's daughter. Didn't I mention her last time we met?'

'I don't think so. But then, I was in a state that night, wasn't I? Too much alcohol on an empty stomach. I'd just found out that my sister was pregnant. I was the one doing all the talking – you probably felt like you were still at work listening to me!'

'It wasn't a problem.' Julia turned gratefully to the waiter as he arrived with two steaming plates. 'Thank you, that looks delicious! More wine?' She reached over for the green bottle.

'Please.' Clare shook out a white napkin shaped into a fan. 'So this Grace is your niece, I suppose?'

Julia nodded, topping up their wine glasses.

'Another family member for you to get to know.' Clare stabbed at a king prawn. 'You say she's a single parent?'

'Yes. How's the risotto?'

'Good. How old is the baby?'

'Four months.'

Clare nodded, looking pensive.

Julia guessed her sister-in-law was once again regretting her childlessness. 'There's still time for you, Clare,' she said quietly.

Clare's face darkened. 'No thanks to your brother! When I think of all the years I wasted on him... Have you seen him since he got back?'

Julia took another sip of wine before she replied. Clare's attitude towards James had clearly hardened during his absence. She aimed for a light tone, attempting to steer the topic of conversation into a less contentious direction. 'He called at the office today. You haven't been in yet, have you? So much better than the old school, though a bit cramped. Pete wants to move on at the end of the tenancy, find somewhere bigger, but I'm not sure we can afford it yet. We could really do with a receptionist—'

'James is staying at your mother's cottage again, isn't he?' Clare broke in.

'Yes. Just till the sale goes through. About a month, the solicitors think. I'll be pleased to get the sale finalised, though it feels like losing another part of Mother somehow.' Julia swallowed. Even now, ten months later, the waves of grief could take her by surprise. *Not helped by lack of sleep or the wine,* she reminded herself. She took another gulp of the excellent Valpolicella anyway.

Clare scooped some risotto on to her fork. 'It must be very difficult, but it will be good to get it done.'

Julia looked across at her, again noting her sister-in-law's new detachment. A year ago, Clare would have said something sympathetic in response to Julia's comment. Catching her glance, Clare gave a tight-lipped smile. 'I was checking James is still there because I arranged for my solicitor to send the papers today. It only occurred to me afterwards that he could have moved on.'

Julia looked at her blankly. 'Solicitor's papers?'

Clare nodded. 'Yes. For the divorce. I held off during his sabbatical.'

Julia chewed a floret of broccoli slowly. There suddenly seemed to be too much garlic in the pesto. She set her fork down. 'I didn't realise you were at that stage yet.'

Clare looked at her unblinkingly. 'Didn't you? I told you earlier in the year that I'd decided to move on after James's affair.'

'I know. But James...' Julia twirled some linguine round her fork, not quite sure how to go on.

'But James what?' Clare sat back in her chair and picked up her wine glass, her eyes narrow. 'He can't give me a child, can he?'

'Well, no,' Julia conceded. James's sadness over his infertility that morning had been tangible and she was certain that it had contributed to his affair. Not that it excused it in any way, but she felt she must say something on his behalf. She chose her next words carefully. 'From what he said when he called this morning, I'm sure he's truly sorry about his affair. Maybe, if you talk to him, give him a chance to explain—'

'Absolutely not!' Clare banged down her glass. A few drops landed on the white tablecloth. Clare dabbed at the crimson stain ineffectually with her napkin. 'I'd have thought you of all people would understand, after Greg leaving you for another woman, and your regrets about being childless at fifty. Surely you realise I have to take my chances whilst I still can?'

Julia winced, even though there was no denying the truth of her sister-in-law's words. 'Of course,' she said. 'You were good together though, you and James, weren't you? Doesn't that count for something?'

Clare shook her head, her coral mouth set in a firm line. 'I get it. Strange how blood is always thicker than water, isn't it?' She extracted her final mussel.

'It's not like that,' said Julia. 'I'm sure James is sincere, that's all.'

Clare shrugged. 'Not my problem.'

Julia took her last forkful of pasta as Clare lined her cutlery up on her empty plate. 'But—'

'There are no "buts", Julia. Why this sudden sympathy for James? When we split, you promised that we would stay friends. You were appalled by James's affair. He goes away, comes back feeling sorry for himself, and you're trying to encourage me to take him back, though that goes against my best interests.' She leant forward, almond eyes stony and accusing. 'If you were a true friend, Julia, you'd be urging me to get on with the divorce as fast as I can.'

The room seemed to swim around Julia, who was suddenly engulfed by fatigue. 'I do want to remain friends, Clare,' she said quietly. 'I understand everything you've said. James behaved appallingly. But I honestly believe he regrets it.' She pushed a loose strand of hair behind her right ear. 'I think he still loves you. For what that's worth,' she added as Clare rolled her eyes.

'Too late, Julia.' There was ice in Clare's voice. 'It's too late. You can tell him that, if you like. If you're finished, shall we get the bill and go? I've lost my appetite for dessert.'

Julia nodded wearily as Clare signalled to Giuseppe. She had tried her best for James and couldn't blame Clare for her decision. But the revelation of her sister-in-law's new implacability chilled her as much as the wind which drove her back home up the hill.

7

Emmeline's wails again assaulted Julia's ears when she reached home ten minutes later. She groaned as she pushed the door closed against the wind. It had been a long day. All she wanted to do was settle into her armchair with a mug of green tea and watch some undemanding TV. No chance.

Grace emerged from the kitchen. Her thick strawberry blonde hair lay in a damp tangled mass above her white and pink floral Laura Ashley bath robe. From upstairs Emmeline's cries grew louder.

'Thank goodness you're back! Emmeline just won't settle. I put her down at eight and had a shower. She hasn't stopped crying since I came downstairs.'

Julia hung her coat on the stand and stepped out of her boots before replying.

'Have you thought of bringing Emmeline downstairs with you?'

'No. The advice is that it's best to leave babies when they're crying, not to keep picking them up. I thought I'd told you that?'

Julia kept her voice neutral. 'You did. Isn't that the advice in the book written by the woman who's never had a child herself?'

Grace frowned. 'Yes, but she's a midwife with lots of experience of babies. More than either of us have!'

Julia's stomach clenched. She did nothing to keep the tartness from her tone as she replied, 'Midwives would have most experience of newborns, wouldn't they? Emmeline is four months old.'

Grace gathered her hair into a ponytail over her right shoulder and squeezed, dripping water on to the parquet floor. 'I think we need whatever help we can get.'

Julia registered herself baulking at the 'we'. She transferred her irritation to the drops of water on the hall floor.

'I don't think that's a good idea, do you?'

'What? Following the midwife's advice?'

'Squeezing water over the floor.' Julia indicated the drips. 'Though I'm not sure about the midwife's advice either,' she added, raising her voice as Emmeline's screams rose in volume.

'Sorry. I wasn't thinking.' Grace yawned and turned back into the kitchen, emerging with a terry tea towel. 'Did you enjoy your meal?' She bent to wipe the floor, her hair curtaining her face.

'Yes, thank you,' lied Julia. The question of whether to warn James that Clare had instructed her solicitors to issue divorce papers had preoccupied her on her walk home. Now she pushed it from her mind, confronting the immediate issue of whether or not to intervene as Emmeline's wails reached a new level. Surely Grace wasn't just going to ignore her daughter and let her cry herself out because of some wretched book?

'Don't you think it's worth checking Emmeline is OK? Could she need a feed, or changing?'

'I changed her before I put her down.' Grace rose, scrunching up the tea towel. 'She's had lots of milk today.'

'Maybe she's still hungry, having a growth spurt?'

Grace rubbed her hand wearily across her forehead. 'It's possible, I suppose. Would you mind going up to see what you can do? I must get more reading done tonight. I'm seeing my supervisor tomorrow, and I wasn't very well prepared last time.'

Responding to the plea in the cornflower blue eyes, Julia moved towards the spiral staircase. 'Isn't it worth asking if you can take longer for maternity leave? I'm sure Dr. Forrester will understand.'

Grace's pale face crumpled. 'But I really want to get on with my research,' she said. 'It's at such an interesting stage. I might lose the thread if I delay. I've not got much done today. Emmeline has been crying and crying. I have to be ready for tomorrow.' She wiped a tear from the corner of her right eye with her dressing-gown sleeve. 'Please, Aunt Julia.'

Julia sighed. 'All right. Would you put the kettle on for me?'

Grace nodded. Julia trudged up the stairs. As soon as she switched the light on in the bedroom shared by Grace and Emmeline, the baby's screams subsided to a more bearable level. Julia went over to the white cot, stepping carefully over the jumble of clothes, toys and board books.

'Shh... shh...' Julia wrinkled her nose. 'I think your nappy needs changing, doesn't it, sweetheart?' *So much for Grace changing her before she put her down. Babies don't poo to order.* She lifted the little girl gently from her white cellular blanket and held her against her shoulder for a moment. Why on earth hadn't Grace been up to check the obvious?

Resisting the temptation to call Grace upstairs, Julia pulled the changing mat out from beneath the cot. As soon as she was lying on the familiar plastic, Emmeline stopped sobbing. She gazed up at her great-aunt. Emmeline's eyes had been blue at birth and had since darkened. Grace had smiled tightly when Julia had commented on this, leading Julia to wonder if the colour was inherited from Emmeline's father, whoever he was. Grace had remained resolutely silent on the subject of Emmeline's paternity since she moved in. So far Julia had avoided the subject, concerned not to put further pressure on Grace whilst she was grieving for her mother and struggling with Emmeline.

Julia tutted as she removed the soiled nappy. Emmeline's small bottom was red. The nappy rash had surely been aggravated by the delay in changing her. Julia wiped her gently, and was rewarded by a smile.

'That's better, isn't it, sweetheart?' Julia murmured softly, bagging up the dirty nappy.

Emmeline kicked her little legs in the air, beaming when Julia tried to echo her gurgles. 'Is Auntie Julia making you laugh? Is she?'

Julia fastened on a clean nappy before picking up the baby and giving her another cuddle. Emmeline nuzzled into her neck. Julia threaded across the cluttered floor to the light switch and flicked it off. After a few minutes in the darkness, Emmeline's small body relaxed against her great-aunt's. Julia lay the child gently back in the cot and covered her with the blanket. Then she tiptoed out of the room and downstairs, taking the nappy bag outside to the wheelie bin.

Back inside, Julia paused on the doormat and surveyed the spacious dining kitchen. She compressed her lips. Dirty dishes, cutlery, saucepans and baby bottles were stacked by the sink. Balanced precariously on top of the overflowing bin was a plastic takeaway tray. It contained a mess of puréed green vegetables mingled with congealed rice and unidentifiable globules in a red sauce. The odour of stale food and spilled milk permeated the kitchen, turning Julia's stomach. Grace didn't look up from the table where she was typing notes on her laptop. Six books lay open in front of her along with three mugs half-full of cold coffee. Cornflakes crunched beneath Julia's stockinged feet as she went across to the kettle. It was cold to her touch and empty.

'Couldn't you even put the kettle on?' The words were out before she could stop them.

Grace paused in her typing and raised her head slowly, her long fingers hovering above the keyboard. 'Sorry?' Her eyes were unfocused, her mind elsewhere.

'It doesn't matter.' Julia kept her face averted as she went over to the sink and ran water into the kettle. 'Emmeline's settled, by the way.' She kept her voice light, but hoped the 'by the way' might elicit a reaction. *By the way, if you're the least interested in your baby's wellbeing.* She shook herself, trying to dispel her frustration.

Grace didn't pick up on the implied criticism. With a muttered, 'That's good,' she resumed her typing.

Julia felt something cold beneath her left foot as she replaced the kettle on its base and switched it on. Looking down, she saw she had stepped on to a mashed teabag. She stooped to pick it up, her indignation rising along with the kettle as it came up to boil. She took a few deep breaths as she poured the water.

Taking her green tea over to the table, Julia moved some post from a chair opposite Grace. In addition to the usual junk mail, there was a cream envelope addressed jointly to her and Grace. Alongside the Norwich postmark, it bore the blue frank of a solicitor's firm. Julia recognised the name of Linda's solicitor. She placed it on the table. It would keep until she had spoken to her niece.

Grace had stopped typing and was flicking through a hefty grey hardback. Julia felt a moment's compunction as she took in the younger woman's pallor, the dark shadows beneath her eyes. But something needed to be said.

'Could I have a quick word, Grace?'

Grace rubbed the bridge of her nose. 'Can't it wait until tomorrow? I'm going to be up at least another hour. I *have* to get this reading done for my tutorial.'

Julia took a sip of tea before replying. It was still too hot and scalded her mouth, adding to her irritation. 'No. I'm afraid it won't wait.'

Roused by the unaccustomed sharpness in Julia's tone, Grace at last peeled her eyes away from her book. 'There's nothing wrong, is there? Emmeline is OK, isn't she? You said she'd settled.'

Finally, some concern about her daughter. 'Emmeline is fine, apart from some nappy rash. She had a dirty nappy.'

'Oh, just after I'd changed her too!'

'That's babies, isn't it?'

Grace's heart-shaped jaw tightened at the implied criticism. 'Yes, but... Anyway, you've changed her now, and the nappy rash will clear, won't it?' She transferred her gaze back to her book.

'It should do, if you change her when necessary.' Julia was aware of laying slight emphasis on the 'you'. 'Before you get on with your studying, I think we need to sort out a few things about our living arrangements.'

Puzzlement spread over Grace's wan face. 'Do we?'

'Yes.' Julia laced her fingers round her china mug, willing herself to stay calm. 'It's been a long day for me too, you know, and I am very tired. So it's not great coming back to *this.*' She waved her hand round the chaotic kitchen.

Grace glanced round. 'It's a bit of a mess,' she said. 'But we can clean up tomorrow, can't we?'

Julia blew on her tea. 'I've rearranged my clients so I can look after Emmeline whilst you go to your meeting with your supervisor at nine. As soon as you come back, I have to leave for the office. I've got clients till five. So if you're here with Emmeline again for most of the day…'

'I've got nowhere else to go, have I? It's not like I can go and get on with my research at the uni library, is it?'

Julia set her mug down. 'Of course not. I'm not expecting you to go anywhere else to study. It's just that it would help if you could clean up as you go during the day, so things aren't in this state at this time of night. We've got your grandfather coming next week too.'

'But it's so *difficult.* Emmeline is so demanding, and I need to study whenever I can. The only time I get is if she has a nap in the afternoon, or when she goes down at night. She was so noisy tonight, I couldn't concentrate. That's why I really must get on now, can't you see?'

Grace's little girl voice had taken on a plaintive note which might have elicited Julia's sympathy on another occasion. But at half past nine on a day which had been emotionally taxing, the older woman sensed the final shreds of her patience disintegrating. 'As I said, Emmeline needed her nappy changing,' she said crisply. 'If you'd gone up to her instead of following the advice in a textbook written by a childless woman, you could have changed her and had a peaceful hour with your books.'

Grace tilted her pointed chin defiantly. 'But you'd have wanted me to spend that "peaceful hour" washing up and cleaning, wouldn't you, whilst you were out enjoying yourself? Then you could have come home to a tidy house and carried on relaxing. You don't care about how late I have to stay up reading!'

Somehow Julia maintained her self-control. 'Of course I'm concerned about you getting enough sleep. And I do want you to make progress with your PhD. But I also have to make sure that I have enough sleep, so that I can give my clients my full attention.' She paused. 'You know how important that is.'

Resentment flashed across Grace's face. 'Can't you forget counselling me? It's months ago. My focus now is my research. It's fascinating, thinking about how Mary and Elizabeth were influenced by their parentage, what impact that had on their lives.' Her eyes brightened. 'Mary's early life was relatively secure by comparison with Elizabeth's, you see. Henry VIII didn't divorce Catherine of Aragon until Mary was seventeen, although of course his affair with Anne Boleyn began before that. So Mary had a settled upbringing. Imagine the impact on Elizabeth of knowing her father had arranged for her mother to be executed when she wasn't even three years old! I've found this really interesting book' – she tapped the grey hardback – 'which touched on the psychology of the relationship between the half-sisters years ago.'

Julia's mind wandered as Grace rattled on about her research. It was good to see the younger woman's enthusiasm, the colour returning to her pale face. But however fascinating, the study of the psychology of the relationship between the Tudor half-sisters wasn't going to help with the practicalities of childcare and housework.

Still only partly listening, Julia finished her green tea and went over to the sink. She ran some hot water into the bowl and was squeezing some washing-up liquid in when Grace mentioned a name which drew her attention.

Julia turned, the washing-up liquid bottle suspended in mid-air, the citrus fragrance sharp in her nostrils.

'Mark Smeaton? What about him?'

Grace frowned, resenting the interruption. 'Nothing, just that he was named as being one of Anne Boleyn's lovers. He was a court musician. Why?'

'No reason.' Client confidentiality meant that Julia couldn't disclose the names of her clients. It was a coincidence that Grace should mention the name in the context of her research, conjuring up the image of the client who had unsettled Julia that morning. She shivered as the wind rattled the sash windows. They were in need of replacing, but that was an expense she couldn't afford at present. She went across to the boiler and turned up the thermostat.

The boiler clanked into life. At the table Grace had buried her head in her book again. Julia rinsed out Emmeline's milk bottles and plastic bowls before tackling the saucepan. Scrubbing at the crusted green purée, she wished that Grace had at least thought to soak the pan.

In the hall the phone rang. 'I hope it doesn't wake Emmeline.' Julia stooped to find a fresh scouring pad in the cupboard below the sink.

Grace didn't look up, her fingers clicking on the keyboard. 'I won't go. It'll probably be for you. This scholar was way ahead of his time!'

Julia bit her lip and peeled off her yellow washing-up gloves, cursing under her breath as one fell into the water.

She picked up the call just before the answerphone clicked in. 'Hello?'

'Jules?'

'Hi, Pete. Oh-h-h...' She groaned in exasperation as Emmeline began to wail upstairs.

Faintly, above the noise of the squalling baby, she heard him say, 'Is everything OK?'

'No,' she said bluntly. 'You've woken Emmeline. I'm sorry, I'll have to go. See you tomorrow.' She hung up without waiting for his reply.

Her heart was beating fast as she stalked back to the kitchen. She stood on the threshold. When Grace didn't look up, she said, 'Emmeline's crying, Grace. Surely you heard her?'

Grace stopped typing. 'Can't you go? Please? I've nearly finished this book and don't want to lose my train of thought.'

There was a pause. Above the roar of the boiler, Julia heard the shed door slam in the wind. Something else which needed fixing along with the ageing sash windows. She pressed her fingers to her temple, aware that Grace was still looking at her expectantly.

'No. I'm sorry, Grace. Not this time.'

Grace slammed the cover of the laptop down, making Julia jump.

'I get it,' hissed the younger woman. She pushed past Julia in the doorway, hard enough for the door jamb to dig into Julia's right shoulder blade. 'You just don't want me to progress my research, do you?'

Julia rubbed her shoulder. 'Of course I do!'

'No. You don't.' Grace paused at the foot of the stairs. 'And you don't really want us to stay. You wish you'd never asked us now, don't you?'

'That's not true.' Julia moved towards her and placed a placating hand on her arm.

Grace shook off Julia's hand and began to climb the stairs, tears streaming down her face. 'It *is* true! You only invited us because you thought you owed it to my mother!

It makes you feel good about yourself, like your counselling, doesn't it?'

'No, Grace…' Julia's voice trailed off. She sank down on the bottom stair as Grace reached the top, her noisy sobs mingling with Emmeline's.

Julia was close to tears herself. Pete's words from the morning echoed in her ears. *'How well do you know her?'*

8

It wasn't only Emmeline's sporadic crying which kept Julia awake that night. Grace's angry accusations that she had only taken them in because she felt she owed it to Linda had hurt her deeply. For the first time since Grace and Emmeline had moved in, Julia steeled herself not to go to their room and offer to take the baby to relieve Grace.

Pete's question *'How well do you know her?'* had sown a seed of doubt in her mind which had taken root with Grace's outburst. However much she told herself that the last few months had been traumatic for Grace, Julia was aware of a growing disquiet with her niece's absorption in her research. She didn't need her counselling experience to understand that Grace might be focusing on her research to distract her from her grief at losing her mother. What concerned Julia was that Grace's PhD was impinging on her care of Emmeline. Allowing the baby to cry herself out seemed cruel, however little experience Julia had of such matters.

It had been a challenging day altogether. Tossing and turning beneath her duvet in her king-sized bed, Julia found herself replaying the other difficult conversations with Pete, James and Clare. The wind continued to rise into the early hours, rattling against the sash windows and shaking the latched oak doors inside the early nineteenth century cottage. Finally she gave up on her quest for sleep and switched on her bedside lamp. The vintage brass alarm clock showed it was half past three. She picked up her book, a psychological thriller. After reading a few pages, she set the novel face down on the duvet. Something about the story of a man stalking a young woman was scrabbling at her subconscious. Something from yesterday… It came back to her as the kitchen door slammed in a fresh gust of wind. She jumped, and the book crashed to the floor. The jolt recalled her shock at Mark Smeaton's unannounced appearance in her office the previous morning. It was his comment which the novel had evoked: *'I know where to find her.'*

Shuddering, Julia pulled the duvet up around her shoulders. Even as she chided herself for her uncharacteristic negativity towards her new client, the unease she had felt in his presence assumed more concrete form as the wind roared around the old house like a hungry predator. *'I know where to find her.'* Weren't those the words of a potential stalker? Her hands shaking, she reached down to pick up the novel and laid it back on the bedside cabinet. Thinking back over the meeting, it crossed her mind that Mark Smeaton's refusal to entertain the possibility that his ex-girlfriend didn't agree that they were destined for one another was a sign of possible obsession. Julia switched off the lamp and settled back under the duvet. Worn out by the contemplation of her complicated personal and professional relationships, she sank into a deep sleep.

Rain was hammering against the sash window when she woke to the sound of Emmeline wailing. Grace padded past her room, the baby's cries receding as they went downstairs. Glancing at her clock, Julia saw that it was already eight. Grace would need to leave for her tutorial at the university in ten minutes.

Julia used the loo and washed quickly before pulling on black trousers and a red roll neck sweater. Her brunette bob was less sleek than usual after her interrupted night's sleep, but there was no time to wash it. She ran a brush through her hair, tutting to see the grey roots beginning to show through. She'd cancelled a hair appointment to attend Linda's funeral and hadn't yet rearranged. She fastened on a smile as she went into the kitchen, hoping it didn't look as artificial as it felt. Emmeline was sitting at the table in her new high chair, her feeding bottle half-full on the tray in front of her.

Julia planted a kiss on top of the child's head. 'Isn't Emmeline hungry? She usually has all her breakfast bottle.'

Grace didn't reply. Nor did she turn from the counter where she was spreading butter on to a slice of wholemeal toast with rapid strokes.

Julia ran water into the kettle and tried again. 'Did the wind keep you awake?'

Grace gave her a sideways glance as she sliced the toast in two. 'Emmeline kept me awake. Didn't you hear her?'

Julia chose to ignore the underlying question: *'Why didn't you come to help?'* The shadows beneath Grace's eyes looked darker than ever under the spotlights.

'I did. With the wind howling around, her crying probably didn't sound as bad in my room.'

'Lucky you.' Grace nibbled at her toast.

Julia pretended not to hear the disgruntled mutter as she flicked on the kettle. Hearing a clatter, she spun round.

‘Oh, *Emmeline!* I haven’t got time for this!’ Grace’s voice wobbled.

Emmeline began to wail. Milk from her upended Peter Rabbit feeding bottle pooled across the terracotta tiles.

‘It’s OK. I’ll clean it up. You go.’ Julia pulled two squares of kitchen towel off the roll and moved across to wipe up the spillage.

‘Thanks.’

‘No problem.’

Grace grabbed her checked tweed coat from the back of a chair and slid into it. She hefted her rucksack on to her slim shoulders before moving round the table to kiss Emmeline. The baby had stopped crying and was looking down at Julia with interest. Grace paused in the doorway.

‘I’m sorry,’ she said quietly. ‘About last night.’

Julia nodded as she rose from the floor. ‘We were both tired,’ she said. ‘Now go, or you’ll miss the bus.’

Grace managed a smile. ‘Thank you. I’ll be back by ten thirty.’

‘See you later.’

Julia rinsed out the Peter Rabbit bottle and poured fresh milk into it. She released Emmeline from her straps and sat her on her lap, savouring the faint scent of baby soap which lingered on her skin from last night’s bath. ‘You smell so good,’ she murmured. The little girl guzzled her milk greedily.

Julia’s eyes fell on the cream envelope addressed to her and Grace from Linda’s solicitor. She’d left it unopened on the table the night before. Shifting Emmeline on to her left knee, she reached for the envelope and slit it open with her right thumb. She smoothed out the thick cream paper, smiling slightly at the outdated font. She had met Linda’s solicitor once at the hospice. Ralph Purvis was a semi-retired sole practitioner, a grave, portly man with a deferential manner who had struck Julia as belonging to a previous era. He had dealt with Linda's family's affairs for over forty years. The old style typeface suited him well.

Julia had to read the letter twice before its meaning sank in. She set it down on the table, her pulse skittering. Linda had divided her estate in equal shares between Julia and Grace. Mr. Purvis explained that the estate comprised the old farmhouse in North Creake where Linda had lived, together with savings of some £300,000. Linda's artwork was also included, but had not yet been valued. The late artist had made a specific bequest of the 'Open Door' series of paintings to Julia. Julia's eyes misted over at this, visualising the pictures featuring her late mother's cottage which Linda had painted during Emily's final months.

Emmeline squirmed in her lap. Julia removed the empty bottle gently from her mouth and carried her through to the sitting-room with the letter. She lay the little girl down on her back in the jungle baby gym. Emmeline kicked her legs happily as Julia read the letter a third time, struggling to take in her sudden good fortune.

Money had been a problem since her ex-partner Greg had left the previous year, especially as he had failed to tell her that he had defaulted on the mortgage payments. Pete's generosity in paying the arrears had helped, but Julia hadn't liked borrowing from him. Now she had a share in a second property. She set the letter down on the coffee table.

Her mind raced as she tried to absorb the ramifications of the inheritance. She had had no idea of the extent of Linda's wealth. Mr. Purvis had explained that Linda had inherited around half of the capital from the couple who had brought her up as their own daughter when Emily's mother had forced Emily to move to

Norfolk during her pregnancy and leave her illegitimate baby with them.

The rest of Linda's money came from the sale of Linda's early paintings. Julia remembered how modest Linda had been about her art. *'I'm an artist, you won't have heard of me,'* she had said during their first phone conversation. Now Julia, Grace and Emmeline would all benefit from Linda's talent. Their future was financially secure with Linda's savings, let alone the money from the sale of the Norfolk farmhouse.

If they sold it, thought Julia, picturing the rambling grey stone property in its peaceful surroundings. Emmeline began to grizzle. Julia went over and knelt in front of her, idly swinging the plush animals on the arch of the jungle gym. Emmeline chortled. Julia beamed down at her, mentally running through the possibilities for the farmhouse. The outbuildings could be converted into a counselling office, and a reflexology suite for Pete, if Grace agreed... and if he wanted to join them. Julia rocked back on her heels, wondering how Pete would react to her news of the inheritance. Emmeline squawked in protest at her aunt's inattention. Julia leant forward and nudged the brown and cream giraffe, but Emmeline had already screwed up her face and begun to cry.

Picking up the whimpering child, Julia wandered over to the window. Heavy raindrops drummed against the glass, beating a steady rhythm which seemed to soothe Emmeline. Julia turned the child in her arms so that she was facing outwards.

'Not a good morning for a walk, is it?' She jiggled the baby up and down on the window sill. 'Now who's this, anyone we know?' Julia watched the person push open the wrought iron gate and walk briskly up the path. The hem of a black skirt poked out beneath a red waterproof. The woman's face was hidden inside her hood.

Seconds later there was a firm rap on the doorknocker. Julia settled Emmeline on to her left hip. The grandmother clock chimed the half hour as she unlocked the front door. Julia clicked her tongue against her teeth. Hopefully the caller would be a salesperson whom she could send on her way. It was already half past nine and she needed to make a start on cleaning the kitchen.

'Hello?'

'Hello! You must be Julia. I'm so pleased to find you at home. Such a dreadful day, isn't it?' The woman smiled brightly, lowering her hood in the shelter of the porch. She wore large-framed, black glasses.

'It is very wet,' Julia agreed, frowning at the woman's knowledge of her name. 'Do I know you?'

'No. But Grace might have mentioned me. Is she in?'

'No. She should be back at—'

'And this must be Emmeline!' Without waiting for Julia to finish her sentence, the woman bent towards the child. Emmeline buried her face in Julia's side. Julia took a step back into the hall. 'How sweet! Is she shy?'

'She's only four months old. Rather difficult to tell at that age.' Julia compensated for her tartness with a strained smile. She spotted the gold band on the woman's ring finger. 'Shall I tell Grace you called, Mrs...?'

'I could wait, if that would be convenient.'

Julia gripped the door as Emmeline shifted restlessly. 'I'm sorry. It's not a good time, I'm afraid. Grace won't be back for over an hour, and I have some jobs to do before I go off to work.'

'Perhaps I could mind Emmeline? I am practically her grandmother, after all!'

Julia detected a nervous note in the woman's laugh. Her brown eyes widened as she looked more closely at her visitor. 'You're Frances? Grace's stepmother?'

The woman nodded, her corkscrew salt and pepper curls dancing around her wide face. 'That's right! Grace *has* mentioned me then?'

'Yes. She has.' Julia smiled tightly. Grace had spoken extensively of Frances in the counselling sessions she had undertaken with Julia before they knew they were related. Julia had formed an unflattering picture of an over-powering, manipulative woman who had undermined the shaky confidence of her young stepdaughter. But remembering Pete's comment that it would be unfair to judge the woman according to Grace's assessment, Julia realised that this unexpected visit gave her an opportunity to form her own opinion. Cleaning the kitchen would have to wait. She stepped back into the hall. 'Please, come in.'

'Thank you.' Frances followed Julia inside. 'What a sweet cottage!' She tilted her head back as she unzipped her waterproof, gazing up at the beamed ceiling.

'Thanks.' Julia hoisted Emmeline on to her shoulder. 'Can I get you a tea or coffee?'

'Oh, a cup of tea would be lovely! Shall I hang my coat? I don't want to drip all over your beautiful wooden floor!'

Without waiting for a reply, Frances slipped out of her shoes and hung her coat on the stand. Water puddled beneath.

'And how nice to be so close to the city's historic quarter! Though I must say, the castle always strikes me as particularly grim in bad weather like today. Thinking about the poor souls who were imprisoned there, especially those who were executed, makes me shiver.' Frances shuddered theatrically as she followed Julia and

Emmeline into the kitchen. 'Doesn't it bother you, living just below it?'

'It can be a bit forbidding on a day like this,' admitted Julia. 'It's lovely in the summer though.'

'Mm.' Frances didn't look convinced. 'Anyway, let's not talk about such gloomy things with the little one here! Perhaps I could have a cuddle?' She held out her arms eagerly.

Julia handed the baby over, registering a reluctance which made her feel guilty as she flicked on the kettle. As Frances had said, she was effectively Emmeline's grandmother.

Emmeline raised her hand towards Frances's glasses. The woman laughed as she ducked her head out of the way. 'Babies are always so fascinated by glasses, aren't they? I remember Suzanne was just the same.'

'Suzanne is Grace's half-sister, isn't she?' asked Julia. 'How old is she now?'

'Twenty-seven,' said Frances. 'I don't know where the time has gone. They grow up so fast.' She smiled a little regretfully. Emmeline continued to bat her hand in the air, trying to reach the elusive spectacles.

'Shall we go into the sitting-room? Emmeline's toys are in there.' Julia poured the boiled water into the teapot before leading the way into the sitting-room. Frances set her down in the jungle gym.

'She's so adorable!' the woman gushed. She straightened up. Behind the oversized glasses, her brown eyes darted around the room. 'What a comfortable room! Laura Ashley curtains, aren't they?' She went across to the window and fingered the curtains. 'Personally, I would associate that floral pattern with a bedroom. It's quite chintzy, isn't it? But I must say, the curtains work well in such a quaint sitting-room, don't they?'

'I'm glad you think so,' said Julia dryly. 'I think the tea should be brewed now. Milk and sugar?'

'Just milk, please.'

Julia returned to the kitchen and was pouring the tea, when the phone rang. Muttering under her breath at a further interruption, she went out into the hall and picked up.

'Hello?'

'Hello. Julia?'

'Ray!' Julia recognised the Canadian accent of Grace's grandfather immediately. She pressed the fingers of her free hand to her temple. Ray was due to arrive from Norfolk the following week, and she was looking forward to his visit, but she would have to do some extensive cleaning before he came. She must remember to buy some new sheets for the sofa bed in the sitting-room... 'How are you? Are you still able to come next week?'

'Yes, everything is fine. I will arrive on Thursday as planned.' The old man paused for breath, and Julia frowned. His breathing had undoubtedly become more laboured since Linda's death. She thought she would arrange an appointment for him with her doctor when he came up. 'I just thought I would check that you are quite certain you can accommodate me as well as Grace and Emmeline.'

'Of course! It will be a bit of a squash, but we'll manage.'

'It's very kind of you, my dear. I don't expect it will be for long.'

'No. You mentioned the bishop is arranging some retirement housing. But you know you are very welcome here for as long as you like.'

There was a pause before Ray spoke again. 'Thank you.' He chuckled. 'But perhaps that won't be for long either. Who knows at my age?'

'Ray!' A lump formed in Julia's throat. In the short time she had known him, she had become very fond of the elderly priest. As she had told Pete in the office, she genuinely wanted to look after him during his latter years, as she was sure Linda would have done if she had survived the brain tumour. Their short time together seemed a tragedy to her, however much Ray said that their reunion was one of God's miracles. 'I have missed you,' she said sincerely.

'And I you,' said Ray. 'I'm very much looking forward to seeing you all.'

'It will be lovely,' said Julia. 'You can probably hear Emmeline crying, so I'd better go. Bye for now.'

'Goodbye, Julia. Tell Emmeline her great-grandpa needs peace and quiet, won't you?'

His quiet chortle made her smile as she hung up. Back in the kitchen, she closed her eyes as the chaos hit her once again. No chance of making a start on cleaning during Frances's visit. With a sigh, she laid a milk jug and sugar bowl alongside the mugs of tea and placed them on a tray. Kicking the door of the sitting-room open with her foot, she saw Frances start beside the coffee table. A piece of cream paper fluttered from her hand.

'I was just about to read 'Hairy Maclary' to Emmeline.' Frances picked up the board book. 'I saw the letter from the solicitors.' She stooped to retrieve it and returned it to the coffee table. 'What marvellous news for you, Grace and Emmeline!'

9

Julia didn't respond to Frances's reference to the inheritance as she advanced across the sitting-room to the coffee table. Frances stepped aside to give Julia space to set the tea tray down.

'I didn't mean to pry!' insisted Frances. 'I couldn't help noticing the letter.'

Somehow Julia bit back the retort that Frances could have helped herself reading it. 'I hope your tea isn't cold,' she said, placing a mug on the side table by the blue fabric sofa. 'I had to take a phone call.' She sat on the edge of her usual armchair.

Frances hesitated. Julia suspected she was going to say something else about the inheritance. But after a moment Frances lifted her mug and drank. 'Perfect!' she breathed. 'I do like a cup of strong tea on a rainy day, don't you?' She flashed her teeth again.

Julia shrugged non-committally. Frances's smile disappeared. She went across to the jungle gym and lifted Emmeline from the mat. Seating herself on the sofa, she beamed down at the child wriggling under her right arm. 'Now then, Emmeline, would you like Granny to read you a story?'

Julia's hand froze around her mug as Frances began to read. *Granny.* The woman hadn't seen her stepdaughter for months, had never even met Emmeline before today.

What did she mean, turning up out of the blue, swanning into Julia's sitting-room, making comments about the cottage and décor, and now asserting grandmother's rights? Julia could just about cope with Frances pointing out that she was effectively Emmeline's grandmother, but recoiled from hearing the woman calling herself 'Granny' so soon.

Julia comforted herself that Emmeline's attitude towards their visitor wasn't one of unqualified welcome either. She usually loved 'Hairy Maclary', especially when Julia acted out the parts of the other canines encountered by the dog on his urban walk. But as soon as Frances began to read, Emmeline started to cry again. Undeterred by the baby's rising wails, Frances read on to the end of the book.

'A bit grumpy this morning, aren't we?' she said brightly. She put the board book down on the arm of the sofa. A small fist promptly knocked it to the floor. Emmeline raised her arms towards Julia.

Frances's smile finally wavered as she passed the baby over. 'It will take time for you to get to know Granny, won't it? But what fun we shall have!'

Emmeline snuggled her downy head into Julia's shoulder, her cries subsiding immediately. Settling back in her armchair, Julia rubbed Emmeline's back beneath her maroon cord pinafore. The action soothed her as well as the little girl. She decided it was time to be direct.

'I'm wondering what brought you here today, Frances?'

Frances blinked. 'I came to see Grace and my granddaughter of course!'

'Why now, after you haven't seen Grace for so long? I think I'm right in saying this is the first time you've seen your *step*-granddaughter?' Julia remembered that Grace had told her about Frances's lecture about 'immorality' when Grace had disclosed her pregnancy to her stepmother.

Frances frowned. 'But hasn't Grace told you? She rang me yesterday evening, saying how much she wanted to see me, and how she was longing for me to meet Emmeline.' Frances leant forward, eyes wider than ever behind the large glasses. 'She thinks I might be able to help with childcare so she can carry on with her studying. I'm sure that will be a relief for you too, won't it? It must be such a struggle, trying to keep house as well as working and helping Grace look after Emmeline.'

'We manage,' said Julia coolly.

Frances sighed. 'It's no secret I was shocked when Grace told me she was expecting a baby.' She grasped the plain silver cross pendant which nestled in her ample bosom. 'Her late father would have been most disappointed that Grace isn't married, let alone that she isn't in a settled relationship with the child's father, whoever he is.' She shook her head. 'But Emmeline is here now, and every child is a precious gift from God, aren't they?'

She paused. Julia sipped her tea without replying.

Frances sniffed. 'I'm not quite sure how to put this.' She smoothed her black pencil skirt over her knees. 'Shall we say that there are different degrees of managing? I mean, I can see from your kitchen – I hope you don't mind me saying this – that you are only barely coping. It's so important a kitchen is clean, isn't it, to avoid germs, especially when there's a baby in the house?'

Julia stared at her. Frances raised a palm.

'I'm sorry. I didn't mean to give offence. I realise how difficult it is with a small child.' She raised a forefinger to her mouth, apparently undecided about her next words. 'I know too how difficult Grace can be to live with.' She screwed up her eyes. 'Or perhaps I shouldn't have said that?'

A beat passed before Julia found her voice. Emmeline lay still against her right shoulder, emitting an occasional snuffle.

'No, I don't think you should. I also don't think that you should have come here uninvited, passed comment on my house and its cleanliness, or read my private correspondence!' The pulse in Julia's neck had begun to throb. She took a steadying breath.

Frances held up both hands. 'Please, I didn't come here to argue. Perhaps I should have phoned you, but I assumed Grace would have told you about our conversation.' She took another sip of tea, then looked at Julia earnestly over the rim of her mug. 'I believe the Lord is asking me to help Grace and Emmeline,' she said in a rush. 'This is very difficult for me. Grace and I haven't had the easiest relationship. As you know, the poor girl's mother was certified and placed in an asylum. I'm afraid Grace's separation from her mother when she was a baby damaged her.' She sighed. 'I don't know what Grace has told you, but she found it very difficult to accept me when I met and married her late father.' Unexpectedly, her face crumpled and she began to cry. Groping in the sleeve of her pink blouse, she extracted a tissue.

Julia looked away tactfully, her irritation with the woman's high-handedness giving way to sympathy. 'I'm sorry for your loss.'

'Thank you. I still miss Philip dreadfully.' Frances twisted the tissue in her hands.

'Of course.' Julia waited a moment, making sure Frances had fully regained her composure, before continuing, 'But I can assure you that Grace knows she and Emmeline are welcome to stay for as long as she wishes, and that I will help as much as I can with looking after Emmeline.'

'Are you quite sure Grace knows that?' Frances leant forward again, stuffing the tissue back into her sleeve. 'She sounded overwrought when she phoned last night, worried about her studying. I could hear Emmeline crying in the background, poor little one.' She cast a fond glance towards the baby, before transferring her gaze back to Julia. 'I think you were out, weren't you?'

If this was intended as a barb, Julia chose to ignore it. 'It was never going to be easy for Grace to balance her studying with looking after a small baby,' she said. 'I've suggested she could extend her maternity leave from university, but she doesn't want to.'

Frances raised her ginger eyebrows. 'Naturally you don't know my stepdaughter very well after such a brief time. Let me tell you, as the one who brought her up, that studying is Grace's passion. When I first met her as a little girl, she was always reading.' She pursed her lips. 'I've sometimes wondered if it was because she couldn't deal with the real world that she buried herself in her books. That can happen, can't it?'

'Maybe,' replied Julia neutrally. 'Although I would suspect the obvious explanation is that someone has a genuine love of reading.'

Frances made a fold in her skirt. 'I have wondered,' she said, her tone tentative, 'whether Grace's intense focus on her studying might be similar to her mother's obsession with her art. What do you think?'

'I think there is a difference between passion and obsession,' said Julia quickly, not wanting to agree that the thought had occurred to her. 'If people have talents and interests, it's natural that they will want to pursue them.'

Frances shrugged. 'Well, you are the counsellor. You would know more than I do about mental illness running in families, I suppose.' She hesitated, twisting the wedding ring she still wore around her finger. 'If Linda *did* suffer from mental illness,' she went on, almost to herself. She looked across at Julia. 'That's the current diagnosis according to human wisdom, isn't it?'

Julia frowned. 'What do you mean?'

Frances leant further forward and lowered her voice. 'There are often spiritual dimensions to these conditions, aren't there?'

'Really?' Julia injected as much scepticism into the two syllables as she could.

'I realise this will be difficult for you to understand, since you don't share my faith.' Frances fingered her cross again and ran her tongue over her cerise lips. 'Perhaps I should be clear. My belief is that Linda's illness was a symptom of demonic manifestation.'

Julia knew from Grace that this was Frances's interpretation of Linda's illness. She found it difficult to believe that anyone could hold such a view in 2002. Hearing the words from the other woman, and seeing how earnest she was, Julia struggled to suppress a shudder.

'I am certain that Linda suffered from postpartum psychosis after Grace was born,' she said firmly. The pulse in her neck was throbbing again. 'It was a misunderstood condition in the late 1960s. What happened was tragic, for Linda and for Grace.' She paused. 'And no doubt for your late husband too.'

Frances's eyes narrowed. 'It was undoubtedly a difficult experience for Philip,' she said stiffly. 'One he came to see as a necessary trial on his route to knowing the Lord.'

'Is that right?' Julia held the other woman's gaze. 'What about Linda, taken into psychiatric care, separated from her baby? Grace too, for that matter?'

'Grace's mother was clearly a danger to herself and her family,' replied Frances. 'Grace was very fortunate to be brought up in a Christian home after the disadvantages of her infancy.' She raised her square chin, daring Julia to contradict her.

Julia found herself lost for words.

'Philip and I were so blessed when Suzanne came along,' Frances went on. 'She never caused us a moment's concern.' She sighed and fiddled with the pleat in her skirt. 'Not then, anyway.'

'Oh?' asked Julia, curious about any problems caused by Suzanne. Grace had always presented her sister as the favourite.

'I'm sure it will blow over.' But Frances's flickering smile led Julia to suspect that the woman wasn't at all certain that her concerns about Suzanne would be resolved easily. Frances returned to the subject of her stepdaughter. 'Grace has always been a worry though.'

Julia raised an eyebrow, remembering Grace describing how she had been sidelined when Suzanne was born. Emmeline squirmed suddenly against her shoulder. Glancing through the window, Julia saw her niece coming up the path. As Julia watched, Grace kicked at a pile of sodden brown leaves, her head lowered beneath her umbrella. Its white polka dots on the lilac background struck Julia as pathetically defiant against the hammering rain.

From Grace's body language, Julia suspected that the tutorial hadn't gone well. How would she react to finding Frances here? She might have called her stepmother out of desperation last night, but that didn't mean she was prepared to see her this morning.

'Grace is back,' she said. 'I'll let her know you're here.'

'No need!' Frances leapt to her feet with surprising alacrity for a stout woman. 'Let me surprise her!' She almost ran out of the sitting-room.

'Grace! It's so good to see you!' Frances opened her arms in welcome as her stepdaughter came through the door, dripping on to the doormat.

Grace's blue eyes widened. 'Frances?' She shrugged off her rucksack and laid it down alongside the open umbrella. Unbuttoning her coat, she leant forward briefly into Frances's embrace. 'I didn't expect you.'

'I felt I had to come after you phoned last night. You sounded so upset! Besides, I so wanted to meet this little one!' Frances turned to Julia, grasping Emmeline's ankle and swinging it against Julia's hip. The baby arched her back and began to cry.

'Tea, Grace?' Julia moved towards the kitchen as Grace hung her coat on the stand.

'Please.'

'I'd love another,' chimed in Frances. 'We'll take Emmeline whilst you make it.' She followed Julia to the door of the kitchen, arms open.

Julia handed the child over. Emmeline's cries intensified. Julia couldn't help smiling to herself as she re-filled the kettle with fresh water, whilst simultaneously berating herself for her uncharitable attitude. Emmeline was no doubt grizzly after her disturbed night, and not in the mood to cope with an unknown visitor.

As Julia prepared the tea, she pondered her impression of Frances. Grace had painted an off-putting picture of her stepmother. She was certainly overbearing, and Julia could imagine she had favoured her own daughter

Suzanne over her bookish stepdaughter Grace as they grew up together. But the woman's grief for her late husband appeared genuine, and she did seem to have visited out of concern for the welfare of Grace and Emmeline following Grace's phone call the previous evening.

What had most irritated Julia though, was Frances's interest in the correspondence from Linda's solicitor. No doubt she would have passed on the news to Grace by now, even though she had no business doing so.

Julia's suspicion was proved correct. As she took the mugs of tea into the sitting-room, Frances beamed towards her from the jungle gym. Emmeline was batting the plush parrot on the arch above with a small fist. 'I hope you don't mind that I've shared the good news with Grace. I couldn't wait!'

Julia deposited the mugs on the coffee table without replying. Grace was standing by the window, head bent over Mr. Purvis's letter.

'Your father and I always told you the Lord provides, didn't we, Grace? Oh, I'm so thrilled for you, and this little one!' She knelt beside Emmeline, extending her forefinger. The baby ignored it, turning her head away from the parrot towards the monkey. 'So many decisions to make!'

Grace looked up from the letter, a small cleft in her forehead. 'Decisions?'

'Yes! What you're going to do with your late mother's house, where you will live... I expect you'll want to sell it, won't you, so you can buy somewhere of your own in Lincoln?'

Grace pushed her plait over her shoulder. 'I don't know,' she said. 'It's a lot to take in.'

'Of course. But it struck me immediately that's the obvious decision, isn't it?' Frances stood and turned to Julia. 'How wonderful for you too. You'll be able to make some home improvements, won't you?' She gave a little laugh which set Julia's teeth on edge. 'I couldn't help noticing the kitchen looks rather tired, and the double glazing is breaking down in that sash window, isn't it?' She pointed towards the left window of the pair which overlooked the front garden. Condensation had misted it over. 'Fortunately, Philip left me very well provided for. Our house is in excellent condition, isn't it, Grace?'

Grace darted a quick glance at Julia, then away again. She bit her thumb. The childishness of the gesture made Julia catch her breath. *Stand up to her, Grace,* she thought, but the younger woman only nodded meekly.

'It is a lovely house,' she agreed. 'Very comfortable.'

'So spacious,' purred Frances. 'I have ambitions to add a conservatory too. There is always so much scope with a house, isn't there? Especially a sizeable one. I'm assuming you have just two bedrooms here, do you?'

'That's right.' Julia spoke through gritted teeth.

'So Grace and Emmeline are sharing. And didn't you say there will be another visitor next week, Grace?'

'Yes. My grandfather.'

'Of course. You did say.' Frances wrinkled her nose as though she had smelled something unpleasant. It crossed Julia's mind that Emmeline must need changing, but she had the impression Frances's distaste related to the complicated family history. 'Very elderly of course, so he'll be staying down here, I suppose?'

'Yes,' said Julia. She indicated the blue sofa. 'This opens into a sofa bed.'

'I see.' Frances put her finger to her lip thoughtfully. 'It is going to be rather cramped, isn't it? I'm just wondering…' She turned towards Grace, palms open. 'Grace, dear, I know we've had our differences, but you would be very welcome back at home. You could have your old room back. And then there is the spare, which would be just perfect for a nursery. I can see it's rather cramped here. With only Suzanne and me in our four bedrooms, we do rattle around! What do you think?'

Grace chewed the end of her plait. Julia swallowed back words assuring Grace that she and Emmeline could stay at the cottage as long as they liked, sensing how important it was that Grace should answer for herself. Beneath the jungle gym, Emmeline had become very still, as if she too were awaiting her mother's decision with bated breath.

'That's kind, Frances, thank you.' Grace's voice was thin and tremulous. 'But Aunt Julia has made me and Emmeline very welcome here. It would be nice to spend some time with Grandpa too.'

'I see.' There was undisguised disappointment in Frances's tone. 'I do understand you feel obliged.'

'It's not that—' began Grace, but her stepmother raised her hand.

'You don't need to explain yourself. Just bear in mind that I could help with childcare, since I'm in the fortunate position of not needing to work.' Frances flicked a glance towards Julia. 'There is also the advantage that if you had your own room, you might get more sleep. I've never been sure it's a good idea for a baby to sleep with their parents. Suzanne never did. Don't some of the experts think there's a risk it can hamper independence?'

Grace looked down at the floor. 'I'm not sure,' she mumbled. Her demeanour was that of a child who didn't know the answer to a simple question and feared a scolding from their teacher.

'I believe so. Obviously, you're not in a position to do otherwise in the circumstances here. Do remember, if you change your mind, the offer is there.' She squatted beside Emmeline, taking her tiny hand and shaking it. Emmeline screwed her face up and Frances hastily stood again. 'It's been so wonderful to meet you, darling. I'm sure Grace will bring you to visit Granny soon, won't you?'

'Yes,' said Grace obediently.

Frances picked up her black shoulder bag. 'Thank you for the tea,' she said to Julia. 'Do get in touch if you would like me to recommend someone for the window. We had a very good contractor when we replaced ours three years ago.'

'I'll bear that in mind.' Julia led the way to the front door.

Frances zipped up her waterproof and addressed Julia in a stage whisper. 'She doesn't look well to me. Very pale and tired. Do ring me if you need any help. Remember what happened to her mother!' She nodded meaningfully, eyebrows raised above the oversized glasses.

Despite the driving rain and the wind which slammed the kitchen door behind her, Julia watched every step Frances took through the gate and along the street. It was only when the woman had plodded out of view that Julia closed the door and breathed again.

10

Julia leant against the front door after Frances's departure. She shook her arms and dusted herself down, acting again upon the advice to dispel the 'bad vibes' left behind by difficult clients. The physical action was refreshing. She returned to the sitting-room as the grandmother clock chimed the half hour. She was cutting it fine to get to the office in time for her first client, but she wanted to speak to Grace before she left.

Grace was sitting in the armchair, bouncing Emmeline up and down on her lap. The little girl gurgled in delight. Grace's smile was strained as she stifled a yawn. Observing from the doorway, Julia felt a twinge of sadness, wishing that Grace could enjoy this precious time of her young daughter's life more fully. She pasted a smile on her own face as she advanced into the room.

'Someone seems happy!'

'Now Frances has gone, you mean?' Grace's expression was unreadable.

'No. Although Emmeline didn't seem very settled whilst Frances was here.'

'She's never settled, is she? This is unusual. Look.' Grace stopped jumping the baby up and down. Emmeline screwed up her face immediately.

'Maybe she just wants to keep playing with her mummy?'

Grace jiggled Emmeline again. Sure enough, the baby's smiles were restored. Grace's brow puckered.

'I don't have time to play with her all day. I'm already behind with my research schedule.'

'Is that what your tutor said?'

Grace turned her head away. 'He didn't need to.'

Julia perched on the edge of the sofa. It was still warm from Frances sitting there. Julia instinctively inched further along.

'So what gives you the impression you're behind with your research?'

Grace stood abruptly, prompting a flurry of cries from her startled daughter. Grace paced the floor, rubbing Emmeline's back.

'I can see from my schedule.'

'Is that your original schedule, or the adjusted one you came up with during your maternity leave?'

Grace's mouth tightened. 'The original one.'

'So you are on track with the revised timetable? That sounds pretty good to me.'

Grace chewed the inside of her cheek. 'I suppose so. The thing is, I saw one of the women who started at the same time as me earlier. She's on to her fourth chapter. I've barely written anything yet, just the beginning of chapter one. I'm still ploughing through books and articles.'

'I'm assuming this woman hasn't had a baby?'

'No. But I did better than her in my master's. I was awarded a distinction. She got a merit.'

Grace's voice had assumed the whining tone which was becoming all too familiar to Julia. It was an effort for the older woman to keep the impatience from her voice. 'So you're finding it difficult to see her moving ahead now?'

Grace rolled her eyes. 'Obviously!'

Julia blinked at the vehemence, struggling to maintain her encouraging attitude in face of her niece's abrasiveness. 'You will get there, Grace. Surely it doesn't matter whether it's in two or three years. It isn't a competition.'

A flash of anger darkened her niece's face. 'That's what you don't get, Aunt Julia. There are only a limited number of jobs in academia, and there's a research post coming up at the uni next year. It's the kind of opportunity I dreamed of when I decided to quit teaching sixth form and do my thesis. If Anna finishes her PhD, she'll go for it. I know she will.'

'I see.'

'But you don't, do you? I'm stuck here with Emmeline most of the time. I just can't get on! I'm going to get left behind, struggle to find a job. I'd love to work as an academic.' She laid Emmeline down in the jungle gym. Her back to Julia, she continued, 'Maybe Frances is right. If I go back to hers, she could look after Emmeline during the day. She hasn't had to work for years. My father earned plenty, and he's left her comfortably off.'

'How fortunate for her.' Julia regretted her acid tone as Grace turned and stared at her. 'Sorry. Some of us women work because we enjoy it, you know. That's what you just said you wanted, isn't it?'

Grace glanced towards Emmeline. From the baby's half-hearted flick at the plush parrot dangling from the arch above her, it looked as though she was about to take a nap. 'Of course. That's why the sooner I can finish my thesis, the better.'

'I understand that.' Julia attempted a smile, hoping to lighten the tension in the room, which felt as oppressive as the lowering sky outside. Rain continued to cascade down the sash windows. 'You're not seriously thinking of going to live with Frances, are you?'

Grace shrugged. 'It's a possibility.'

'Right.' Julia looked from Grace to Emmeline, who had suddenly become very still. She was gazing at Julia wide-eyed, as though she understood their discussion would have an impact on her.

Julia's stomach contracted as she realised how much she would miss seeing the baby every day. She pushed the thought away, telling herself that her main concern had to be Grace's well-being and not her own wishes. 'After all you've told me about Frances! How overpowering you find her. Are you sure it would be good for you to go back there?'

Grace pulled at her plait. 'I don't know. But it might be better for my thesis. And Frances does mean well. It was kind of her to come round this morning after I phoned her last night. It's so difficult with Emmeline.' On cue, the baby began to wail. 'There you go! Isn't it past your morning nap time, Emmeline?'

Julia took a deep breath. 'Babies do sense tension, Grace. I don't think your raised voice is helping.'

'What would you know? It's not as though you have the experience, is it?'

Julia stared back without replying.

Grace broke the eye contact as she sank down in the armchair. 'I'm sorry,' she said, her voice small. 'I shouldn't have said that. I don't know what came over me.' She looked up at her aunt, wide blue eyes bright with unshed tears.

'Apology accepted,' said Julia quietly. She paused, conscious of the grandmother clock steadily ticking away the minutes to her eleven o'clock appointment in the hall. But she sensed that she couldn't let this further verbal attack pass. 'Grace, I know you're struggling, and that it's difficult juggling Emmeline and your thesis. I'm not your punch bag though, OK?'

Grace nodded miserably. 'I am so sorry,' she repeated. She turned her head away. 'It's not an excuse,' she continued, her voice low. 'Something else happened at uni.'

'What was it? What happened?'

Grace dashed away a tear with the back of her hand. 'I bumped into my ex-boyfriend. I'd popped into the library to look at a journal article, and he was there by the river when I came out. He said he'd seen me going in and decided to wait.'

'Did you tell him about Emmeline?' ventured Julia cautiously.

Grace frowned. 'No. Why would I?'

Julia stood and went over to the jungle gym. Emmeline smiled up at her sleepily. Julia framed her next question carefully. 'Wouldn't it be better for Emmeline to have her father in her life, Grace?'

'No.' Grace shook her head vigorously, her plait bouncing from side to side. 'I don't want anything to do with my ex. You don't know what he's like!' She crossed her legs, jiggling her right foot up and down.

Julia crouched beside Emmeline, idly swishing the plush giraffe on the arch above the jungle gym. It was clear from their conversation that Grace wanted nothing more to do with the man, whoever he was, but Julia couldn't help agreeing with Pete that he should be made aware of the child's existence. However, she didn't have time to pursue the matter now. Nor did she want to alienate Grace who was clearly stressed about her thesis.

Her right leg numb beneath her, Julia stood unsteadily and rose up and down on her toes, gazing unseeingly through the misted window. Maybe it would be simpler for Grace and Emmeline to move in with Frances after all, much as she would miss them, Emmeline in particular. With Frances clearly enthusiastic to offer child care, it would relieve Grace so that she could progress her studies.

The grandmother clock chimed the three quarters, breaking into her thoughts. She groaned. 'I really have to go. Sorry. Shall we talk more later?'

'I don't think there's anything left to say.' Two red spots flamed in Grace's cheeks. 'I'm not telling my ex about Emmeline, and that's the end of it.' She glared at Julia, daring her to contradict her.

Julia bent to plant a quick kiss on Emmeline's strawberry blonde head. She wrinkled her nose as the unmistakable smell of ammonia wafted upwards. 'I think Emmeline needs changing, don't you?'

'Probably.' Grace didn't stir from the armchair. 'I'll do it in a minute.'

Julia dashed into the kitchen to pick up her handbag and laptop from the table. She shook her head at the mess which she had been unable to clear because of Frances's unexpected visit. No doubt if Emmeline took a nap, Grace would take the opportunity to get on with her research rather than tidy up, despite their conversation the previous evening.

Inside the Mondeo, Julia switched on the radio, tuned to Classic FM. Strains of Vaughan Williams's 'Lark Ascending' were a welcome reminder of spring, and of the peace which seemed so elusive in her household at present. Despite her lateness, Julia leant back against the headrest, allowing the soaring notes of the violin to soothe her. After a moment she reluctantly flicked on the indicator, glancing automatically over her right shoulder to check her blind spot.

Her left hand jerked on the steering wheel in response to a sudden movement on the opposite side of the street. Through the slanting rain, she could make out someone squatting in a black coat behind a lamp post. The person was evidently tying their shoelaces. Julia smiled wryly as she pulled out on to the quiet street. Frances's visit and another tense exchange with Grace had jangled her nerves more than she had realised.

It was five past eleven when she entered the office, windswept and wet from the short walk from the car park. She registered relief in Pete's smile as she unzipped her waterproof.

'There you are!' He glanced towards her client who was seated ramrod straight on one of the four functional chairs.

'I'm so sorry, the traffic was heavy. The weather always makes it worse, doesn't it?'

Julia's client didn't return the pleasantry. She eyed her watch pointedly before following Julia into her office. Julia had established a good rapport with the middle-aged woman during their previous six sessions. Her client had admitted at their first meeting that she was suffering a particularly bad case of empty nest syndrome after her youngest child had gone to university. Having given up her teaching career to be a homemaker, the woman had sought Julia's help to 'look for a new direction'. Julia had expected today's session to be straightforward, but where her client had previously been enthusiastic about possible voluntary work and college courses, she spent most of the fifty minutes talking herself out of various options.

It was a relief when the session drew to an end, although Julia was sufficiently self-aware to know that she had found it unusually tedious because of her lateness and domestic difficulties. Alone in her office after she had seen her client out, she sank down in her chair and closed her eyes. The faint sound of panpipes drifted through the wall which separated her room from Pete's. He must have taken a client in during her session.

The vibration of her mobile roused her. Fishing it out from the front pocket of her black handbag, her heart sank when she saw the caller was James.

'Hi, James. How are you?'

'If you want the truth and not the standard response, pretty bloody awful.'

Julia stifled a sigh. 'I'm sorry. What's happened?'

'Divorce papers.'

'Oh.'

'You don't sound surprised. Don't tell me you knew.'

Julia hesitated. 'I did see Clare last night.'

'Great. So you didn't think you should warn me?'

'Well, no. I didn't want to worry you.'

'You didn't want to worry me? After I'd made it clear I hoped we might get back together? Didn't you think it was worth letting me know so I could try to speak to her?'

Julia focused on the wall clock above the filing cabinet. Her next client was due in ten minutes. 'The papers were already in the post,' she said. 'Maybe I could have warned you, but I'm not sure it would have helped.'

'Surely I'm the judge of that! Why is it you always think you know best?'

'It wasn't like that. Clare seemed to have made up her mind.'

'All the more reason to warn me then, surely?'

'James, it was only last night. I've not had the chance to contact you.'

'Too busy with lover boy?'

If only. 'No, actually. Other things.'

'Too many troubled souls? Shouldn't you make sure you've got time to help those closer to home in their distress?'

There was no mistaking the sneer in James's voice. Julia finally snapped. 'Maybe if they didn't bring problems on themselves, disappear for months and then expect me to pick up the pieces, I'd be more ready to help.'

There was a pause before James said sulkily, 'I *had* to go. Sabbaticals don't come round that often. I have to make the most of research opportunities. If I don't get something published soon, my job might be axed in the next round of cuts. Between that and Clare...'

Julia heard the tremor in his voice. 'I'm sorry, James, I had no idea you were under pressure at work as well.' She plucked a speck of lint off her black trousers. 'Look, you will take it easy, won't you?'

'What do you mean?'

It would have been better if they were face to face. Julia plunged on anyway. 'I realise you've got a lot to deal with. But when you called in yesterday, I could smell the alcohol.'

There was no reply as the line went dead.

Julia was still staring at her phone when Pete knocked on the door and poked his shaved head round.

'Hi. It's not like you to be late. Everything OK?'

Julia leant forward to replace her phone in her handbag. 'Not great. That was James. He hung up on me.'

'Ah. Something you said?'

Julia sighed. 'I did mention his drinking. But he's upset because he's got the divorce papers from Clare.'

Pete grimaced. 'She's made her mind up fast, hasn't she? Not wasted any time since he got back from sabbatical.'

'No. She made her decision when he was away. That was clear when I saw her yesterday. James isn't happy that I didn't warn him.'

'Would you have told me when I rang last night?'

There was a casualness in Pete's tone which made Julia look at him more intently. She had forgotten about their truncated phone call.

'Probably. Sorry I couldn't speak. Emmeline was crying.'

'So you said.'

Julia rose from her armchair and stifled a yawn. She steered the conversation away from the topic which had led to their disagreement the day before. 'I had an unexpected visitor this morning. Frances turned up.'

'Wow. Was she as bad as you expected from Grace?'

Julia chewed her lip, thinking. 'Probably not,' she admitted. 'Rather domineering, but missing her late husband. She seemed genuinely concerned about Grace and Emmeline. She was nosey though,' she added, picturing Frances reading the letter from Linda's solicitors. She found that she didn't want to mention the inheritance to Pete yet, not until she'd thought further about the possibility of them living and working together in Norfolk. 'She suggested Grace and Emmeline should move to hers so she could help with childcare.'

'What did Grace say?'

'She said she would think about it. She's worried about her research.'

'Doesn't sound a bad idea to me.'

'I knew you'd say that.' Julia rubbed the bridge of her nose and yawned. 'I'm not sure it's the best thing for Grace personally. She seemed quite overpowered by Frances.'

'It would help her with Emmeline though. Could be a good short-term solution, until Grace finishes her thesis.' Pete paused, blue eyes scanning Julia's face. 'You know my feelings. It would help you – *us* – too.' He touched her lightly on the shoulder.

Julia looked down. 'Let's not get into all this again,' she said quietly.

Pete withdrew his hand. 'All right. How about nipping out for lunch? My next client isn't due till two.'

'Sorry. I've got one in a few minutes.'

'This evening then?'

'I'd love to, but I was out last night with Clare, and Grace seems really tired. I don't feel I should go out again today.'

Pete held up his right hand. 'OK. I get it.' He smiled, but she had heard the edge in his voice.

'I'm sorry. Why don't you come over on Friday for dinner?'

He raised an eyebrow. 'That'd be with you, Grace and Emmeline?'

'Well, yes.'

'Not exactly romantic, is it?'

She flushed beneath his gaze. Looking at him properly for the first time during their conversation, she noticed that he too looked tired, his face tinged with grey, uncharacteristic dark shadows beneath his eyes. Thinking back to their interrupted phone call the night before, she steered the conversation on to safer ground. 'Everything is all right with you, isn't it?'

He fiddled with his ear stud, then opened his mouth. The buzzer on the reception desk sounded. 'That'll be your client.' He backed out through the door. 'Catch you later.'

'Pete...'

He turned towards her on the threshold of his own office, his usual crinkly-eyed smile in place. 'Everything's fine, Jules.'

She smiled back uncertainly, wishing she believed him.

11

It was 4.15 p.m. when Julia left the office on Friday after her last client failed to show for an initial session. It wasn't unusual for people to miss first appointments, and after a hectic week, the extra hour was welcome. Pete would be pleased with the early finish too. He had voiced misgivings about her being in the premises alone, even offering to forego a training course he had booked on to months previously.

Julia had laughed off his concern. Now, with the light already fading after another wet and windy day, she found herself glancing over her shoulder as she locked up. There were few pedestrians around, although the street was busy with traffic. One reason she and Pete had chosen the location was that the rent was lower away from the main shopping area around St. Mark's Square. They had redecorated the unit before moving in, and it looked cheerful enough on a sunny day. But in the gathering gloom of a late October afternoon, the rundown atmosphere was palpable.

Julia hurried along, head down against the driving rain. In the distance she heard the warning noise of the level crossing barrier. Traffic ground to a halt. Diesel fumes from an ancient bus caught in her throat. Nauseated, she turned away. Faint notes of a treble recorder reached her ears above the sound of the idling engines and the crossing siren. She recognised the haunting tune of 'Memory' from the Lloyd-Webber musical 'Cats' and swallowed. Her late mother Emily had loved the song. Julia had taken her to the West End show one Christmas. A sudden vivid image of her mother dashing away tears as the soprano's voice soared came to her. It struck Julia that the lyrics must have held great poignancy for Emily, recalling her wartime love affair.

Julia slowed as she drew alongside the recorder player. He was sitting in the doorway of a boarded up former café, and wore an oversized donkey jacket and battered trilby. His grimy fingers moved deftly over the wooden instrument. Julia scrabbled in her pocket for some loose change to add to the coppers and silver in the polystyrene cup in front of him. Then, as the final notes soared to their plaintive conclusion, and with her mother's face still clear in her mind's eye, she impulsively opened her shoulder bag. Digging out her purse, she extracted a five pound note.

As Julia stooped to place the cash in the cup, the man looked up at her. Instinctively she took a step backwards. The left side of his face was red and blistered, the eye so tiny that it was barely visible. For a moment he held her gaze with his good right eye, before lowering his head over the well-worn recorder.

'Thanks, duck,' he said gruffly. He coughed before embarking on another poignant tune. Julia moved off, identifying 'Annie's Song' just before the music was drowned out by the train rattling along the track towards the city station. It wasn't only the song she knew, she realised, weaving across the road through the stationary traffic. It was the man's voice and his cough. It was the same man whom she had spoken with near 'Giuseppe's'. She recalled Clare's disapproval that she had asked his name. *Derek.* She wished she hadn't recoiled at the sight of his burnt face, although the poor man must be used to that reaction.

She turned down the side street leading to the car park, pondering the coincidence of coming across him so soon after their last encounter. But how many people were there in this city whom she saw every day without any mutual recognition? Meeting Derek again wasn't so unexpected; the number of rough sleepers in Lincoln was relatively low compared to other cities. She decided to mention it to Ray when he came to visit – the retired priest was convinced that individuals come into our lives for a reason. The agnostic Julia didn't share his view, although she found it interesting. Looking back over the last week, it was hardly an appealing perspective. There had been the unsettling initial session with Mark Smeaton on Tuesday, and she had ambivalent feelings about Frances's unexpected visit.

She remembered how spooked Grace had been bumping into her ex at the university too. Julia had avoided the topic after their difficult conversation about Emmeline's paternity on Wednesday morning. Yesterday Grace had heard that some books she had requested had been returned to the university library. Julia had offered to take care of Emmeline whilst Grace collected them. Given Grace's concern to finish her thesis as quickly as possible, Julia had been surprised when Grace had said that she would leave the books at the library for a few days.

'I don't want to risk seeing him again.' Grace tugged at her plait in the way she did when stressed. 'Not so soon after yesterday. He's too pushy. Did I tell you he asked me to go for a coffee? He said he had things to tell me, hinted he wants us to get back together. I just don't want to know.'

Seeing how determined Grace was to avoid any further chance meeting with her ex, Julia hadn't pressed her to collect the books. But she did feel that Grace was over-reacting, and that this was another sign of the younger woman's fragile mental state. Pete had a point when he talked about paternity rights, and Julia was uneasy about Grace's refusal to allow Emmeline's father any part in her life.

She thought that she might discuss the matter with Ray. Grace was very fond of the grandfather she had only known for eight months. If anyone could persuade her to reconsider her decision to keep Emmeline's father in the dark about the child's existence, it would be him.

As Julia turned into the car park and extracted her car key from her coat pocket, she wondered if Grace had thought any further about Frances's suggestion that she and Emmeline should move in with her. The more Julia considered it, the more certain she was that it would help Grace in terms of progressing her research. With Frances available and enthusiastic to look after Emmeline, that would relieve Grace of trying to juggle childcare and study. On the other hand, Julia hadn't been able to shake off misgivings about the rapidity with which Frances had sought to draw a parallel between Grace's fervour for her studies and Linda's passion for her art. Julia was fearful that Frances might be too quick to jump to the conclusion that Grace had inherited her mother's psychiatric illness. But that possibility was much more acceptable to Julia than the woman's suggestion that Linda's condition was a symptom of demonic manifestation. That was so alien to Julia's perspective that she had dismissed it outright.

‘Excuse me.’ A man’s voice behind her startled Julia. She dropped the car key into standing water in front of her Mondeo. ‘Sorry, I didn’t mean to frighten you.’ The voice was vaguely familiar.

Julia stooped awkwardly over her laptop case and bag to retrieve the key, trailing her coat sleeve in the puddle. Then she turned to face the man, shaking water from the key. Her heart skipped a beat when she saw that it was Mark Smeaton, the client who had disturbed her during their first meeting earlier in the week. She had the uncanny thought that she had spirited him up after thinking about him a few minutes earlier.

‘It’s you,’ he said, sounding surprised.

Julia could just make out his smile in the fading light. She summoned a smile in return. She was suddenly conscious that no-one else was around. There were only around a dozen cars left on the car park, which was mainly used by office workers.

‘Hello.’ Julia kept her voice even with an effort. ‘How can I help?’ She clutched the key and took a couple of steps backward towards her car.

‘No chance you have a pound coin, is there? Machine spat mine out.’ He jerked his head in the direction of the ticket dispenser by the entrance.

‘I might have. Let me see.’ Telling herself that there was no reason for her unease, Julia flicked the remote and opened the rear door of the Mondeo, placing her bag and laptop on the floor behind the driver’s seat. Her purse was in her bag, but she was reluctant to take that out in the deserted car park. She barely knew this man. She closed the rear door.

Fishing in her coat pocket, Julia extracted some loose change. She found a pound coin and slipped the rest of the money back into her pocket. Mark Smeaton moved a few paces forward, extending a coin between his thumb and forefinger. 'I guess I'm lucky that you came along, aren't I?'

Julia muttered something non-committal and held out her palm. He dropped his coin into it and took hers in exchange. His fingers brushed her hand briefly. She forced herself not to recoil from the contact.

Mark Smeaton didn't move away, but glanced around the car park. 'Deserted here at this time, isn't it? Don't take this the wrong way, but it doesn't seem the safest place for a woman on her own.'

Julia reached with her left hand for the handle of the driver's door, still facing the man. 'I've always felt perfectly safe,' she said, annoyed to hear the tremor in her voice.

She suspected her client heard it too, as she saw his lips twitch into a smirk.

'Pleased to hear it,' he said. 'You struck me as the independent type at your office.' He paused. 'But you never know who's around, do you?' The smirk disappeared and his dark eyes bored into hers.

Somehow Julia managed a careless shrug of her shoulders, even though her heart was banging against her rib cage. 'Excuse me,' she said. 'I need to get home.'

'Of course,' he said smoothly. 'Enjoy your weekend. Any plans?'

'Nothing in particular.'

'Just chill-out time then. Do you have family at home?'

Julia opened her car door. 'I'm afraid I don't share personal information with clients,' she said stiffly.

He held up his hands. 'Apologies. I forgot.' He turned away at last. 'I'll see you on Monday.'

Something in the way he alluded to the appointment made it sound like a threat to Julia. She opened her car door and sank into the driver's seat. Her legs were shaking so much that she wasn't sure she would manage to operate the pedals. Turning the key in the ignition, she flicked on the windscreen wipers. The familiar sound of the engine and the swish of the wipers were reassuring. She took a deep breath, slipped the car into gear and moved forward. She avoided glancing towards the ticket machine which was situated near the exit, having no wish to see Mark Smeaton again.

The journey home through the rush hour traffic was slower than usual in the heavy rain. By the time Julia pulled up on her street below the castle, the cathedral clock was chiming the quarter. She tutted to herself. The benefit of her early finish had been lost thanks to her encounter with Smeaton. There was definitely something unsettling about the man, and it was an effort to shut him out of her mind. But she was home now and it was the weekend.

Glancing towards the cottage, she saw through the condensation on the passenger window that the kitchen light was on. Grace had mentioned visiting a friend this afternoon, but she and Emmeline were evidently back. Julia felt guilty as she realised how much she would have preferred to be alone with Pete this evening after the difficult week.

She let herself into the cottage and called a greeting. She had just hung her coat when there was a clatter from the kitchen, then a screech from Emmeline. Grace came running downstairs carrying several books and followed Julia into the kitchen.

'Oh, Emmeline! What a mess!' Grace added the books to the pile on the table and stooped to pick up the baby's Peter Rabbit bowl and spoon from a pool of orange mush.

'Probably wanting attention. You really shouldn't leave her alone in the high chair.' Julia bent to take a cloth from the cupboard below the sink.

'It was only for a minute!' Grace banged the bowl and spoon down on the table.

Julia closed the cupboard door. 'That's all it takes for an accident.' Her voice was sharper than she intended. She saw a flicker of resentment cross Grace's face. 'We just need to be careful,' she said more gently. She glanced round the kitchen. Evidently Grace hadn't made any progress with cleaning.

'I was just fetching these books. I thought she'd be all right.' Grace stepped back to give Julia space to clean up the mess on the floor.

Julia knelt wearily and mopped up the worst of the vegetable purée from the tiles. Emmeline arched her back in her high chair, screwed up her face and began to cry.

'All right, don't start whinging!' Grace unstrapped Emmeline and held her against her shoulder. Emmeline continued to moan.

Julia stood. 'Shall I take her?'

'She's fine with me.' Grace went across to the window, rubbing Emmeline's back. Entranced by her reflection in the glass, the baby fell quiet. The rain had subsided to a mild patter.

Julia rinsed out the cloth under the tap, dripping orange splodges into the sink. She filled the kettle, then rifled through the boxes of assorted teas in the cupboard. She extracted a green box. 'Have you tried sencha tea? I can make us a pot if you like before I go to the supermarket.'

'No thanks. You said Pete's coming round later, didn't you?'

'Yes.' She glanced round the cluttered kitchen again. 'Do you think you could tidy up in here a bit whilst I'm out?'

'I suppose so. I guess you'll want the table cleared, won't you?'

'Well, yes.' Julia kept her back to Grace and spooned tea leaves into the infuser, ignoring her niece's sigh. She placed it inside her china mug and added the boiled water. She took the mug across to the table and sat down. 'Did you visit your friend?'

'No.' Grace carried Emmeline back to the table and plonked herself down in the opposite chair. Emmeline reached towards a small blue knitted teddy lying on a pile of Grace's books. Grace handed it to her. 'I thought I should stay at home, try to get some work done. But Em's been difficult this afternoon. She wouldn't go down for a nap. I've not been able to get on at all.'

Julia took in her niece's peaky face. 'Maybe a couple of hours out might have been good for you both?' She extracted the infuser and set it in the grimy Peter Rabbit bowl. 'The fresh air might have helped to get Em to sleep.'

Grace shrugged her slim shoulders inside her cream mohair sweater. 'Oh, I don't know,' she said wearily. 'I still wouldn't have had long. I can't believe how much I used to get done in a day compared to now.'

Julia fiddled with the infuser. 'That's the reality of babies, I suppose.'

Grace shot her a resentful glance, then asked, 'What time is Pete coming?'

'About seven thirty.' Julia blew on her tea and took a few sips.

'I hope he's not going to ask me anything about Em's father again.' Grace's voice was sullen. 'It's none of his business.'

Julia bit her lip. 'I don't think Pete will mention it again,' she said carefully. 'But, since you raise the subject, don't you think your ex has a right to know about Emmeline?'

'No, I don't,' she snapped. 'We went through this on Wednesday, and I made it very clear I want nothing to do with him.'

Emmeline dropped the teddy and began to howl. Grace retrieved the toy from the floor, but the baby carried on moaning.

I could join her, thought Julia. She drank the rest of her tea, then tried again. 'I understand you might not, but what about Emmeline? Wouldn't it be better for her to have her father in her life? Think about it practically. He could share the childcare.'

Grace raised her chin. 'It's my decision and no-one else's.'

Julia closed her eyes, too tired to pursue the discussion. 'I realise that.' She hauled herself to her feet. Feeling light-headed, she steadied herself against the table, aware that she was hungry as well as tired. 'Please let's not argue, Grace. It's been a long day.'

Grace shrugged, which Julia took as assent. Relieved, she turned to practical matters. 'Right, I'd better get off to the supermarket.'

'OK. I'll give Emmeline her bath and then do some tidying,' muttered Grace. She walked towards the doorway and retreated upstairs, Emmeline wailing on her shoulder.

The rain reflected Julia's mood as she drove across the northern edge of the city. She felt tired and dreary. Even the prospect of Pete coming over didn't lift her spirits after yet another difficult exchange with Grace. Her niece seemed to be incapable of thinking about anything or anyone beyond her research and Emmeline, and their domestic arrangements were proving much more stressful than Julia had anticipated. Perhaps Pete had been right when he had expressed his reservations.

Lost in her thoughts, and regretting not making a shopping list, Julia made haphazard progress around the supermarket. On her way to the till with a trolley full of produce which she had uncharacteristically flung in without considering a menu plan, she realised she'd forgotten the mince after all. Turning abruptly, she rammed into the newspaper stand at the end of the toiletries aisle with such force that it moved several inches into the path of an oncoming trolley.

'I'm so sorry!' The apology was out before she saw who was pushing the trolley.

'Julia?' Greg bent over the green trolley handle, clutching his midriff.

'Greg!' Julia closed her eyes. Could this disastrous evening get any worse? 'Are you OK?'

Greg straightened up. 'I'll live,' he said coolly. 'At least it was accidental this time.'

Julia's cheeks glowed. She took a deep breath. 'I am so sorry about what happened in the shopping centre,' she said, not quite meeting his eye. She straightened some newspapers dislodged in the collision.

'Right,' he said. 'It was totally out of order. But having thought about it, I understand you were upset.'

Patronising git! 'Upset' didn't come anywhere near covering the tide of devastation which had swept over her the day she had seen him and Lisa baby shopping.

An older woman in a cherry red anorak was trundling down the aisle. She halted her trolley in front of the incontinence pads, blocking Julia's passage. Greg showed no sign of moving. He seemed to be waiting for a response.

'How are Lisa and the baby?' she asked stiffly. She wondered if Lisa had told him about their meeting by the castle car park.

'Well enough when I left the house,' he said. 'Nathan was screaming the place down. Coming here was an escape.'

He smiled ruefully, the boyish smile which had charmed Julia when they first met. She bent over to rearrange the contents of her trolley.

'What's with all the baby stuff?' he asked.

'It's for a friend,' she said shortly.

'Oh? Who?'

'No-one you know.' Julia glanced past Greg. The old lady's hand hovered indecisively over a packet of pads.

He hesitated. 'Not Clare then?'

'No.'

'Pity.' Greg had known how desperate Clare was to become a mother. 'I heard she and James have split. How is he?'

'Not too bad,' she said curtly.

'Anyway, give him my best when you see him.'

'Will do,' said Julia, with no intention of doing so. She offered an internal prayer of thanks as the old lady finally placed a blue packet of pads in her trolley and shuffled towards them. She drew alongside Greg and peered into both of their trolleys with undisguised curiosity. She pointed at the incontinence pads in her own trolley with a swollen forefinger.

'Daylight robbery. Just like them nappies. Profiting from toilet issues both ends of life. Disgusting!'

She rattled off. Despite herself, Julia caught Greg's eye. They both spluttered with laughter.

‘Anyway…’ Julia said, recovering herself.

‘Yes. Best be getting on.’ Greg rested his hand briefly on her shoulder as she steered her trolley past him. ‘Good to see you, Jules,’ he said quietly.

‘And you,’ muttered Julia.

She could still sense the pressure of his hand as she wove her way back to the meat refrigerator. ‘Damn,’ she said aloud, staring down at the array of pink and grey mince in bloodied plastic packets. How was it that Greg could still make her nerves fizz after all these months?

12

The cathedral clock was chiming the half hour as Julia hoisted three bulky carrier bags out of the boot of the Mondeo. Her hand tensed around the car key after she had activated the central locking system. The cottage was ablaze with light. A memory plucked the edges of her subconscious. She stood for a moment with the bags wedged against the boot, but the memory remained submerged. She made her way down the path, skidding on some sodden leaves. The front door was flung open, revealing a wild-eyed Grace, her face strained beneath the light cast by the porch lantern.

'Have you seen her?'

'Who?' Julia already knew the answer. But until Grace said the name, she could fool herself she didn't.

'Emmeline!'

'No. I've just got back.' Julia raised the bags, her chest tight.

'She's not here!' Grace stepped back into the hall, raking her hands through her tangled wet hair. 'I've looked everywhere!'

Julia followed her inside. 'But she must be here.'

'She's not! I left her in the kitchen and went for a shower. I came downstairs and she's gone!'

'Grace, that's not possible.' Julia tried to speak calmly, although her heart was hammering against her rib cage. 'If you left her in the kitchen, she must still be there.'

'She isn't. You can see for yourself!' Grace stood back to let her pass.

In the kitchen Julia dumped the bags on the table, scanning the room despite Grace's words. Her right wrist ached from the weight of the shopping. She massaged it distractedly.

'Maybe you took her upstairs with you?' Julia spoke slowly, in the voice she would use when counselling a distressed client.

'I didn't! Don't you think I'd remember?'

'Shall I go and check anyway?' Julia stepped towards Grace in the doorway.

The younger woman shook her head. 'She isn't up there! I told you, I left her here in the pram.' She looked frantically round the untidy kitchen as if the buggy might suddenly materialise.

Julia paused mid-step. 'In the pram?'

'Yes, after our walk.'

'I thought you'd taken Emmeline up for her bath when I left? Weren't you getting her ready for bed?'

Grace shook her head, dripping water on to her grubby dressing-gown. 'I took her out after her bath, just along to Bailgate. It had stopped raining and I thought it might settle her as she was grizzling again. I needed to clear my head too. That's not the point, is it? She's missing!' Her voice rose to a near-shriek.

Julia took a deep breath. 'I understand you're worried, Grace. But Emmeline must be here somewhere. Could you have taken her into another room and forgotten?'

She pushed past the younger woman and went into the sitting-room. It was empty. 'You must have taken her up to your bedroom,' she said firmly. *Please,* she prayed, as she ran towards the stairs. *Please let that be what's happened.*

Grace collapsed on the bottom stair and began to sob. 'I told you, I've looked in every room, and she's *not here!'*

Julia half-tripped her way up the stairs, her mouth dry. All the doors from the landing were open. First she checked the bedroom which Grace shared with Emmeline. Her heart sank when she saw that the cot was empty, the white cellular blanket neatly folded back. Only then did she acknowledge to herself that however unlikely it might be, she had been hoping that Grace had made a mistake and had somehow forgotten putting Emmeline down for the night. She bent to look under Grace's bed and was unsurprised to see nothing there except a jumble of Grace's books, files and shoes, and her purple suitcase patterned with cream roses.

Julia's breath was coming in sharp gasps as she turned into her own bedroom. It was just as she had left it that morning: duvet tidy on the king-size bed, fluffy cream slippers protruding from the side, straighteners resting on the bedside cabinet alongside the thriller she was reading. Knowing it was pointless, she glanced under the bed before poking her head into the compact en suite. No sign of Emmeline.

Finally, her mind racing through the possibilities, Julia darted into the bathroom across the landing. The air was heavy with moisture and Grace's white musk shampoo. Condensation clouded the mirror above the sink. She went over to open the window and started when Grace spoke from the threshold.

'Well? She's not here, is she?'

'No.' Julia realised that she was shaking uncontrollably. She leant back against the window sill for support. Looking at her niece's fraught face, she suddenly realised what the illuminated cottage had reminded her of: Linda setting fire to the farmhouse when Grace was a baby. She shuddered even more, digging her nails into her palms.

Grace noticed her tension. 'What is it? What do you think has happened?'

'I don't know.'

'What are we going to do?'

'We'll have to call the police.' Julia paused. 'You're quite sure you didn't leave Emmeline in the garden?'

'Of course not! It's so damp and windy!'

Hardly the weather to take Emmeline out in anyway. Julia bit back the words, asking instead, 'You didn't go into a shop?'

Grace stared at her, cornflower blue eyes wider than ever in her wan face. 'And leave Emmeline behind? What kind of mother do you think I am?'

Julia looked down, the image of the burning farmhouse still vivid in her mind's eye. She remembered how fearful Grace had been that she might inherit her mother's postpartum psychosis in the later stages of her pregnancy, and Frances's parting words: 'She doesn't look well to me... Remember what happened to her mother!'

'Well?' demanded Grace. 'What are you saying? That I took Emmeline out and left her somewhere?'

She advanced into the narrow bathroom. Julia instinctively moved backwards on the window sill, knocking a can of hairspray on to the vinyl floor.

'No,' she said hesitantly. 'We do need to cover all the possibilities before we contact the police.'

'All the possibilities!' echoed Grace furiously. 'I told you, I brought Emmeline home and left her in the kitchen! Why don't you believe me?'

A bead of perspiration rolled down Julia's back. She hadn't taken her coat off in her frantic search of the house. Her clammy hand slid over the buttons as she tried to unfasten them. 'I'm thinking of questions the police are likely to ask.'

Grace moved forward again. 'That's why you're asking them, is it?' She thrust her head forwards so that her face was only inches away from Julia's. 'Is that the only reason?'

'Of course,' said Julia quickly.

Grace's eyes narrowed. 'You're lying.'

'You've been so tired,' countered Julia. 'We can all get confused when we're tired.'

'So tired and confused that I'd forget where I left Emmeline?'

'Well—'

Grace cut in. 'You do think I'm like *her*, don't you? Like my mother? That I'm ill like she was.'

'No. I don't think that, Grace.' But even as Julia said the words, she wondered if they were true. She shifted awkwardly on the narrow window sill, pressing her palms to her forehead to try to dispel the persistent image of the burning farmhouse.

'Don't pretend, Julia! You think I've inherited my mother's illness! Surely you don't think I'd harm Emmeline, do you?' Grace's voice broke suddenly on a strangled sob.

'No, no.' Julia shook her head vehemently, as much to dispel the doubts in her mind as to reassure her niece.

Grace slumped to her knees on the tiled floor. 'You do!'

Julia leant forward and placed a hand on the younger woman's shoulder. She chose her words carefully. 'I know you would never deliberately harm Emmeline.'

Grace buried her head in her hands. 'But you think I might accidentally?'

Julia didn't reply immediately.

Grace began to cry. 'You do, don't you? You think I took Emmeline out and didn't bring her home.' She looked up at Julia. 'Is that what you think happened?'

'I—' Julia bit her lip. There was another possibility which seemed outlandish and too terrible to contemplate, but she needed to raise it. 'You didn't see anyone you knew when you were out, did you?'

Grace rocked back on her heels and reached for some loo roll. She blew her nose, frowning. 'I don't think so. Like who?'

'I'm not sure. Just a thought.'

Julia pinched the bridge of her nose between her thumb and forefinger. It was difficult to believe anyone would snatch Emmeline, yet what other explanation was there if Grace's version of events was true and she had left the baby in the kitchen? But was Grace to be believed? Julia thought how frustrated her niece had been earlier, unable to progress her research even though she had cancelled her meeting with her friend. Once again Pete's question echoed in her mind: *'How well do you know her?'*

A squall of wind gusted rain through the window on to the back of Julia's neck. She jumped up off the window sill. 'We must call the police,' she said, turning to close the window. Then she froze, her fingers on the handle.

'What is it?'

'Shh!' Julia stood on tiptoe, straining to listen through the aperture. There it was again, faint but unmistakable. A baby's cry. 'Emmeline! It sounds like she's in the back garden! Quick!'

The two women sped downstairs and into the kitchen. Julia noticed that the key wasn't in its usual place in the lock of the back door.

'Where's the key?'

'I don't know,' said Grace. 'The phone was ringing when we got back. I left Emmeline in the kitchen and dashed through to pick up. I couldn't see the key when I came back. I used the spare.'

Grace yanked out the drawer under the kettle which housed a paraphernalia of spare batteries, sellotape, picture hooks, pins and instructions for various household appliances, and grabbed the spare key from the front corner. She ran across to the door, fumbling with it in the lock. She groaned. 'It won't turn.'

'Let me.' Julia reached round her. She tried the handle. 'It's already unlocked.'

She flung the door open and dashed outside. Grace followed, muttering, 'I'm sure I locked it.'

'Where is she?' Grace's voice was plaintive as they scanned the small cottage garden. They could see the shadowy outlines of bushes and shrubs and the shed in the rear corner, but there was no sign of the pram. Rain was falling again, slanting silver needles below the security light. A gust of wind was accompanied by a familiar repetitive thud, followed by Emmeline's muffled cry.

'The shed!'

Grace covered the short distance faster than Julia and threw back the timber door. 'Emmeline!' She scooped the child from the buggy and clasped her to her shoulder. 'Oh, Emmeline!' She spun round, her face indistinct in the darkness. 'I didn't put her out here, Aunt Julia, I swear!'

Julia bit her lip. 'Let's not worry about that now,' she said eventually. 'The important thing is that Emmeline is safe. You take her inside. I'll close the shed.'

She stepped off the gravel path to let Grace and Emmeline pass. The heels of her boots sank into the sodden lawn.

Grace hesitated. Emmeline began to cry more loudly.

'She'll be hungry,' said Julia. 'We all are. You both need to get in out of this drizzle.'

On cue, the rain increased in intensity, bouncing noisily on the corrugated roof of the shed. Emmeline's cries intensified. Grace ran back with her to the shelter of the warm kitchen.

Julia decided to wait until the rain eased before taking the pram back inside. She closed the shed door as well as she could. It had swollen in the recent wet weather, and she made a mental note to ask Pete to take a look at the rusting hasp. Unlike her, he was good at DIY, and would know whether it could be fixed or should be replaced. She wheeled the recycling bin round the corner of the shed and wedged it against the door. At least it would stop the door banging in the wind.

Back in the kitchen, Grace was warming a bottle of milk for Emmeline. The little girl was sitting in her high chair, stuffing bite-sized slices of banana into her mouth with avid concentration.

Julia took off her dripping coat and hung it on one of the coat hooks beside the back door. She felt bone-weary, and the prospect of frying mince for the bolognese seemed suddenly beyond her. She rooted through the drawer under the sink and extracted the glossy green and red menu from the local Italian.

'I'll ask Pete round another evening. Shall we order pizza? I don't have the energy to cook, and I don't expect you do either.'

'I'm not really that hungry. Not like this one.' Grace set the bottle down on the table before unbuckling

Emmeline's straps and lifting her from her high chair. Nestling against her mother in the chair alongside, Emmeline sucked noisily.

'I'll get one anyway.' Julia went out to the hall to call Pete and phone through the order.

Conscious that Grace would be able to hear what she said from the kitchen, Julia avoided mentioning Emmeline's temporary disappearance to Pete. 'I'm really sorry, but we've got a lot going on here,' she said. 'Do you mind if we postpone tonight?'

'Shall we go out instead?'

Julia massaged her throbbing temple. She was still shaking from the shock of Emmeline's disappearance. 'I'm sorry,' she said in a small voice. 'I think I'm starting with a headache.'

There was a silence. 'OK,' Pete said eventually. 'I'll see you tomorrow at Mum's.' He hung up without saying goodbye.

Julia was close to tears as she rang the Italian takeaway. She could tell Pete was disappointed, and so was she. But she couldn't contemplate telling him what had happened until she had processed it herself, knowing his reservations about Grace. Her mind scrambled for an explanation. Could Grace have put Emmeline in the shed and forgotten in a moment of aberration? Or had she done it deliberately? Was there any other possibility? It was a relief when a bored-sounding young female voice broke into her thoughts. 'Antonio's. How can I help?'

Julia made the order and returned to the kitchen. 'Twenty minutes.' She unpacked the shopping, then sank down into the seat opposite Grace and Emmeline. The baby's eyes were almost closed. 'Emmeline looks none the worse for her adventure.'

'Thank goodness.' Grace looked at Julia directly for the first time since coming in from the garden. Julia saw the younger woman's face was pinched and wan under the ceiling spotlights. 'You do believe me, don't you?' Her naturally high-pitched voice took on the characteristic little girlish note which signalled stress. 'I didn't leave Emmeline in the shed, I swear.'

Julia clasped her hands together in her lap and looked down at them. 'So how do you think Emmeline got there?'

'I don't know,' conceded Grace. 'All I know is that I left her in here in the buggy when I went for my shower. She was asleep, and I didn't want to wake her by taking her upstairs.' Grace gently extracted the nozzle of the bottle from Emmeline's mouth and shifted her daughter on to her shoulder.

'You said you locked the door after you took the phone call and used the spare because your key was missing?'

'Yes. I ran through to get the phone. It was my sister, Suzanne. She rang to tell me she's started seeing someone, and that Frances isn't happy about it. She sounds head over heels with the man. She must be, to have bothered to call me. You know we're not close. I thought I'd left the key in the outside lock, but it wasn't there. I suppose it must have fallen out, but it was too dark to look for it. I locked the door with the spare, like I said. I remember double-checking it because of leaving Emmeline in here whilst I had my shower.'

'Ah.' Julia wondered briefly if Suzanne's boyfriend was the problem that Frances had hinted at the day before. But she had more pressing concerns. 'The door was unlocked when we came down,' she pointed out. She stood and went across to the cupboard where she kept the torch.

Grace rose and began to pace the floor, patting Emmeline's back. The baby burped.

'I know I locked it. Why won't you believe me?'

Julia glanced towards the table strewn with Grace's books and laptop. Grace followed her gaze.

'No! You can't seriously think I'd leave Emmeline in the shed so I could get on with my research!'

'I don't know what to think.' Julia opened the back door and shone the torch around. There was no sign of the key. She closed the door and leant against it, facing Grace. 'But you *have* been worried about your research lately.'

'Not so worried that I'd shut my baby in the shed!'

The women looked at one another for a long moment. Then Julia said slowly, 'None of this makes sense. I'm sorry, Grace, but you must see that the most likely explanation is that you forgot what you were doing. Perhaps it began to rain when you got home from your walk? Maybe you put Emmeline in the shed to shelter her whilst you looked for your key?'

She was aware the suggestion sounded feeble, but it was preferable to the alternative, that Grace had deliberately left Emmeline in the shed to have some quiet time to study.

Grace stared at her, eyes wide with disbelief and anger. 'So I either forgot where I left Emmeline, and fantasised about locking the back door to keep her safe, or I was so obsessed with my research that I put her in the shed?' She sank back down on to her chair, Emmeline nodding on her shoulder. 'You *do* think I'm ill like my mother, don't you?'

'I'm not saying that,' said Julia quietly. 'You must see we're struggling here though.' She waved her hand around the disordered kitchen. 'I can't do all the cleaning myself,

Grace. You have Emmeline and your studying, and I understand that. But I'm working.' She paused. 'And I need time with Pete. For this living arrangement to work, we need to share the chores. For me to come home from shopping and find Emmeline missing, somehow in the shed, with you not knowing how she got there... You have to see that's a worry.' She took a deep breath. 'I want my home to be safe. Especially for your baby.'

There was a long silence, broken by a rap at the front door announcing the arrival of the pizza.

Grace leapt to her feet, jolting the table and Emmeline, whose eyes snapped open. The baby began to wail. 'Fine! If we're not welcome here, we'll go to live with Frances! At least she wants to look after Emmeline!'

Julia rose and followed them out to the hall. Grace dashed up the stairs with the crying baby. Julia found she was too tired to argue as she took delivery of the pizza. Again she heard Pete's voice as if he were there beside her. *'How well do you know her?'*

13

Grace was distant over breakfast the next morning. She told Julia that Frances would be over to collect her and Emmeline in the early afternoon. Julia didn't try to dissuade her from the move. Mulling over the situation during a sleepless night, she had reached the conclusion that it would be for the best. She could no longer deny that there were concerns about the baby's well-being, especially after the events of the previous evening. Since Frances didn't work, she would be able to look after Emmeline when Grace was studying. However unpalatable she found the idea, Julia had to acknowledge that the most likely explanation was that Grace was responsible for putting Emmeline in the shed. She shied away from the more disturbing thought that her niece might have inherited her mother's mental illness.

Julia wanted to be at home when Grace and Emmeline left. She hoped this would ensure the parting could be as smooth as possible, desperate as she was to avoid any further rift in the relationship with her niece. Much as she hated to admit it even to herself, she was also uneasy about leaving Grace alone with Emmeline in the cottage for any period of time. But staying at home meant that she wouldn't be able to join Pete and his mother for lunch to celebrate Brenda's birthday. She phoned him and gave her apologies, explaining that Grace and Emmeline were leaving. Again, she omitted telling him anything about Emmeline's temporary disappearance. 'I do feel I should be here when they go,' she said. 'I am sorry, but please wish your mum happy birthday from me, won't you?'

'Sure.' Pete hung up.

Julia sighed as she went back into the kitchen to begin some much-needed cleaning. She wondered about inviting Pete round for Sunday lunch, then decided it would be better to give him some space over the weekend. She felt bad letting him down again after cancelling dinner on Friday evening. But there would be more time for the two of them once Grace and Emmeline had moved out. She hoped that Pete would understand this when she saw him at the office on Monday. He was usually so easy-going; she was sure he would come round.

An hour later Grace came downstairs and tentatively asked Julia if she would mind Emmeline. She wanted to go to the university to collect the books she had postponed picking up after bumping into her ex earlier in the week. Julia enthusiastically agreed, seeing the request as an olive branch following the frosty start to the day. She was also only too pleased to have the chance to play with the baby. She pushed away the guilty thought that she would miss Emmeline more than Grace when they left.

When Grace returned from the university, Julia prepared a simple lunch of soup and sandwiches. Emmeline enjoyed a purée of mixed vegetables. Conversation between the two women was stilted, but they had made some progress after their argument the evening before. Julia was sure that she had made the right decision in passing on Brenda's birthday lunch in order to spend time with her family.

Julia was washing up the lunch dishes when the doorbell rang a few minutes before two. Grace was upstairs with Emmeline finishing her packing. Julia peeled off her rubber gloves and went through to the hall. Grace called down that she would be ready in ten minutes.

Frances was accompanied by a young woman with strawberry blonde hair hanging loose around her face and cascading down the back of her denim jacket. The plump build and square jaw belonged to Frances, the hair to Grace. So this was Suzanne, Grace's sister.

'Julia, let me introduce my daughter, Suzanne. Suzanne, this is Julia, Grace's... relative.' Frances flashed her large teeth at Julia, revealing a spot of cerise lipstick on an upper front canine. 'Such a complicated relationship, isn't it?'

Julia tilted her chin. 'Do you think so? I'm Grace's aunt.' Julia turned towards Suzanne.

'Hi,' said Suzanne flatly.

Julia stepped back and the women followed her into the hall. Julia noticed that Suzanne was looking around much as her mother had done on Wednesday. 'Grace is just finishing packing,' she said. 'Would you like a cup of tea whilst you wait?'

They both declined, and Julia showed them through to the sitting-room. Frances took a seat on the sofa. Suzanne wandered across to the window and looked out over the small front garden.

'So how have Grace and Emmeline been since Wednesday?' asked Frances. 'I was surprised when Grace rang last night to say she would like to come and live with us after all.'

Julia had prepared herself for such a question. She had thought carefully about whether she should tell Frances about Emmeline's temporary disappearance, and concluded that she should leave that for Grace to explain. Suzanne turned from the window and looked at Julia directly for the first time, her brown eyes watchful. This reinforced Julia's decision. Suzanne might have phoned to confide in Grace about her new boyfriend, but Julia knew that the relationship between the sisters was difficult. She offered a heavily edited answer. 'Grace is quite anxious about her research. I think she's realised that your help with childcare will mean she can progress her studies more quickly.'

Frances nodded, apparently satisfied. 'That sounds very sensible,' she said. 'Suzanne is looking forward to meeting Emmeline, aren't you?'

Suzanne's expression brightened. 'I am. I love babies. I work in a nursery.'

'The little ones love you, don't they?' beamed Frances. 'I'm sure Emmeline will do too. And here she is!' she said, as Grace entered the sitting-room carrying the baby. 'Can Granny have a cuddle?' She held out her arms and Grace handed Emmeline over. Grace withdrew to the doorway.

Suzanne left her post by the window and joined her mother on the sofa. The two women cooed over the baby, who gurgled and smiled adorably. Looking on, Julia felt a moment's regret that she had encouraged the move, but then chided herself for being selfish. She was convinced that Emmeline would be safer at Frances's.

Suzanne swivelled round to look at Grace. 'Emmeline has such dark brown eyes, hasn't she? Not your cornflower blue.'

Grace stared back at her sister, her expression inscrutable.

'Are her father's eyes brown?' Suzanne persisted.

Julia held her breath. Grace's jaw tightened, but all she said was, 'Maybe,' before she turned towards her stepmother. 'Could I have the car key please, Frances? I'll start taking my bags out.'

'Of course. We must get on.' Frances bounced Emmeline on her lap and then said, with a sensitivity which surprised Julia, 'Suzanne and I can help, so Julia can have a few moments with Emmeline.'

'Thank you.' Julia smiled at Frances and stepped forward to take Emmeline.

Suzanne started to cough. She recovered sufficiently to ask for a glass of water, and trailed Julia into the kitchen whilst Frances and Grace began to load the car. The young woman's eyes roved around the kitchen as she drank. Julia wondered if her mother had told her about its chaotic state during her visit earlier in the week, and was pleased she had begun to make inroads on tidying it that morning. She asked herself why she should mind what the young woman thought. Apart from her enthusiasm to meet Emmeline, Suzanne hadn't made a very favourable impression so far. She had clearly been needling Grace for information with her question about the eye colour of Emmeline's father. Julia cuddled Emmeline more tightly to her chest.

The water seemed to have alleviated Suzanne's cough. 'Has she told you anything about him?' she asked abruptly, setting the glass down on the counter.

Julia stalled. 'About who?'

Suzanne narrowed her eyes. 'Emmeline's father.'

'Very little.'

'Oh.' Suzanne moved forward and gazed down at the baby in Julia's arms. 'He really has a right to know, don't you think?'

Julia didn't respond immediately. On balance she agreed, but to admit that would feel like a betrayal of Grace. After all, she, Julia, didn't know Emmeline's father, and her niece seemed to have developed strong feelings against him. 'I think that's for Grace to decide,' she said with as much firmness as she could muster.

But Suzanne had noticed the hesitation. She gave a small smile. 'Do you really?' she asked.

Fortunately, Frances and Grace returned to the hall at that moment. Julia hastened out of the kitchen, grateful to be spared any further questions from Suzanne.

'All done!' Frances turned to her daughter. 'Cough gone, darling?'

Suzanne nodded.

Julia broke what could have been an awkward silence by moving forward and handing Emmeline over to Grace. 'Come and see me soon, won't you?'

'Yes.' Grace leant forward briefly into Julia's hug. 'Thanks for everything,' she mumbled.

Julia forced a smile and ducked her head, surprised by a lump in her throat.

Perhaps Frances intuited something of Julia's sadness, because she said that Julia would be very welcome to visit any time. Julia nodded gratefully as she waved them off. Back in the kitchen, it occurred to her that Pete had been correct to suggest that she shouldn't be swayed by Grace's judgement of Frances and should form her own opinion. Julia had half-expected the woman to gloat about Grace's decision to move in with her, but Frances had shown more sensitivity than Julia would have credited her with. Julia hoped this might mean that they would be able to support Grace and Emmeline together going forward.

Julia had just finished vacuuming the bedroom Grace and Emmeline shared when the phone rang. She hoped it might be Pete, calling after his mother's birthday lunch, and sped down the stairs. But it was James who returned her greeting.

'James. How are you?' It was an effort to keep the disappointment from her voice.

'Been better.' There was a hubbub of chatter and TV in the background, then a clink of glasses.

Julia's heart sank. 'Are you in the pub?'

'Yeah. Drowning my sorrows.' He paused. 'Clare wants the house.'

Julia groaned. 'Have you heard from the solicitors again?'

'Yeah. Today. I thought she'd let me buy her out with Mum's inheritance. I'd have to take out a mortgage, but I could just about manage it. Apparently, they reckon they can make a substantial financial claim against me, including the house.'

'Oh, James. I am sorry. I know how much you loved that house.' Julia's mind turned to her own inheritance from Linda. She'd been thinking about it intermittently since the letter arrived. 'Listen, I might be able to help,' she said impulsively.

There was a loud cheer in the pub.

'What did you say?' James asked. 'Football's on; I couldn't hear.'

Julia tried again. 'Linda left me some money, quite a lot, and a share of her property in Norfolk. I— '

But her brother cut her off. 'I'm sure that's great for you,' he snarled. 'Congratulations. Here am I practically homeless and soon to be divorced. Meantime, you've got lover boy and now a nice inheritance. Remind me not to ring you again when I'm looking for support, won't you?'

The line went dead. Exasperated, Julia replaced the handset. It occurred to her that if she had asked James which pub he was in, she could have gone to meet him and make her offer of financial help in person. But a less charitable part of her thought it would do no harm to let him stew after his verbal assault. She would give him a few days before phoning with her suggestion.

14

Julia passed the rest of the weekend quietly. Pete didn't contact her. It took all her resolve not to get in touch herself. She thought it would be better if they cleared the air face to face, and arrived at the office on Monday with some trepidation. She was reassured when he greeted her with his usual warm smile as she shook her umbrella over the doorstep.

'Did your mum enjoy her birthday? I'm so sorry I didn't make it,' she said immediately.

A shadow passed over his face. 'Yeah. We had a good day, thanks.' He turned to the coffee machine. 'Coffee?'

'Please.' Julia placed her umbrella under the umbrella stand and joined him behind the desk. She watched him run water into the jug, then laid a hand on his arm. 'Pete, I do wish I hadn't missed your mum's birthday lunch. I felt I should be at home when Frances collected Grace and Emmeline.'

He shrugged off her hand. 'Yeah, I know. I'd better get on with this. I've got a client due soon.'

'Of course.' She tried to keep the hurt out of her voice as she brushed past him on the way to her office.

She switched on the light and opened the blind, blinking away sudden tears that blurred her vision. Gathering herself, she extracted her notes for her first appointment from her filing cabinet. *Mark Smeaton.* Not a prospect to lift her spirits following last week's initial difficult session. She had still not shaken off her unease following their encounter on the car park on Friday evening either.

She heard the front door open and close, and Pete saying, 'I'll tell her you're here.' The rest of his words were drowned out by a lorry thundering past. Julia checked her watch against the wooden wall clock. Ten to nine.

Pete came through a moment later with a steaming mug of coffee. He pulled the door to with his free hand. 'Your client's here,' he said, his voice low. 'I told him you'd take him in at nine. He asked if you could see him now, made some sarky comment about your coffee. What shall I tell him?' He set the mug down on the low beech Ikea side table which stood between the two matching armchairs.

'I'll let him wait,' said Julia. 'He was early last week as well. I need to make sure I set the ground rules.'

'Yeah.' Pete ran his hand over his shaved head, frowning. 'I think I'll stick around reception till you're ready. There's something about him...' He half-smiled. 'Sorry, I know that doesn't fit in with your non-judgemental approach.'

'That's fine. But what about getting ready for your client?'

Pete shrugged. 'I'm ready, and she won't mind waiting if she's early. We do need to think about a receptionist, don't we?'

'Yet another thing to sort out.' Julia stifled a yawn.

'Can't be put off for ever. I'm not too happy with you being here on your own as the nights draw in.'

'You're generally around though, aren't you? Friday was unusual.'

He looked down at his feet. 'You never know what might come up, do you?'

Julia tried to focus on her notes from last week's session as she sipped her coffee, but Pete's parting comment niggled. She remembered her misgivings that all was not well with him the previous week. Was he keeping something from her? He had seemed unduly disappointed that she hadn't made it to his mother's birthday lunch on Saturday. She resolved to ask him more as soon as they were both free.

'I know where I'm sitting this week.' Mark Smeaton smirked as he seated himself in the chair furthest from the door. 'I worked it out. You sit in the chair nearest the door for personal security, don't you?'

'That's the advice we're given in training,' said Julia stiffly.

'Mm.' He nodded and cocked his head on one side so that the light reflected off his glasses, obscuring his eyes. 'I guess you never know, do you?'

'Never know what?'

'Who you're letting in.' He paused. 'You must meet all kinds of people in your line of work.'

He lowered his head and surveyed her intently. Julia willed herself not to inch backwards in her chair.

'It's an interesting job,' she said coolly.

'That's how you see it, is it? A "job"? There was I thinking counselling was more of a calling.' He steepled his fingers, tapping the tips together. 'A vocation, wouldn't you say? A calling. Rather like the priesthood.'

Julia puckered her brow. Her ex, Greg, had once likened counsellors to secular priests. Although he had tended to be patronising about her work, she had found the comment insightful.

'Don't you think so?' her client persisted. He leant forward in his seat, dark eyes fixed on her face.

'Possibly.'

'Definitely, I'd say.' He pushed his glasses on to the bridge of his nose.

'It seems that's important to you?'

He nodded. 'It is. I was worried when I left last week that with our different frames of reference you might not be able to help me. This gives us some common ground, doesn't it?'

'I suppose so. Although as I explained last week, even if we have different views—'

He held up his hand. 'I know. I understood what you told me. As the counsellor, you try to move around in my world, see things from my perspective. That's the idea, isn't it?'

'More or less. Now…'

'I've been reading up on Carl Rogers.' Smeaton settled back in his chair with a smile, legs splayed wide. Julia unconsciously crossed hers. 'Doing my homework.'

'Right.' Julia decided it was time she took control of this session, and ploughed on when he opened his mouth again. 'So you'll know that I'm seeking to offer you a safe space to explore your thoughts and feelings. One thing we began discussing last week was your understanding of "The One" and how that's impacting your relationships.'

The smile disappeared. 'One relationship,' he said slowly. 'The one that matters.'

Julia's palms were damp. She tried to wipe them discreetly on her bootcut black trousers. 'OK.' She matched his tone, drawing out the two syllables. 'The relationship which you view as particularly special and which ended recently after your infidelity.'

His eyes narrowed. 'I thought you aspired to being non-judgemental?'

'I do.'

He folded his arms. 'I find the phrase "your infidelity" pejorative.'

'It wasn't intended to be. In using it, I intended to state a fact.'

Even as she spoke, Julia asked herself if this were true. Greg's unfaithfulness had shocked her to the core. Looking back, she was ashamed to think how she had once been contemptuous towards those who stayed with unfaithful partners. When Greg had finally come to collect his belongings from the cottage months after their separation, she had been shocked to realise that she would have taken him back if he had said he had made a mistake with Lisa. She wondered how they were getting on after that row she had witnessed by the castle car park... Mark Smeaton was speaking again and she dragged her mind back to the session.

'There are usually reasons for infidelity, wouldn't you agree?'

Julia took a sharp intake of breath. It was the question that she had tormented herself with after Greg had left her for Lisa. 'What do *you* think, Mark?' she parried.

'Oh, I'm sure of it.' He nodded his dark head for emphasis. 'There's the classic case of the middle-aged man trading in the woman of a certain age for a younger model, for example. Driven by attraction and fertility.'

Colour flooded Julia's cheeks. Her heart begin to beat faster beneath his unblinking gaze.

'That must be upsetting, mustn't it?' he went on. His dark eyes scanned her face. 'You look a little uncomfortable. I hope it's not something you've experienced yourself.'

Julia held his gaze, making every effort to remain expressionless. 'As you might have found out from your research between sessions, person-centred counselling provides the client with the opportunity to explore their thoughts and feelings. It's not a place for the counsellor to share their experiences.'

The corner of his mouth lifted in a sneer. 'Touched a nerve, have I? Sorry about that.' His smirk belied the apology. 'At least I've got a reaction.'

For a moment Julia didn't trust herself to speak. She inhaled deeply. 'I think you might have misunderstood the process,' she said, struggling to keep her voice level. 'The counselling I offer is to help my clients find their answers to the issues which they want to explore. My personal life is, metaphorically, left behind at the door.' She turned her head in the direction of the door, not so much to emphasise her words as to avoid his mocking face.

He raised an eyebrow but didn't reply.

Julia decided to try one last time. 'So, getting back to where we were, you mentioned your conviction that there are reasons for infidelity. I'm wondering whether you would like to consider your reasons, especially as you were so certain that your ex-girlfriend was "The One"?'

He blew out his cheeks. 'Not *was*,' he said. 'She *is* The One. I've told you that already.'

He spoke quietly. Julia shivered again.

Smeaton settled back in his armchair and folded his arms. 'I made a mistake. At the time she was preoccupied. Her mind was on other stuff outside our relationship. She'd had a bereavement, but I don't think that was the whole of it. She shut me out. And this other girl, what can

I say?' He shrugged. 'I knew she fancied me. Still does.' He licked his lips. 'Not bad in bed, to be fair.'

Bile rose in Julia's throat. She swallowed hard. Mark Smeaton seemed to be too immersed in contemplating his sexual prowess to notice her disgust.

'I guess I used her, the other girl. Made her happy enough at the time.' He smiled lasciviously. 'It was only the once back then. Unfortunately, my girlfriend found out. She wouldn't accept she'd been distant, refused to listen to me. I tried to explain, said I was sorry, and I was. Like I said last week, I thought she'd come round eventually, because we were so good together.' He stroked his moustache. 'Then, as I said, she disappeared for a while.'

Julia's attention was caught by his last sentence. 'For a while? I understood you'd lost contact after she moved and changed her mobile number?'

'That's right. But I told you I knew where to find her, didn't I?'

Julia gripped the arms of her chair to suppress her shudder. 'Yes, you did,' she said steadily. 'I'm guessing you've seen her?'

He nodded. 'I have.'

Julia glanced towards the window. The strip of sky visible above the roofs of the terrace opposite was charcoal grey. Seconds later hailstones thudded against the glass. Julia's shoulders tensed as she turned back to her client. He was still watching her with his intent dark gaze, seemingly oblivious to the hailstorm.

Had it been any other client, Julia might have waited for them to speak. But there was something unnerving about this man. 'So you saw your ex? Would you like to tell me more about that, Mark?'

He chewed his lower lip. 'She didn't get it,' he said.

'Didn't get it?'

He shook his head. 'Didn't get that we should be together again.'

'Ah. It sounds as though for her your relationship is over.' Julia let a beat fall. 'How do you feel about that?'

His face flushed. 'Is that the best you can do? Trot out your person-centred questions asking how I feel when it's bloody obvious?'

Julia blinked. 'I can't second guess any of my clients' emotions, Mark,' she said. 'I encourage my clients to name their feelings so that we can explore them together.'

He rolled his eyes.

'I'm very clear that I practise person-centred counselling,' Julia went on. 'It might not suit all clients, and if not, they – you – may wish to access counselling elsewhere.'

He clapped his hands slowly. 'Well done,' he said. 'I can see what an effort it was for you to recover your self-control there.'

She stared at him, once again speechless.

'But you know, I still can't shake off the idea that counselling should be a two-way process, like any relationship.' He leant forward, his hands on his knees. This time Julia was unable to stop herself from shrinking back in her chair. He spat out his next words. 'Do you honestly think your pathetic reflective listening is going to help me to bare my soul to you, you supercilious middle-aged cow?'

A fresh flurry of hailstones battered the window. Blood drummed in Julia's ears. In her seven years of counselling she had never experienced such a venomous verbal attack. She opened her mouth. No words came. Her client sniggered.

'Don't you like to be the one to break it up, Julia? Would it make you feel a failure?' He stood abruptly.

Noticing Julia start in her chair, he grinned as he looked down at her. 'Don't worry, I'm not going to attack you. You might want to think about some security measures, you know. I've noticed you don't have a receptionist, and with the dark nights coming... And that car park was pretty deserted last Friday, wasn't it?'

He took two steps forward, drawing alongside her. She froze.

Bending over her, he leant in close, his moustache tickling her cheek. 'Like I said, you never know who you're letting in, do you?'

The window reverberated as he slammed the door behind him.

15

'That does it. We have to get a receptionist.' Pete paced the floor of the reception area. His final client of the day had left ten minutes ago. This was the first opportunity they had had to discuss Mark Smeaton's angry exit.

Julia took a sip of her water. 'I agree,' she said. 'But I thought we planned to wait a bit longer, see how the business goes, before taking one on?'

'It's a security issue,' said Pete firmly. 'Not one we needed to worry about in summer so much. I said I didn't like the look of that character, didn't I?'

'You did. I've never had such a hostile client before.' Julia set her glass down on the desk, not wanting Pete to see that her hands were trembling. She had been shaking sporadically since the altercation with Mark Smeaton.

'Obviously you can't tell me the details. But I wondered what the hell was going on. It certainly put an end to my client getting any benefit from her session.' Pete had come racing into Julia's office when he heard the door slam behind Smeaton, abandoning his client in the middle of a foot massage.

'I know. I'm sorry. Do you want me to cover the refund you gave her?'

'Don't be daft. At least she was a regular; she'll be back next week. What about him? He won't show his face again, will he?'

'He made it clear he has no intention of coming back. I wouldn't see him again anyway.'

'He didn't scare you, did he?' Pete stopped his pacing and moved round the desk towards her.

Julia was tempted to deny it, but found herself nodding under his concerned gaze.

'Something he said?'

'Yes.' Julia shivered, hearing again that whisper, *'You never know who you're letting in, do you?'* Unconsciously, she touched her cheek where Smeaton's moustache had brushed against it.

Pete's jaw set into a firm line. 'Did he threaten you?'

Julia hesitated, thinking about Smeaton's comments about office security and the car park. 'What he said was... unsettling.'

Pete swore under his breath and clenched his fist. 'If I ever see that scumbag again—'

Julia's eyes widened. 'You couldn't say or do anything to him,' she said. 'You know that.'

Pete rubbed his cheek. 'I know. Client confidentiality and all that. You shouldn't have to put up with behaviour like that though, Jules.'

'I guess it goes with the territory. I must have been lucky all these years. I'll talk it through with my supervisor, I promise. That will help.'

'All right,' said Pete reluctantly. 'Meantime I'll work on an ad for a receptionist.'

Julia frowned. 'Can't we wait till the new year like we said? We're not really making enough money yet, are we?'

'It's security,' Pete repeated. 'If I'm not around, I don't want to be worrying about you here on your own. I've got to take the day off tomorrow as it is.' He twiddled the gold stud in his right ear.

'What is it?'

'Nothing. Anyway, how was Grace when she left? Was it a sudden decision? I haven't had the chance to ask.'

Julia was apprehensive about telling Pete that she had returned home from shopping on Friday evening to find Emmeline missing, but knew that she should be open and divulge what had happened. He was shocked when she told him that Emmeline had been found in the shed and that Grace couldn't explain how she had got there.

'I'm sorry to say you have to consider the possibility that Grace might have inherited her mother's illness,' he said as soon as she had finished the story. 'Did you tell Frances?'

'No. I didn't have the chance on Saturday afternoon,' said Julia. She ran a finger round the top of her glass, creating a faint ringing sound. She sighed. 'I didn't really want to, I suppose. Frances is home most of the time, so she'll be able to keep an eye on Emmeline. With Grace having been so tired, she could have been confused. Or maybe something else happened…' Her voice trailed off. Try as she might, Julia hadn't been able to come up with a plausible explanation for how Emmeline had come to be in the shed. She chose not to mention how much Grace had been stressing about her research.

Pete raised an eyebrow sceptically. 'I think you need to tell Frances, Jules. This is a baby's safety you're talking about.'

'I know.' Julia pushed her hair behind her ear. 'I plan to visit later this week, so I'll see how things are then and decide if I should mention it to Frances.'

'Mm.' Pete's expression was serious. 'Are you sure you're not trying to save your relationship with Grace when it's Emmeline who should be the main priority?'

Julia looked down at the carpet. 'I don't know,' she said honestly. 'But I will get in touch soon.' Recalling their exchange earlier, she continued, 'This was why I wanted to see Grace and Emmeline off on Saturday, to make sure we parted on good terms. If Grace is struggling, and if things don't work out for her living with Frances, I don't want her to think my door is closed to her.' She glanced up at him. 'If it hadn't been for all this, I would have come over for your mum's birthday. I am sorry I missed it, Pete. Truly.'

Pete's clear blue eyes searched hers for a moment. He raised a hand towards her arm, then dropped it. 'Yeah. I know.'

Julia caught her breath. 'Pete. Are you sure there's nothing wrong?'

He looked down and rubbed his chin, the grey stubble silver under the fluorescent light. 'I'm going to have to take a bit of time off over the next few weeks. That's why it's important we find a receptionist.'

Julia frowned. 'Are you going away? You hadn't said.'

'No. I wish I were. It's Mum.' His voice was thick.

'Your mum? What's the matter with her?'

He darted her an agonised glance. 'She's got lung cancer,' he said bluntly.

'Oh, Pete, I'm so sorry.' She moved forward to put her arms around him. He stiffened and backed away. She let her hands fall and turned to pick up her glass from the desk.

'The thing is, I'm not dealing with it too well. And I'm not sure... at the moment...'

Her stomach contracted with a premonition of what he was about to say. She set the glass down without drinking from it. Her hand was wobbling so much that water spilled over the top.

'I'm not sure I can manage our relationship,' finished Pete bleakly. 'Not as it is.'

'Not as it is?' she repeated tonelessly, reaching for the tea towel from the hook by the sink.

'No, Jules. It's just too much, don't you see? I was going to tell you about Mum on the phone last week, that evening when you had to ring off because Emmeline was screaming the house down. We'd seen the consultant that afternoon, had the confirmation we'd been dreading.' His voice cracked and he inhaled deeply before going on. 'I suggested lunch one day, but you had a client. Then I planned to tell you when I came over on Friday evening, and you cancelled. I can see you've been worried about James since he showed up, as well as Grace and Emmeline. Like I said, there's never time for us, is there?'

'But we can make time!' She blinked back tears as she turned towards him. 'I will, Pete, I promise. If I'd had any idea about your mum...'

'You'd still have all this other stuff to deal with though, wouldn't you? These people, their problems?'

'Well...'

He leant forward and placed a finger on her lips. 'It's good you care so much, Jules, but I think you've taken on too much recently. I'm not just saying that because of us, because of our relationship.'

'But with Grace and Emmeline at Frances's, that will make things easier for us, won't it? Surely these things aren't reasons for us to break up.' Her voice caught.

He looked deeply into her eyes. 'That's not what I'm saying,' he said gently. 'I'm talking about us taking some time out. Temporarily.' He took another breath before continuing gruffly, 'Have you thought about where all this has left us, Jules? Do you remember when we were last together?'

She turned away and concentrated on wringing out the sodden tea towel over the sink. 'I haven't thought... I'm sorry. I've just been so caught up in everything.'

He moved round the counter and resumed his pacing. 'Yeah. It was when we were in Norfolk.' He ran his hands over his head. 'I don't want to pressure you, Jules. I want to support you. There doesn't seem to be any time for us as a couple though. Now I want to be with Mum as much as I can.' His voice broke. 'She's not got long, you see.'

'Pete, I am so, so sorry. I had no idea. Please, can't we talk this through?'

He went over to the coat stand and lifted off his leather jacket. Willing him to answer, 'Yes,' she held her breath. Pete pulled on his jacket and went across to the door. Still with his back to her, he said quietly, 'Maybe another day. Not now. I promised Mum I'd go for tea. I'm sorry, Jules.'

With that he disappeared into the drizzle of the late October afternoon, leaving Julia staring numbly after him. She mechanically rinsed out her glass and collected her laptop and bag from her room. Locking the door, she made her way up High Street to the car park in a daze.

If asked, she would have been unable to describe anything of the drive home. It was only when a driver honked behind her as she drew up in front of the cottage that she came to herself. Belatedly she realised that she hadn't indicated she was pulling in. She held her hand up to the driver in apology as he went by. In the semi-darkness she saw him shake his head, mouthing some obscenity. She began to tremble, and gave in to her pent up tears. After a few moments she found a tissue in her bag and blew her nose before stepping out of the car.

The rain had eased, but the wind was gusting as strongly as ever, whipping the leaves from the cherry blossom tree. The tree had been stripped almost bare over the last few days. Beyond the side gate the shed door banged rhythmically. She shuddered, thinking of Emmeline abandoned inside on Friday evening, and wondered whether Pete was right with his advice that she should tell Frances about the incident. But if she did, wouldn't Grace lose trust in her?

Julia had just unlocked the door when the phone began to ring. She flicked on the hall light before picking up.

'Julia Butler.'

'Hi, Julia. It's me, Clare.'

'Oh. Hi.'

Clare seemed not to notice the flatness in Julia's tone. 'How are things with you?'

'OK,' lied Julia. 'And you?'

'I'm fine.' Clare let a beat fall. 'Feeling better now I've got things moving with the divorce.'

Julia thought of James's despondent phone call from the pub on Saturday. 'Right.'

'I'm sure you'll understand. You're always encouraging people to move on in your job, aren't you?'

Julia glanced around the hall, missing the clutter of Grace's footwear and Emmeline's pram. Without Grace's outerwear alongside, Julia's waterproof and summer coat looked bereft on the coat stand.

'Aren't you?' pressed Clare.

'It depends,' she replied. 'Sometimes it's better to stay where you are.'

'So you won't be moving then?'

Julia's hand tightened on the phone. 'Me?'

'When you get the inheritance.'

Julia tucked a strand of hair behind her ear. 'How did you hear about that?'

'From James. He spilled it when he turned up here on Saturday night. You've done rather well out of your mother's estranged illegitimate daughter, haven't you?'

'Now hang on.' Julia couldn't let Clare's disparaging reference to Linda pass. 'It isn't fair to say that Linda was estranged from my mother. Mother was too young to stand up to my grandmother when she sent her away pregnant to Norfolk. Linda understood that when she traced Mother last summer.'

She looked at her parents' wedding photograph hanging on the wall above the phone. It might be her imagination, but ever since Julia had found out about her mother's doomed wartime relationship, she had imagined she knew the reason for her mother's stiff pose in the photo. She was sure that Emily had wished she was marrying Ray. She couldn't keep the quiver from her voice. 'Mother was heartbroken.'

'Whatever.'

'What do you mean?'

'Don't dress it up as some glorious love story, Julia. It was just a sordid affair.'

'How dare you?'

Clare laughed mirthlessly. 'Because it's true,' she said. 'Anyway, back to this inheritance. I thought you should know that my solicitors will be making enquiries about this woman's will. I notified them about it today.'

'Why? Why would your solicitors be interested in it?'

'Surely you can understand why? James is Linda's brother, you're her sister. Why should you benefit and not him?'

'But Linda didn't know James. She and I were—' Julia swallowed. 'We were close in her last few months.'

'What difference does that make? He might still be able to make a claim. If he is entitled, you should know that it will be taken into account in the divorce settlement. So you'd better not make any plans about how you're going to spend it yet.'

'What—?' Julia began. But Clare had already hung up. Julia replaced the phone in the cradle, her hand shaking.

In the kitchen she automatically ran water into the kettle. Reaching for the sencha tea in the cupboard, she changed her mind. A large glass of red was called for. She poured the remains of a bottle of merlot into it and sank down on to a dining chair, her mind churning.

So much had happened in the last few days that she had barely thought about her unexpected inheritance from Linda. James's resentment about it had been obvious, but she didn't expect him to try to make a claim himself. Besides, she intended to offer him some money from her share. Thinking it through as she sipped her wine, Julia suspected that Clare's solicitors wouldn't get far, although their 'enquiries' would probably cause a delay in the settlement of Linda's estate. This wasn't a problem to Julia, but she worried it would adversely impact Grace and Emmeline. Until Grace came into her inheritance, she would be unable to afford childcare if she lived independently. But perhaps that was no bad thing; if Grace wasn't well enough to look after Emmeline properly at present, the two of them were better staying with Frances.

There was no point sitting brooding and drinking wine. Julia got to her feet and set about some chores. She gathered the weekend newspapers for recycling. Reaching into the scallop shell on the window sill by the back door for the key, she felt nothing. Peering inside, she saw that the key wasn't there. She frowned, realising that she had forgotten to look for it after Grace had told her it had disappeared when she brought Emmeline back from her walk on Friday. It was too dark to scout around outside now, so Julia retrieved the spare from the drawer, unlocked the back door and dumped the newspapers in the recycling bin.

Back in the kitchen, she switched on the radio, tuned into Radio 4 as usual, and began to wash the breakfast dishes. The American author Donna Tartt was being interviewed about her new novel, 'The Little Friend'. Julia shuddered when she heard that the storyline concerned the unsolved murder of a nine-year-old. She'd been more sensitive about any stories containing violence towards children since Emmeline's birth. But as she listened to the description of the subsequent fallout within the fictional victim's family, she found herself intrigued, her mind turning inevitably to the complexities within her own extended family.

She emptied the water. It gurgled down the sink, drowning out the radio interview. Then she started when she heard a man's voice behind her. She spun round, dish brush in hand. Greg's broad frame filled the doorway to the garden.

'Greg! How did you get in?' Drips of water spattered the floor from the brush.

'Through the door?' he said, his tone ironic.

'What about the gate?'

He shrugged. 'It wasn't bolted. I knocked at the front but didn't get an answer, so I tried the gate.'

'I didn't hear you above the radio.' Julia reached across the counter to switch it off. She frowned. 'I always keep that gate bolted.'

'I can assure you it wasn't.' Greg half-smiled. 'I didn't climb over it to get to you.'

Julia's cheeks grew warm. She turned and unhooked the tea towel which hung alongside the sink. She hoped

Greg wouldn't notice her hand was trembling as she took a plate from the dish rack. Presumably Grace had forgotten to bolt the gate when she returned with Emmeline on Friday evening.

'Aren't you going to invite me in?'

Julia set the plate down on the work surface and began to dry another. 'Why are you here, Greg?'

'I...' The uncharacteristic hesitation led Julia to look at him properly. There was a twitch in his right cheek, a telltale sign of tension with him. 'It would be easier if I came in.'

'OK.'

He wiped his feet on the doormat, then bent to unlace his shoes.

'Take a seat.' Julia gestured towards the table. It looked bare without Grace's books scattered over it. But she'd left behind Emmeline's Peter Rabbit cup. Julia had washed it and left it on the table, ready to take when she went to visit her niece.

Greg hung his waterproof over a chair and nodded towards the cup. 'Does that belong to your mysterious friend's baby?' He pulled out a chair and sat down, long legs stretched out in front of him.

'Yes,' said Julia shortly. 'Coffee?'

Greg looked pointedly at the empty wine bottle and glass on the table. 'Wouldn't mind a glass of red if you're having another.'

Julia hesitated. 'I wasn't, but go on. Would you open a bottle whilst I dry the rest of this? The corkscrew is—'

'I know where the corkscrew is.'

Greg brushed past Julia on his way to the drawer beside the gas hob. Warmth spread through her. *After all this time.* She dried some spoons vigorously.

'Another merlot?' Greg was examining the contents of the wine rack.

'Fine.' Julia flung the spoons into the cutlery drawer and took another wine glass from the cupboard above. She set it down on the table. 'So, are you going to tell me the reason for your unexpected visit?'

Greg kept his eyes fixed on the bottle, apparently concentrating on extracting the cork. He poured out the wine and pushed a glass towards Julia. 'Should I have phoned?'

Julia looked at him sitting at the table where they had eaten so many meals and shared countless bottles of wine during their six years together. Greg didn't seem to have considered the possibility that she might not want his company.

'Yes. You should.'

He shrugged and took a sip of wine. 'OK. Sorry. I thought maybe you wouldn't mind after we bumped into each other the other evening in the supermarket. Literally, in your case.' The corner of his mouth lifted as he met her eyes.

She couldn't help smiling back as she sat down opposite him. 'Even so...'

He opened his palms. 'Fair enough. I wasn't really thinking where I was going. When I found myself outside the castle, I thought I might as well drop in.'

'Right.' Julia considered this as she sipped her wine. 'So you were just driving around?'

'Walking.'

'OK.' Julia nodded, waiting for him to continue. She realised she had already drunk half her glass of wine, and set it down on the table.

'Yeah. The thing is, me and Lisa, we... things haven't been going too well. Since we had Nathan, it's all got...

complicated. We had a bit of a row tonight.' He stared down into his glass, sloshing the wine around.

Julia pondered his words. In the early months after their separation, she had longed for him to come back home, to tell her that he had made a terrible mistake in leaving her for Lisa. Now here he was, admitting he was struggling in the relationship, especially since he had become a father, and she felt nothing, no sense of satisfaction or vindication. The irony wasn't lost on her.

'This is excellent.' Greg raised his glass. He smiled, the smile which she had once found so beguiling. 'You always had good taste in wine.'

'Thanks.' Julia found herself taking another couple of sips. *Don't be drawn in,* she told herself. 'So you had a row, went for a walk, and found yourself here? I'm wondering why, Greg?'

He looked across at her, the tic starting up again in his right cheek. 'I'm not sure I can answer that,' he said. 'You're the counsellor, Jules. Why do you think I made my way here?'

There was a long silence, broken by the grandmother clock striking nine in the hall. Julia waited until the last chime died away. 'I don't know,' she said. 'But I think it's time you went home to your partner and son, don't you?'

He hunched over his wine glass. 'I guess.' He tipped his head back and finished the rest of his wine in three gulps. 'It's good to be back.' He held her gaze.

'Is it?' Julia rose abruptly from the table and reached for his glass. She willed herself to walk in a straight line as she took it across to the sink.

'Yes,' he said. 'Sometimes I wonder…' His voice tailed off.

Julia kept her back to him, her hand clamped to the faucet. 'What do you wonder, Greg?'

'If, you know...' The legs of his chair scraped the tiles.

Julia turned on the tap and rinsed out the glass, setting it down carefully on the draining board. She turned to face him, folding her arms across her small bosom. 'If what?'

The peal of the doorbell tore through the silence.

Greg gave a crooked smile in which Julia detected relief. 'You're busy tonight. I'd better go.' He led the way into the hall and paused, his back to her. 'Would you mind if I call by again? It would be good to think we could be... friends, wouldn't it?'

'You think so?' Julia slipped past to get to the front door before him.

He placed a hand on her shoulder as she turned the key. 'I'm sure of it.'

Julia opened the door. 'Pete?' She shrugged off Greg's hand, aware that his grip had tightened slightly.

It was impossible to read Pete's expression in the shadows of the porch, but there was no mistaking his acid tone. 'I didn't realise you had company.'

'I was just leaving,' said Greg smoothly. He held out his hand. 'It's Phil, isn't it? We met years ago when I was helping Julia move into her old office.'

Julia suspected that Greg was pretending that he hadn't heard her greet Pete by name. Pete didn't bother to correct the mistake. He rammed his hands into the pockets of his leather jacket, turned and walked rapidly down the path.

'Pete!' Julia called after him. 'Aren't you coming in?'

He raised a hand at the gate. 'I don't think so. Catch you at work.'

'What's his problem, I wonder?' Greg stepped out into the wet night. 'I didn't know he was in the habit of calling on you outside work hours.'

Julia didn't reply, her eyes still on Pete. He was climbing into his Fiesta, parked behind her Mondeo. Her head was pounding. With a screech of tyres, Pete drove off up the street.

'You'll make sure you bolt your side gate, won't you?' Greg called over his shoulder. 'You never know who might be around.'

16

Julia woke unrefreshed on Wednesday morning after another fitful night's sleep. She spent longer than usual over her make-up, applying concealer to the dark shadows beneath her eyes and blusher to her sallow cheeks. She had considered phoning Pete the previous night to explain that Greg had turned up unexpectedly on Monday evening and ask how his mother's hospital appointments had gone, but decided it would be better to have the conversation face to face. More than anything, she wanted to reassure him of her support during his mother's illness. The knowledge that her preoccupation with family problems had led to him delaying telling her about Brenda's cancer weighed heavily on her conscience.

As usual, the aroma of fresh coffee greeted her when she arrived at the office. But Pete wasn't in the reception area. Julia hung her coat beside his leather jacket on the stand and was disappointed to find barely a quarter of a cup of coffee left in the jug. A knot of tension formed in the pit of her stomach when she saw that his door was closed. It would be unusual for him to have a client so early. She pressed her ear to the door. Hearing no voices inside, she knocked lightly and pushed the door open, with a bright 'Morning!'

Pete was standing on the far side of the reflexology table which occupied most of the windowless office. He didn't look up from the roll of disposable paper in his hands, offering only a curt greeting in return.

'I wondered if there might be more coffee going?'

He ripped a piece of paper from the roll and laid it on the table. 'I've got a client at nine.'

'I'll make myself a tea then. I really should learn how to work that coffee machine!'

Pete didn't reply, bending to smooth creases Julia couldn't see from the paper.

'About Monday night—' she began.

He studied his watch. 'I've not seen this client since we moved here. I need to check her details.' He turned his back on her to open the metal filing cabinet which was squeezed into the far corner of the room.

'Of course. I just wanted to explain that I wasn't expecting Greg. He turned up out of the blue.'

'There's nothing to explain.' Pete riffled through some folders and extracted one. 'Would you cover reception in case my client arrives early? I'd like to read through this.' He waved the red folder at her, still not making eye contact.

Julia hovered whilst he took his reading glasses from their case on top of the cabinet. He opened the folder and began to read the contents.

'But—'

He didn't look up. 'Can I just get on?'

Julia spun round and went back to reception. She ran water into the kettle. Pete had never spoken to her so coldly. It was ridiculous of him to react so badly to Greg turning up. It wasn't as though anything had happened between them, was it?

So far, she hadn't allowed herself to ponder whether Greg had been about to say he regretted his affair with Lisa when Pete had arrived. It had seemed disloyal to Pete to speculate. Now, taking a teabag from the canister in the cupboard, she found herself replaying their conversation. A surge of triumph accompanied her certainty that Greg would have acknowledged his mistake. *And then what? What if Pete hadn't come round?* Julia slammed the cupboard door, shutting out further musings of how the scene might have developed if Pete hadn't turned up.

Pete's client swept in on a waft of Chanel. She was a slim woman in late middle age. Her appraising glance around the office reminded Julia of Frances evaluating the cottage. She wondered fleetingly how Grace and Emmeline were getting on.

The woman unzipped her grey Joules gilet. 'I didn't realise you were so far along High Street.'

'No? I hope you didn't have too far to walk.' Julia poured the boiled water into her mug and removed the teabag.

'I don't mind walking.' The woman patted her silver bob, immaculate despite the drizzle. 'But I prefer the St. Mark's end of the street.' She glanced out of the window, her crimson mouth downturned. 'Do you always feel safe here?'

'Yes.' Julia dismissed the memory of her unease when she was locking up on Friday afternoon, and tried to silence Mark Smeaton's voice in her head, *'You never know who you're letting in, do you?'*

The woman raised her eyebrows. 'Perhaps it was just the rough sleeper I passed a few doors along who made me uneasy.' She gave a little shudder. 'He had the most dreadful face. Burns, I think.'

'That must have been Derek.'

The woman wrinkled her nose. 'You know him?'

‘A little. He plays the recorder beautifully.’ Julia suppressed a smile as the woman’s plucked eyebrows nearly disappeared beneath her fringe.

‘Oh? Is Mr. Hinds ready, do you know?’

‘I’ll tell him you’re here.’ Julia turned as Pete emerged from his office. He smiled warmly at his client. Julia felt a twinge of jealousy.

‘Great to see you again, Sylvia. I couldn’t help overhearing. It might not be the best area, but you’ve got to admit it’s an improvement on that old wreck of a school.’

The woman’s shoulders relaxed as she slipped past Julia. ‘Absolutely.’

‘I’ll be moving again soon,’ continued Pete, standing back to allow the woman to precede him into his room. ‘Somewhere more salubrious, I promise.’

His client giggled girlishly. Julia’s hold tightened on her mug.

‘Really? Do you have somewhere in mind?’

Pete’s reply was lost as he closed his door. Julia went through to her office. She took a gulp of the tea. It burnt the back of her throat. She set it down on the side table to cool and went over to the window, gazing out unseeingly at the queuing traffic and boarded up premises across the street. Did Pete plan to relocate without her? Had he decided their relationship was not only on hold, but over?

Last night’s headache had returned. She raised the slatted blind. Rivulets of rain trickled down the outside of the window. She rested her forehead against it, soothed by the coolness of the damp glass. Closing her eyes, she drew some calming breaths.

She gasped and took a step backwards when she looked outside again. James was staring back at her, his eyes bloodshot. His navy parka was unzipped, revealing a crumpled polo shirt beneath. His blond hair was plastered to his head. Julia's heart lurched.

'Come in,' she mouthed, and hurried through to reception.

James staggered across the threshold and sank on to one of the blue fabric chairs. Without a word, Julia re-boiled the water and scooped two spoonfuls of sugar into a mug of steaming tea. She splashed in some milk from the mini fridge which stood by the coffee machine. 'You'd better come through.'

He managed a lopsided smile as he dragged himself to his feet and wove his way across the foyer. 'Worried I'll scare the clients?'

'Something like that.'

Julia stepped back to allow James to precede her into her office, where he collapsed into the chair reserved for clients. She set his mug down on the side table before taking her usual seat. She took a sip of tea and surveyed him over the rim of her mug. Close up, he looked more unkempt than ever. Toothpaste mingled with unidentifiable brown stains on the maroon polo shirt. His black moleskin trousers and brown suede loafers were spattered with mud. He badly needed a shave.

'Has something else happened? Is it about Clare and the divorce?' Thinking back to the phone conversation with her sister-in-law, Julia wondered if Clare's solicitors had already contacted James about a claim against Linda's inheritance.

James passed a grimy hand through his matted fringe. 'That was bad enough. It's my job as well.'

Julia's forehead puckered. 'Your job?'

He nodded. His head lolled on to his chest. Julia leant forward and tapped his knee.

'Come on, James.' She glanced at the clock on the wall behind him.

He jerked his head up. 'You in a hurry?'

'I don't want to rush you, but I do have a client at ten.'

His face hardened. 'That's my slot, is it? All the time you can offer me? A measly half hour, when these strangers get what, twice as long?'

Julia took a deep breath. It was an effort to keep calm. 'We can talk again later. I've only got four clients booked in today.' She hesitated. 'What's happened at work? Have you phoned to say you won't be in today?'

His gaze slid towards the window as a passing lorry momentarily darkened the room.

'No need.'

'What do you mean?'

James fiddled with the zip on his parka. 'I've been suspended.'

Julia's hands froze around her mug. 'Why? You haven't tried to go in in this state, have you?'

He grimaced. ''Fraid so. We had a joint symposium over the weekend with some postgrads and lecturers from another university. I was due to give a lecture on Sunday morning.' He picked at some dirt under the nail of his forefinger. 'As you know, I was out drinking on Saturday. I didn't feel like my own company. It was late when I got back to Mum's cottage. I woke up late on Sunday with a nightmare hangover.' He raked his hand through his hair. 'I arrived ten minutes late for the lecture. My Head of Department took one look at me and sent me back home. Then in the afternoon I got the suspension e-mail.'

'Oh, James.' Julia nudged his mug towards him across the table. 'Drink some tea. What will you do?'

His hand trembled as he raised the mug and drank deeply. 'I'm not sure yet. I could get the union involved, I suppose. But I'm not sure they can help. I'd already received a warning last week when I went in the worse for wear. I wouldn't have got in such a state on Saturday if I hadn't heard from Clare's solicitor.' His lips curled. 'News of your good fortune couldn't have come at a worse time either.'

'Now don't try to lay this at my door,' snapped Julia. 'You sounded tipsy when you phoned me.'

He ignored her comment. 'It wasn't what I needed to hear,' he said mulishly. 'Hardly tactful, was it?'

Julia summoned every ounce of patience and bit back a retort. The charming, self-assured academic was unrecognisable in the dishevelled drunken man in front of her. She considered telling him about her intention to offer him part of the inheritance, but she was provoked by his resentment. 'We'll talk about the inheritance another time,' she said. 'For now, I know how upset you are about Clare and the divorce proceedings. Haven't you still got a chance to save your job though? Couldn't you maybe tell your Head of Department that it won't happen again, that it was a one off?' But even as she said it, Julia feared this wasn't true. Each time she had seen her brother since his return from sabbatical, he had clearly been under the influence of alcohol.

James shook his head. 'I'm not begging for my job.'

Julia sighed. She glanced at the clock and drained her tea. 'I'm sorry, James, but I need to get on. Shall I give you a call tonight?'

He didn't look at her as he rose unsteadily to his feet and followed her into reception. She sloshed water into her mug. She knew she should ask James where he was going in his present state, but she felt as wrung out as the dishcloth in her hands. She wanted him out of the office without further delay.

James paused on the threshold, his back to her as he opened the door on to the wet street. Wistful recorder music drifted in. *Derek.*

Straining to identify the tune above the traffic, Julia paid little attention to James's parting words. 'Don't worry. I shan't be bothering you again, sister.'

17

Rain was still falling heavily when Julia's final client left that afternoon. She could hear relaxation music filtering under the closed door of Pete's room whilst she typed up her session notes on her laptop, and guessed he was engaged with a client. She had kept to her office during lunch, eating a banana she had brought from home and catching up on paperwork. After the strained conversation with Pete and subsequent bruising encounter with James, she wanted to avoid any more emotionally charged discussions, fearing these could hinder her work with vulnerable clients. Now she scribbled Pete a hasty note apologising for leaving early because of a headache. Mindful of their discussions about security, she locked the door behind her. It was too windy for an umbrella, so she pulled up her waterproof hood and set off towards the car park.

A familiar figure was hunched in the entrance of the second hand bookshop five doors along, battered trilby pulled down low over his forehead. There were no lights on in the shop behind him. Julia couldn't remember the last time she had seen the elderly man who owned it. She hoped that he was all right. She knew nothing about him, whether or not he had a family who cared for him. She wondered who might look out for Derek. She recalled James's comment earlier, *'I didn't feel like my own company.'* A sudden acute sense of human isolation made her draw to a halt rather than call out a greeting and hurry past.

'Hello, Derek. I heard you playing earlier. "Windmills of your mind", wasn't it?'

He raised his head slowly. Julia braced herself not to react as his burns came into view.

'Very likely.' He coughed wheezily.

'That's a nasty cough. Have you seen a doctor?'

A flicker of amusement crossed his damaged features. 'Doctors can't cure lung damage from smoking and life on the streets.'

Julia's cheeks coloured. 'No, of course not.' She fished in her pocket and found four pound coins. 'Here you are.' She dropped the money into his grubby polystyrene cup.

'Thanks, duck.' He cleared his throat. 'You mind how you go. There's some strange types hanging around.' The right corner of his mouth twitched upwards. 'Present company excepted of course.'

Julia smiled. 'I will. You take care too, Derek.'

He nodded, picking up his wooden recorder from his filthy sleeping bag. Julia identified the first haunting notes of 'Lara's Theme' as she crossed the street. She continued to hum the melody when she could no longer hear the music above the traffic, mulling over Derek's warning. She was more inclined to pay attention to his reservations than those expressed by Pete's well-groomed client that morning. Turning the corner to the car park, she wondered what she would do if Pete relocated his reflexology practice without consulting her. From his exchange with the smart Sylvia, that seemed to be his intention.

She found herself scanning the car park before she crossed to her car, looking out for Mark Smeaton following her unexpected meeting with him there on Friday. She had done so each afternoon. She knew it was irrational to think he might be there again, but the encounter had rattled her. Nor had she recovered from his aggressive departure from the office earlier in the week. She'd told herself that he was just trying to frighten her, but there was something menacing about his words: *'You never know who you're letting in, do you?'*

Thinking of her disgruntled former client quashed the momentary cheer she had gained from her conversation with Derek, and the fading light of the wet October afternoon reflected her darkening mood as she drove home. Schools' traffic impeded her progress, giving her the opportunity to contemplate the problems she had been distracted from by work. Looking up at the cathedral looming to her left, she found herself comparing the difficulties in her relationships with the technological challenge of building the immense structure so that it would endure. She and Pete had taken a guided tour in the spring. They had learnt that whilst most of the existing structure had been completed by the late thirteenth century, the original spires had been removed in 1807 because they were in danger of collapse. Her chest tightened as she reflected how it was much easier to tear down a relationship than to build one.

Back on her street, Julia pulled in outside her gate. She trudged down the path, slick with fallen leaves. The winds of the last two days had whisked off the last of the cherry blossom foliage. Its bare branches looked as bereft as Julia felt. The dark windows of her empty cottage stared blankly back at her as she scrabbled in her shoulder bag for her key. She glanced up at the curtain wall of the castle behind the terrace, a lowering presence in the gathering dusk.

She gave herself a little shake as she unlocked the door. Telling herself that manual work would be a good weapon against self-pity, she ran up to her bedroom and changed from her skirt into an old pair of jeans. She set about cleaning the sitting-room ready for Ray's arrival the following day. She hoovered and dusted and pulled out the sofa bed. On her way upstairs for bed linen, she noticed that the red light was flashing on the answerphone in the hall.

There were three messages. The first was from Ray, confirming he was due to arrive in Lincoln by train at 11 a.m. the following day. Julia clapped her hand to her forehead, remembering Pete's offer the previous week to collect Ray from the station and drive him to the cottage. She'd completely forgotten to check with him. She shrank from the thought of phoning him given the tension between them following Greg's impromptu visit. The answerphone clicked on to the second message. Her heart beat faster when she heard Pete's voice. His message was brief and business-like, confirming that he had remembered about picking up Ray and would do so.

Tears pricked the back of her eyes. Pete was so reliable and dependable. *What must he have thought seeing Greg here on Monday?* He had clearly been in no mood to discuss it earlier, but maybe she should have plucked up courage and stayed on at the office to try to speak to him again after his client left. Again she berated herself for not realising that she had been putting Grace and Emmeline in front of their relationship, so much so that he hadn't felt he could tell her about his mother's illness. Would he forgive her and give their relationship another chance?

Her finger hovered over the delete button when she heard prolonged static at the start of the third message. Then she heard a baby crying, unmistakably Emmeline.

Julia felt a wave of affection, replaced by concern when she heard Frances's voice. From the little Julia knew of her, she thought the woman sounded unusually hesitant. 'Julia, it's Frances here. Would you... would you phone me when you get this message? I think I need your help.'

Frances gave the number, which Julia scribbled down on the pad she kept by the phone. She punched it into the handset, stomach fluttering. She was certain that the other woman wouldn't be seeking her help unless something was wrong.

The person picking up didn't offer a greeting.

'Hello?' ventured Julia after a few seconds.

'Hello. Who is this?'

There was no mistaking the rather strident voice. 'Frances, it's Julia Butler. You left a message.'

'Oh. Julia. Thank you for calling back.'

'You mentioned you might need my help?'

'Yes.' Frances paused. 'It's as I feared with Grace.'

The fluttering in Julia's stomach intensified. 'How do you mean?'

Frances's voice dropped to a stage whisper. 'She says that she and Emmeline were followed on their walk. All in her imagination of course.'

Julia digested this, scrunching up her right foot inside her slipper as her toes cramped. However erratic Grace's behaviour had been recently, she had never shown any signs of paranoia.

'Perhaps I could come over? Talk to Grace?'

'That sounds an excellent idea. We have to be so careful, don't we, for the sake of our precious little Emmeline?'

Julia's heart-shaped jaw clenched. 'Indeed we do.' She wrote down Frances's directions and rang off.

Half an hour later she drew up on the gravelled driveway of a substantial detached house. Frances's home was situated in a leafy cul-de-sac to the south-west of the city. The headlights revealed a modern property with a mock Tudor frontage. This seemed fitting for Grace, whose thesis centred on the relationship between Henry VIII's daughters Mary and Elizabeth.

Julia had barely climbed out of the car when Frances opened the door. 'There you are! I'm so relieved you could come. I've been quite beside myself with worry. Do come in.'

Julia crunched across the gravel and entered the brightly lit hall.

'Let me take your coat.' Frances held out her arms. 'If you wouldn't mind taking off your boots... Mud shows up terribly on this gold carpet. Not a practical colour, but we inherited it when we moved in. Excellent quality though. Axminster, you know.'

Julia declined to comment further on the superior carpet as she slipped off her trench coat and handed it over, then stooped to remove her black ankle boots. She placed them on an expensive looking oak shoe rack to the left of the front door and straightened up. The 'Postman Pat' theme spilled into the hall from a room on the right. Instinctively Julia stepped towards it, but Frances waved her towards the stairs.

'I thought you'd like to go up and see if you can convince Grace that there is no-one watching her before you disturb Emmeline.' The lines on her broad forehead wrinkled. 'I do hope you're able to talk some sense into her.'

'You haven't spoken to her since our call?'

'No. She's been upstairs most of the day. I offered to look after Emmeline at breakfast, so she could make progress with her studies. She was delighted, as you can imagine.' Frances paused meaningfully. 'When she came down for lunch, I suggested she might like to take Emmeline for a walk. She said she would go later, because she was in the middle of some important research.' She pursed her lips, bright with her cerise lipstick. 'When she finally came down, it was already going dark. You know how dull and wet it's been today. But she *would* insist on going. They were out about twenty minutes when I heard hammering at the door. I wondered what on earth was going on!' She fingered the silver cross which nestled above the top button of her indigo shirt. The shirt was too tight, straining across her ample bosom, and exposing a flash of white bra at the third button.

'And?' Julia tapped her car key against her left palm impatiently.

'There she was, shaking like a leaf, saying someone had been following them. Emmeline was very upset after being jolted home in such a rush, poor lamb! I looked around but couldn't see anyone.' Frances sighed. 'As I said on the phone, I'm afraid Grace must have been deluded.'

Julia frowned. 'Surely it is possible someone was following them? After all, no-one would follow them right up to the door. You wouldn't see them in the dark, if they took care to stay out of sight.'

Frances's eyebrows disappeared beneath her ginger fringe. 'Why on earth would anyone follow Grace and Emmeline?'

'I don't know,' conceded Julia. 'But I will go up and speak to her.'

'It's the second room on the left. I do hope you can help.' Frances blinked hard behind her oversized glasses. 'I have grave doubts about the story. As I was saying the other day, we must take into account her mother's history.'

Julia had planted her foot on the bottom step of the oak staircase when a door was flung open above her. From the heavy footsteps on the landing, she knew it wasn't Grace. Suzanne came into view and began to descend the stairs.

The young woman was carrying a pair of high-heeled black ruched boots and a patent black clutch bag. She didn't acknowledge Julia, who removed her foot off the step to let her pass.

'Here's Julia, Suzanne,' said Frances, with an apologetic smile at Julia.

Suzanne avoided eye contact. 'Hi,' she said unenthusiastically. She grimaced as she forced her broad feet into the boots, one hand on the front door for balance.

'Those don't look very comfortable, dear!' There was a forced note in Frances's laugh. 'Are they new?'

'Got them a while ago.' Suzanne straightened up and tugged at the brief skirt of a lacy orange dress which she wore beneath a leopard faux fur coat.

Julia was struck by the contrast with the nondescript denim jacket Suzanne had been wearing on Saturday. So was Frances.

'And I don't remember seeing the coat or dress before. Very… eye-catching, aren't they? You have been on a shopping spree!'

Suzanne shrugged and glanced inside the clutch bag. Satisfied she had everything she needed, she snapped the bag shut and opened the door. The porch light illuminated the heavy raindrops bouncing on the doorstep. Frances moved forwards and placed her hand on the door.

'You have got money for a taxi, haven't you?'

There was a fractional pause before Suzanne nodded. 'What time will you be back?'

'Late. You needn't stay up.'

Mother and daughter exchanged a long look before Frances removed her hand. 'Bye then. Enjoy yourself!'

Suzanne slammed the door without a backward glance.

'Girls!' Frances shook her head with an indulgent smile, though Julia detected a flicker of anxiety in her large brown eyes. She lowered her voice conspiratorially. 'She has a new boyfriend, but is keeping him quite secret. I don't know anything about him at all!'

'I see,' said Julia. She remembered that Suzanne had phoned Grace to tell her about her new man on the night Emmeline had been found in the shed. Given that Suzanne and Grace had a strained relationship, the phone call had struck Julia as surprising. She could understand why Suzanne might not wish to disclose details of the relationship to Frances. From her mother's attitude, Suzanne might have been a teenager rather than a grown woman.

The 'Postman Pat' theme struck up again accompanied by an indignant cry from Emmeline.

'Wanting attention, no doubt! I'll see to the little treasure whilst you go up to Grace.'

Frances turned towards the sitting-room. Emmeline's moans increased in volume above the jangling tune as Julia made her way upstairs.

She tapped on the door of Grace's room. Music filtered on to the landing, and Julia recognised Philip Glass's soundtrack to 'The Hours'. They'd seen it together at the cinema a few months earlier. A lump formed in Julia's throat as she considered how their relationship had unravelled since then. The door opened. Grace looked paler than ever, the dark shadows under her eyes as livid as fresh bruises.

'What are you doing here?'

Julia aimed for a light tone. 'What a greeting! May I come in?'

There was no welcoming smile from Grace, but she did step back. Julia followed her into a spacious bedroom tastefully decorated with duck egg wallpaper. Matching velvet curtains were drawn across two windows. Beneath one window was Grace's desk, her laptop and books scattered across it. A single bed stood against the wall behind the door, made up with ivory duvet and pillows. Against the far wall was an oak wardrobe and matching chest of drawers. Bookcases crammed full of hardbacks and paperbacks lined the wall to Julia's left. From a quick glance, Julia saw children's books mingled with adult novels and history books. She hugged herself, suddenly cold in the virginal room. Something was missing.

'Where's Emmeline's cot?'

Grace knit her brows. 'In the room across the landing. Frances said it was time for Emmeline to sleep on her own.'

'Oh? And what did *you* think?'

Grace turned towards her desk, tugging her plait over her right shoulder. 'It's worth a try. I could do with more sleep. As you know.' Her voice had taken on the aggrieved tone which Julia had heard too often lately.

'But Emmeline has always slept with you so far.'

'She's got to sleep on her own sometime,' Grace flashed back. 'You'd better sit down,' she added ungraciously, indicating an upholstered wingback chair positioned in front of the bookcase.

Julia sat, curling her toes into the thick pile of the azure carpet. Grace took a seat in the high-backed cream leather chair at the desk.

'I'll just save this.' She clicked a few keys on her laptop.

'How's your research been going since you moved in?'

'Not bad. I've managed to do some writing up.' Grace closed the lid of the laptop, laying her palms on it protectively. She tilted her head towards Julia, her strawberry blonde hair illuminated into a flaming halo by the angle poise desk lamp. 'I assume you're not here to talk about my thesis.'

Julia hesitated. 'Frances rang me,' she said cautiously.

Grace's slim shoulders tensed inside her powder blue cashmere jumper. 'Why?'

'She was worried about you saying that someone was following you and Emmeline.'

Grace kneaded her temples with her forefinger. 'I could tell she didn't believe me!' She raised her large cornflower blue eyes to Julia's, entreaty replacing hostility. 'But you do, don't you, Aunt Julia?'

Julia registered the little girlish tone, the contrast with the previous antagonism. Snippets of recent conversations clamoured in her head so insistently that she had to resist a temptation to cover her ears, trying to drown them out. One phrase though echoed loudest. *'How well do you know her?'* Pete had asked. She swallowed the instinctive reassuring words which sprang to her lips and responded with a question of her own. 'It is possible someone was following you,' she said tentatively, 'but why would anyone do that?'

'I've no idea.' Grace shot her aunt a resentful look. 'You don't believe me either, do you?'

'I'm not saying I don't believe you,' said Julia calmly. 'I'm just wondering about the person's motive. Did you see him or her?'

'It was too dark. It began to rain hard soon after we reached the main road, so I turned round to come back. That's when I first saw them standing under a tree on the other side of the road. I thought the person was waiting for someone, or maybe sheltering from the rain. But when I looked across the road again a minute later, they were parallel with us.'

'Then whoever it was might have been sheltering and then decided that it wasn't worth it, surely? It hasn't eased off since.' Julia nodded towards the window. The rain was pounding against it.

'I'm sure they weren't. They stopped when I glanced over. Just stood there.' Grace began to tremble. 'When I moved on, the person did too. Then I began to run, turned into our road. Poor Emmeline was screaming. I dashed down to the house and banged on the door. When Frances opened the door, whoever it was had disappeared.'

'Right.' Julia thought for a moment. Grace's account was quite convincing, but Julia understood Frances's scepticism. Why would anyone follow her and Emmeline? She chose her next words carefully. 'There wouldn't be any point calling the police at this stage. I think the best thing would be to stay vigilant, see if this person turns up again. What do you think?'

Grace tapped her long nails on the desk. 'You're probably right. The police would want more information. I'll wait and see what happens.'

'OK.' Julia stifled a yawn and realised suddenly how tired and hungry she was. She hadn't eaten since her midday banana. She stood. 'I'm going to go home and get some food. Remember your grandfather arrives tomorrow. Would you and Emmeline like to come over on Friday for tea? I've got an early finish at the office, so I could pick you up and we can eat early. Then I can run you both back here so that Emmeline isn't up too late.'

Grace's face brightened. 'That would be lovely,' she said. 'It will be so good to see Grandpa.'

Julia smiled, relieved to sense the tension dissipate. Then she grew serious, thinking of the reason for her impromptu visit. 'And if you have any more worries about being followed or spied on tomorrow, give me a ring, won't you?'

The brightness left Grace's face. 'OK.'

Julia left the room, closing the door behind her. On the landing she heard a creak. Frances was halfway down the stairs. Julia followed. The woman glanced up at her when she reached the hall. Her face was flushed and she was panting slightly. She had obviously been eavesdropping.

'There you are! Did you have a fruitful chat with Grace?'

'I think so.'

'Did you manage to persuade her that she was mistaken about being followed?'

'I'm not sure she was mistaken.' Julia brought her feet together on the bottom stair, wanting to retain the advantage of height. Frances was slightly taller than her at floor level.

'Really?' Frances raised her ginger eyebrows.

'From her description of what happened, I think it's possible someone *was* following her.'

Frances clutched her cross. 'If you're right, we must pray for protection,' she said. 'But I hope you're wrong, that it's a product of her overwrought imagination.' She glanced up the staircase and lowered her voice. 'Not the result of any other influences.'

'What other influences?'

Frances opened her mouth, then closed it again. She lifted her right hand. 'I don't want us to disagree. Not when we both want the best for Grace and Emmeline.' She sighed. 'I realised after we met that we have quite different worldviews.'

Julia frowned. 'I don't understand.'

Frances leant towards her, her broad face centimetres away. 'You remember our conversation at your house.' Her voice was little more than a whisper. 'When I mentioned the possibility of… *satanic influence*.'

Julia jerked her head away. The woman's breath reeked of onions and garlic.

Frances misinterpreted the movement. 'I'm so sorry. I don't mean to frighten you. But it could be an explanation, possibly connected with the poor girl's sad maternal history.' Her wide eyes stared unblinkingly into Julia's.

'I see.' Julia shivered as a draught blew down the stairs. There was a loud bang. Julia jumped. In the sitting-room Emmeline howled.

Frances laid a hand on her arm. 'Dear me, you are nervy, aren't you? Don't worry, it will just be the bathroom window slamming in the wind. Not that you or Emmeline would know that!'

Julia stepped down the final stair, dislodging Frances's hand. 'I'll just pop in and see Emmeline.' She winced to hear her artificially bright tone, but she was determined not to engage with the other woman's reference to satanic influences. It sounded bizarrely medieval to the rational Julia. She steered the conversation on to safer ground.

'I've suggested Grace should ring if she has any more concerns.'

'That sounds like a good idea.' Frances followed Julia into the sitting-room, closing the door behind them. She hesitated. 'I think we need to make a plan, don't you?'

Julia knelt by Emmeline who was strapped into a white rocker decorated with colourful triangles. She was wearing a woodland animal sleepsuit which Julia had bought her. Julia's heart melted as the baby held up her arms towards her. 'Make a plan?'

'Yes.' Frances plodded across the gold carpet and turned off the TV which stood on an oak cabinet in the corner. Postman Pat was waving goodbye, his black and white cat, Jess, resting her paws on the window sill of the Royal Mail van. 'Surely you must see that there are issues here about Emmeline's safety?'

Julia didn't answer immediately. She unstrapped Emmeline and scooped her from the rocker. 'Hello, sweetheart.' She pressed her nose to Emmeline's strawberry blonde head, savouring the aloe vera scent of her baby shampoo before turning to Frances. 'I'm not sure I understand. Obviously if Grace and Emmeline are followed again, we need to contact the police. It could have been a one off, or Grace could have been mistaken, or—'

'No, no.' Frances shook her head. 'You think they may have been followed, but I'm still far from convinced. I am concerned – *very* concerned – about Grace's ability to look after Emmeline adequately. You know as well as I do that she is obsessed with her research, just as her late mother was obsessed with her art.' She compressed her lips. 'Now, suppose Grace imagined that someone was following her earlier?'

'I don't think we can assume that,' said Julia.

'Mm.' Frances managed to inject sufficient doubt into the single syllable to make it clear that she thought otherwise. She looked intently at Julia. 'I don't like to say this, but all things considered, we do have to ask ourselves whether Grace is fit to be looking after Emmeline, don't we?'

Julia became very still. Emmeline nuzzled into her shoulder.

'What are you saying?' Emmeline's small body jerked in response to Julia's sharp tone and she began to whimper quietly. Julia rubbed her back. 'Shh, shh.'

'Shall I take her?' Frances stepped forward. 'She was so nearly settled, weren't you, darling?' She held her arms out.

Reluctantly Julia handed over the baby. Emmeline's whimpers immediately escalated into sobs.

Julia shoved her hands into the pockets of her jeans. 'What do you mean about questioning Grace's fitness to look after Emmeline?'

Frances raised a finger to her mouth. 'Let's talk about it some other time, shall we? I see the thought has shocked you, although I would have thought with your counselling background...' She let the words trail off. The implication that Julia had been negligent not to question Grace's capacity to look after Emmeline was clear. 'Besides, I don't want to disturb this little one any further tonight.' She rocked the baby in her arms, crooning, 'Here you are, darling. Safe with Granny now.' Emmeline's sobs subsided.

Julia stared at them wordlessly, ramming her hands further into her pockets. She had a sudden irrational urge to grab Emmeline and take her home, away from Grace's haphazard mothering and Frances's control.

'Sorry to rush you,' said Frances. 'Please, do think over what I've said and visit again soon.'

She turned from the room. Julia had no choice other than to follow her out into the hall. They exchanged brief farewells after Julia had put on her coat and boots. Emmeline was still crying as Julia went out into the stormy night. The baby's soft moans plucked Julia's heartstrings.

The wind had risen during her visit. Large raindrops spattered the windscreen as she backed the Mondeo out of the drive. On a whim she stopped the car and wound the front windows down at the top of the cul-de-sac. Unsurprisingly, no-one was around in the hostile conditions. But there was no doubt, as she had pointed out to Frances, that the bushes offered a good hiding-place to anyone who might have been following Grace and Emmeline.

Traffic was light as she skirted the west side of the city on the drive home. Even with the heater on, she felt chilled to the bone. Both conversations had disturbed her, especially Frances's suggestion that Grace might not be fit to look after Emmeline. Yet Pete had hinted at the same thing, she recalled, her heart dropping as she thought of him. She wished more than anything that she could ring him up and talk through the situation with him. But after his distance at the office following his disastrous encounter with Greg, she understood that he needed space to think things through. And it would be selfish of her to burden him with another problem when he was preoccupied with his sick mother. Julia's mood was bleak as she pulled up outside her cottage fifteen minutes later.

The cathedral clock was striking eight as she climbed out of the car. A movement in the porch stilled her hand on the wrought iron gate. She recognised the tall, broad figure of Greg stepping down on to the path. He raised his right hand in greeting. Her stomach flipped as she walked towards him, wondering what had brought him back again. The heavy rain made any conversation outdoors impractical. In any event, Greg had already withdrawn into the shelter of the porch. He was stooping to pick up something as Julia approached.

'I'm back sooner than I expected.'

'So I see.' Julia unlocked the door and stepped into the hall, flicking on the light. Greg followed her inside. He held a large black duffel bag in one hand, a white plastic bag in the other.

'What...?'

He twisted his mouth in the ironical half-smile which had once charmed her. 'Lisa's thrown me out. I've nowhere else to go tonight. Would you mind...?'

18

Julia stared at Greg, lost for words. He proffered the plastic bag. A spicy aroma rose from it, making her mouth water.

'I picked up a takeaway. Enough for two, if you haven't eaten.'

Julia bit back suggestions about hotels. He had food, and her stomach was rumbling. The wind was gathering strength, driving the rain into the hall. You wouldn't put a cat out on a night like this. Her thoughts turned to Derek, the rough sleeper. She shivered, hoping he'd found shelter somewhere on this inhospitable night.

As she wavered, a gust of wind slammed the door behind Greg.

'Takeaway would be great.' She unzipped her waterproof. 'OK, you can stay. Just for one night.'

'Thanks. You're a sport.' He rested a hand on her shoulder.

Julia shrugged off his hand without looking at him. She hung her waterproof on the coat stand. 'You can use the sofa bed in the sitting-room.'

The corner of Greg's mouth twitched. 'Of course. Where else?'

Julia chose not to reply as he removed his waterproof and placed it alongside hers, dripping water on to the laminate floor. She remembered they'd bought the waterproofs together one wet weekend in the Peak District. They'd joked that they mustn't buy matching colours, so as to avoid any resemblance to Howard and Hilda from the eighties sitcom 'Ever Decreasing Circles'.

Greg seemed to read her thoughts. 'It was raining cats and dogs that weekend we bought these in Bakewell, do you remember?'

'Was it?' she dissembled. She dipped her head in the direction of the sitting-room. 'You'll find a duvet and sheet in there, ready for another guest tomorrow. Maybe you could make the bed whilst I warm some plates?'

'Sure.' Greg's face fell. Picking up the bag containing the takeaway, Julia smiled to herself. He'd contributed little to household chores during their relationship.

'Who's your next guest, then?' Greg asked ten minutes later. He was pouring wine from the bottle they'd opened on Monday evening into two glasses.

Just like he's never been away. Julia clamped down on the thought, closing the lid on an empty plastic box which had contained her favourite beef in black bean sauce.

'A friend.'

Greg crunched a prawn cracker. 'Anyone I know?'

'No.' Julia wasn't about to explain that her visitor was an octogenarian priest and former Canadian Royal Air Force Wing Commander who had been her mother's lover in 1943. She spooned rice on to her plate and nudged the container towards him. He heaped some alongside his chicken and pork chow mein.

'I hope I didn't put your visitor off last night,' he said, fluffing some congealed grains of rice with his fork.

Julia speared a piece of beef without replying. She put it into her mouth, savouring the piquant sauce.

'Phil didn't use to call round out of hours, did he?' Greg persisted.

‘It’s Pete, not Phil.’ If Julia wasn’t going to fill Greg in on the family history she’d uncovered since their separation, she certainly wasn’t about to tell him about her relationship with Pete. Her stomach knotted. What on earth would Pete say if he saw her and Greg eating Chinese together? Suddenly the beef tasted too salty. It was an effort not to spit it out.

‘Pete then.’ Greg set down his cutlery and reached for his wine. ‘Are you more than colleagues now, if he’s turning up after hours?’

‘He’s not the only one, is he?’ replied Julia tartly.

Greg tipped his glass towards her. ‘Touché.’

She changed the subject abruptly. ‘You said Lisa’s thrown you out?’

‘’Fraid so.’

She took a sip of wine, waiting to see if he would tell her more. When he didn’t, she asked, ‘Are you going to tell her where you are, in case she needs to contact you?’

Greg shrugged. ‘She can ring my mobile. Though I think it’s switched off at the minute.’

‘What if there’s an emergency?’

‘An emergency?’

‘What if your little boy is suddenly taken ill, or has an accident?’

‘He was fine when I left. He’ll be tucked up safely in his cot by now.’ Detecting disapproval in Julia’s face, he added, ‘Don’t worry. I’ll check my phone after we’ve eaten.’

Julia raised an eyebrow, but said nothing further. In the hall the grandmother clock chimed the quarter. Greg jerked his head towards it.

‘I’ve missed that sound, you know.’

Julia concentrated on winding some noodles round her fork. ‘Oh?’

'Yes. Strange what you miss.'

In the silence which followed, the ticking of the clock sounded unusually loud in Julia's ears.

'It belonged to your grandparents, didn't it?'

'That's right.'

'I never used to think about it when I was younger,' Greg went on, helping himself to more rice, 'but I can understand now why you've always appreciated the clock and the bookcase. They're tangible links with your roots, aren't they?'

Julia glanced at him, her brow furrowed. Greg had never been one for analysis. 'Yes, I suppose so. Although as you know, I barely remember my mother's mother, and my grandfather died years before I was born.'

'Even so, you've got something that belonged to them, that was passed down through your family. Is your grandfather's desk still in your mother's cottage?'

'Yes.'

'Will you bring that here too, then? Or do you think James will get it?'

'I don't know. We haven't talked about it.'

It occurred to her that she would like the walnut desk since it matched the grandmother clock and bookcase. The furniture had belonged to her grandparents when her grandfather was vicar in the parish of Scampton, a village six miles north of Lincoln. But she could hardly insist on taking the desk if James requested to keep it in memory of their mother. Her maternal grandmother had bequeathed the clock and bookcase to Julia, the only grandchild she had lived to see. It was only fair that James should have something. From Clare's belligerent attitude, it sounded as though she would make things as difficult as possible when it came to dividing the matrimonial furniture. More expense for James in setting up home again.

Greg was still asking questions. 'Has the cottage sold yet?'

'We've had an offer. The solicitors are dealing with the legal work.'

Greg chewed thoughtfully. 'Pity.'

'How do you mean?'

'It crossed my mind I could have stayed there for a while if it was empty.' Seeing Julia's eyes widen, he added hastily, 'I'd have offered rent of course.'

'Right.' Julia was far from convinced that she believed him. She wondered if money had been the main reason he and Lisa had split. It wouldn't have surprised her, following her own experience of his financial incompetence and the row she'd overheard him having with Lisa by the castle that afternoon.

'Good that you won't have to worry about it over winter,' Greg went on. 'Empty properties can be a problem, can't they; risk of frozen pipes and all that?'

'Mm.' *What would you know?* Greg had never owned a property. He'd rented with a previous partner before his relationship with Julia. Thinking how Pete had covered all the mortgage payments Greg had missed, in order to save the cottage from repossession by the bank, Julia didn't feel hungry any more. She pushed the food around her plate.

'Do you think I could stay there for a week or two, till I find something else?'

Julia swallowed a rude response at his audacity, as a gust of wind drove the rain against the windows with renewed intensity, drawing the attention of them both. Julia reminded herself that Lisa had thrown Greg out on the worst night of the autumn. However insouciant he seemed, he must be anxious about his next move, especially if money was an issue for him as it so often was.

'I'm afraid not. The sale should go through soon.'

He shrugged. 'Fair enough.' He wound more noodles round his fork. 'Nice for you to get an inheritance, even though I guess your mum's cottage is at the lower end of the property market.'

When Julia didn't respond, he said, 'It will be handy for James to come into some money too, won't it?'

'Mm.' Julia reached across the table for a piece of kitchen towel and dabbed her mouth. She should ring James, check he was OK after he'd flung out of the office earlier. He might have taken out his anger on her but she didn't like to think about him drunk and alone.

'Do you think James will have enough to buy Clare out?'

'What?' Julia stared at him.

He smiled. 'Sorry. None of my business, is it? It's just I bumped into Clare recently and she gave the distinct impression that she's after all she can get.'

Julia bit her lip and chose not to reply, prodding at the remains of her beef. There was no way she was going to confide in Greg about her brother's financial situation.

Greg reverted to his previous subject. 'Anyway, I do find myself thinking more about the lives of those who've gone before as I get older. Do you ever imagine what it was like for our parents and grandparents during the wars, for instance?'

Julia's hand became still on her fork. Greg's head was bent over his plate as he stabbed a piece of pork in the chow mein. 'From time to time,' she said.

'When you think of all the things we go through in our lives, the things other people don't know about us, you wonder what secrets they carried too, don't you, our parents and grandparents?'

Despite his blank expression, Julia's heart was beating quickly. 'We're all very complex,' she said non-committally.

He tilted his head on one side, as if waiting for her to say more. When she didn't, he said, 'That's a disappointing answer, coming from Julia the counsellor.'

'What were you expecting me to say?' she temporised.

He shrugged. 'I'm not sure. Just something more... concrete. I mean, did you never talk to your mother about the past, the war years?'

Julia inhaled. It would be so easy to tell Greg about her mother's secret, about Linda and Grace, but she resisted. She realised that she didn't trust him with it. Nor could she bear the thought that he might reduce her mother's wartime relationship to some 'sordid affair' as Clare had described it. If Clare had mentioned it to him, why didn't he just come out with it? Was he goading her? She eyed him narrowly.

'Remembering what your mother told you about the war years?'

'No,' she said shortly. 'We only talked about it occasionally. It was something I steered clear of. I sensed it brought back painful memories for her.' She reached for her glass and took some quick sips of wine.

'Sure.' Greg nodded his blond head, the picture of understanding. He had always been a good listener, and that was one of the things which had attracted her to him in the beginning. She noticed that his hair was beginning to thin at the crown. 'At least you had your mother till this year.' He sighed deeply, setting down his fork and reaching for his own wine. 'When you lose your parents early...' His voice trailed off. He sloshed his glass back and forth, the liquid shining ruby red beneath the ceiling spotlight.

Julia's breath caught. Throughout their six-year relationship, Greg had always closed down any mention of his parents. They'd been killed in a road accident when he was sixteen. 'It was desperately sad for you,' she ventured. 'And I'm well aware how inadequate that sounds.'

'Thanks.' Greg took a slug of wine. 'Sometimes I've wondered if that's why I have commitment problems,' he muttered.

'Commitment problems?'

He smiled wryly. 'That's what Lisa's been telling me since Nathan was born.' He picked up his fork again, loading more rice on to it. 'You know as well as I do how I've struggled to hold down a job, let alone a relationship. That's the main reason I went freelance, so I didn't have an employer to answer to. Don't tell me it hasn't crossed your mind that I might be commitment-phobic.'

Their gazes locked for a long moment. Julia sensed her chest rising and falling rapidly. She broke the eye contact and took another mouthful of chow mein.

'So what does counsellor Julia think?'

Julia set down her fork, undeceived by the levity of his tone. 'I don't think it's wise for me to say.' She paused. 'Maybe it's something you could discuss with an independent counsellor?'

Greg's mouth twisted. 'You always were one for your precious boundaries, weren't you? Can't you offer anything else? You used to encourage me to open up, to talk about my feelings about losing my parents so young.'

Julia lined up her cutlery neatly on her plate. 'You said you were asking me as a counsellor,' she said, cursing the slight tremor in her voice. 'Because of my... personal involvement, my best advice is for you to talk to another counsellor about it.'

'OK.' Greg nodded and took another sip of wine. 'You don't have any words of wisdom for old times' sake?' His voice had taken on a husky note.

He set his glass down, reached suddenly across the table and grabbed her right hand.

For a moment Julia looked at her slender hand in his large one, so familiar with the blond hairs rising on the back, the square clean nails. She pushed away the thought of how many times his hands had touched her, explored her body. She wrenched her hand away.

Greg's hand lay still for a moment before he withdrew it and plunged his fork into a piece of chicken.

'I take it that's a no.' He sounded amused rather than regretful.

She rose and took her plate across to the bin. Her hands shook as she scraped off the leftovers. She angled her body away from Greg so that he wouldn't notice.

'That's right. I'm the last person you should ask.'

Greg clattered his cutlery noisily on his plate. Julia rinsed hers at the sink, turning the tap on so that the water gushed out with unnecessary force. The familiar sound was comforting in the silence.

Greg finished eating and moved his chair back, scraping the tiles and setting Julia's teeth on edge. She picked up the empty takeaway cartons from the table without looking at him and bagged them up inside the white plastic bag. Her movements were jerky and self-conscious. She was certain that he was watching her. But when she turned, he was studying the Chinese menu which had accompanied the food.

He stretched out his long legs and topped up his glass, then waved towards hers which was half-full. 'Aren't you coming back to finish your wine?'

She sat down and took a gulp.

'Food was good, wasn't it? I remembered "The Golden Dragon" was always our favourite.'

Julia looked at him over the rim of her wine glass. 'I prefer the "Hung Wang" these days.'

He raised an eyebrow, the corner of his mouth rising in a mocking smile. 'If that's how you want to play it.'

Julia set down her glass with exaggerated care. Her heart was banging against her ribs. 'I'm not playing games here, Greg. I asked you last night and I'm asking you again: what is it that you want? Why have you turned up after all these months?'

His smile disappeared. 'We were good together, you and I, weren't we?'

Julia swallowed hard.

He leant towards her across the table, gazing deeply into her eyes. 'I know what I did was unforgivable. But if you tell me there's a chance, I'll do my best to make it up to you, I swear.'

Julia closed her eyes, assailed by memories of her grief when he had left her for Lisa, grief compounded by the loss of her mother and then her devastation at being childless. Another image rose before her too: of Pete, turning back down the path the previous evening when he had encountered Greg on her doorstep. Her eyes snapped open.

'It's too late, Greg. There's someone else.'

It was a relief to say the words. Julia jumped up from the table and headed for the door. 'I'm off for an early night. It's been a long day. If I don't see you in the morning, just pull the front door behind you when you leave.' She spun round, struck by the sudden thought that Pete would be bringing Ray here the next morning. She aimed for a casual tone. 'I assume you'll be gone quite early? My guest will be arriving mid-morning.'

He surveyed her a moment. 'Is your mysterious guest the "someone else"?'

'No.'

'OK. Well, I should be out soon after you,' he said smoothly.

'Good.' She smiled sweetly. 'Don't worry about the dishes. I'll do them when I get home from work tomorrow.'

Greg gazed back at her sulkily. Tired though she was, Julia sped up the stairs. For the first time since he had walked out on her fourteen months earlier, she felt free of him.

19

Julia was out of the house early the next morning, determined to catch Pete before his first client arrived. Greg hadn't emerged from the sitting-room and she didn't bother shouting a farewell. She'd said all she needed to say the night before. She only hoped that he would leave soon after her. The last thing she needed was for Pete to bump into him at her cottage when he dropped off Ray.

Grey clouds scudded across the sky. A bright spot behind the cathedral hinted at the presence of the sun. The postman jerked his head towards it as she went out of the gate. 'Change from the rain!'

Julia smiled and thanked him as he handed her a brown envelope which bore the local authority's stamp. She guessed it was about the council tax on her mother's cottage and shoved it into her shoulder bag. It would keep till later.

She'd left early enough to miss the worst of the schools' traffic, and it was only eight fifteen when she walked round the corner from the car park on to High Street. She wrinkled her nose against the diesel fumes from a lorry held up at the traffic lights, jogging across the road just before the lights changed. There was no sign of Derek in the doorway of the second hand bookshop where she had seen him yesterday. She hoped that he had found shelter during last night's storm. Head down against the wind, she was just three doors from the office when she noticed a young man in a cheap grey suit pause on his way past. He seemed to be staring at something in the window.

Julia drew alongside and gasped. The window was emblazoned with the message 'KIDS NEED DADS' in purple capitals.

The young man glanced at her. 'This your place?'

Julia nodded, picking at the letter 'K' with her finger nail.

'That's no use.' Julia detected satisfaction in the man's tone. He tapped on the glass, indicating the brochures on the display unit inside. 'Julia Butler, Counsellor' alternated with 'Pete Hinds, Refloxologist'. 'Looks like you've been targeted. Are you one of those women who's against dads seeing their kids?'

'Certainly not!' Julia rummaged in her bag for her office key.

'Pah! You got any idea how much it costs to go through the courts? My ex always has a last minute excuse why I can't see my two. Now she's got a new fella, she doesn't want me around. Do you know when I last saw them?' He thrust his face towards Julia, close enough for her to smell the mint toothpaste which didn't mask his halitosis.

She shook her head and took a step sideways, hand closing on her key.

'Five months ago!' He eyeballed her as if daring her to contradict him. 'You women don't know the damage you cause.'

Julia didn't want to take issue with this aggressive stranger. It crossed her mind that she should delay opening up in case he tried to follow her into the office. But he lost interest, turning his head and spitting into the gutter before continuing along High Street without a backward glance.

Inside, Julia locked the door behind her and made herself a mug of strong tea. She left the vertical blinds drawn, shutting herself off from the graffiti and the gaze of curious passers-by. Sipping her tea in one of the reception chairs, she dismissed the idea of phoning the police. Graffiti on an office window at the wrong end of High Street would be low on their priority list.

Less shaky after drinking the tea, she was rooting under the sink for the glass cleaner when a key scraped in the lock. She found it and stood up as Pete came in, his face set.

'You've seen it then?'

'Impossible not to.' He didn't meet her eye.

'I'm hoping this will get it off.' She waved the glass cleaner.

'That won't work. The best thing for spray paint is nail polish remover.'

'Oh.' Julia set the plastic bottle down on the desk. 'Shall I go out and get some? I don't have a client till nine thirty.'

'OK. I've got a nine o'clock.' Pete pulled off his beanie and ran his hand over his freshly shaved head. Julia's chest contracted as she took in how tired he looked. Pete had always had a youthful appearance, but under the unforgiving fluorescent tube he looked every day of his fifty-two years. His face was grey and there were dark shadows under his eyes.

'How's your mum?'

He turned towards the window and tugged the cord of the blind. It jerked unevenly upwards. 'Not good.' He fumbled with two tangled slats. 'I need to go up to the hospital after I pick up Ray. She's got an appointment with the consultant at twelve thirty.' He turned from the window, still not quite making eye contact. 'You got my message on the answerphone?'

'Yes, thank you. I really appreciate you collecting Ray. Are you sure you won't be pushed to get to the hospital on time for your mum's appointment?'

'No problem. Did you bring your spare key?'

'Yes.' Julia unzipped the front pocket of her bag and withdrew the key. She placed it on top of the desk.

Pete came over and pocketed it. 'I'm not happy about leaving you here alone again,' he went on. 'I wish we'd sorted out a receptionist.'

'I'll be fine.' Julia wanted to go round the desk and put her arms round him. But the few metres of blue flecked carpet which separated them seemed as wide as the ocean. 'I hope the consultant is able to... help,' she finished lamely, not sure what treatment could be offered to a terminally ill patient.

Pete nodded. 'Thanks.' He touched the gold stud in his right ear. Julia saw his Adam's apple rise and fall. She swallowed a lump in her own throat.

'Will you be back later?' she asked tentatively.

'I'll see how it goes.' He turned back towards the window. 'You said you'll go for the polish remover?'

'Of course.' Julia buttoned up her coat and retrieved her bag from beneath the desk.

'Odd we've been done. I didn't notice any other shops or offices had been sprayed.'

'No.' It was on the tip of Julia's tongue to tell Pete about the hostile passer-by, but something held her back. She told herself her hesitation was because she needed to get the varnish remover, and nothing to do with Pete's view that Grace should have disclosed Emmeline's existence to the baby's father.

‘I hope we’ve not been deliberately targeted.’

‘Why would we be?’

Pete frowned. With a jolt, Julia noticed that even the wrinkles on his forehead appeared to have multiplied and deepened over the last week.

‘I’m not sure.’ He shot her a glance. ‘Is it possible Grace’s ex has found out about Emmeline?’

‘I don’t think so.’ Julia looked down at the grey rubber doormat, noticing distractedly how muddy it was. ‘Grace has seen him at uni, but she didn’t tell him about Em. She’s adamant she wants nothing to do with him.’

Pete grunted as he straightened the brochures in the display unit. ‘You know my thoughts about that.’

A middle-aged woman wearing a light blue fleece paused to peer at the sprayed words. She glanced away when she caught Pete’s eye.

‘Yes,’ said Julia quietly. She bent to pick up a small green button from a groove in the doormat. She slipped the button into her pocket and opened the door. ‘I’m sure it’s just random vandalism. I’ll get the polish remover before your client arrives.’

Without waiting for Pete to reply, she hastened outside. The street was busy now with rush hour traffic. Coming towards her was a young woman with spiky pink hair. Julia recognised her as Pete’s client, arriving early. Julia sighed as they exchanged greetings. Too late for her to be spared the sight of the graffiti.

Fifteen minutes later Julia was scrubbing the office window. Pete was right. The nail varnish remover she had bought at the nearest pharmacy was lifting the purple spray paint with relative ease.

A familiar hoarse cough made her glance round. Derek was standing outside the empty retail premises next door, his filthy sleeping bag bundled awkwardly over his right arm. Three battered carrier bags swung from his hand, their logos long since faded. Julia steeled herself not to recoil from the sight of the red blistered skin on his face. This was the closest she had been to him. Below the battered trilby, his scars were more pronounced than ever in the sunlight.

'Looks like hard work,' he observed.

Julia grimaced. 'At least it's coming off. Did you find somewhere to stay yesterday, Derek? It was a terrible night.'

'Here and there,' he said evasively. He adjusted the sleeping bag and coughed again. 'Have you been keeping a lookout, like I said?'

Julia paused in the action of applying more varnish remover on to the sponge. It had been yellow when she started but now oozed purple paint. 'How do you mean?'

'I told you there are some strange types hanging around.' Derek shuffled nearer. He tapped the window with his plastic bags. 'A couple scarpered when I came along earlier. Could be them responsible.' He cleared his throat noisily.

The phlegmy sound combined with the unsavoury smell of Derek's body odour and stale cigarettes made Julia gag. She turned back to the window. 'Just one of those things.' She thought about the young man who had accosted her earlier. 'Some dad angry that his ex isn't letting him see his children, I expect.'

'Not seen paint on any other windows though. Any idea why you've been done?'

'No.'

'Mm.' In the glass Julia saw Derek raise the hand holding the bags to tug at his unkempt grey beard before he spoke again. 'You've got a business partner here, haven't you? Someone who's around when you're in?'

Julia sighed, her hand still on the sponge. She wondered how much longer she and Pete would be 'business partners', and if they would ever be anything more again. He'd barely been able to look at her before. A tear leaked out of her eye. She dashed it away, rubbing with renewed vigour at the graffiti. 'Pete's usually in when I'm here. He's going out later. I'll be OK.'

'Then I'll be across the street outside the old antique shop. I can keep an eye from there.'

'That's really kind, Derek, but I don't think there's any need.' Julia turned, but Derek was already making his way between the vehicles backed up from the traffic lights. She noticed he walked with a limp. He showed no sign of having heard her. She smiled and shook her head to herself, touched that the rough sleeper was looking out for her. She considered his protectiveness unnecessary, but it did niggle that none of the other buildings nearby had fallen victim to the graffiti artist.

She stood back when she had scrubbed off the last of the paint. Satisfied that it had all been removed, she turned to give Derek a wave across the road. He had set up on the pavement outside the boarded up antique shop and was looking down the street towards the St. Marks shopping centre.

Julia followed his gaze, just in time to see a woman in a leopard print coat darting round the corner into a side street. The sun lit up her strawberry blonde hair. Close on her heels was a man in a black leather jacket. Julia recognised Suzanne, Grace's half-sister, and wondered idly what had brought her to this part of town. She looked as though she was running late. Maybe she worked nearby? It was odd to think that they might have been passing one another in the street every day without either of them being aware that they were connected through Grace.

She glanced over at Derek again, hunched up in the doorway of the former antique shop. He was looking in her direction now and raised his hand. She waved back, then caught sight of her nine thirty client crossing the street towards her. She smiled a greeting at the middle-aged woman. The woman grinned back, and Julia glowed inwardly. The contrast with the depressed figure who had barely spoken in their first four sessions was remarkable. It was when Julia saw clients transform like this over weeks of working with them that she was convinced that her decision to leave a secure teaching job and retrain as a counsellor had been worth it.

Behind her client, Julia saw Derek half-rise from the doorstep of the antique shop, his hand still raised. Assuming he hadn't seen her wave back before, she raised her hand again before ushering in her client. She didn't notice Derek haul himself upright as she closed the office door.

The session went well, with the client suggesting that she felt two more sessions would be enough for her to feel 'brave enough to cope with life again'. After she had seen the woman out, Julia typed up her session notes before her next client arrived.

Client 'J' was ten minutes early. He had been referred by his GP, who had diagnosed symptoms of obsessive compulsive disorder. His early arrival put her in mind of Mark Smeaton. Three days after he had flung out of the office so aggressively, she still tensed whenever she recalled the altercation. But where she was certain that Smeaton had been trying to take control within the counselling relationship by his early arrivals, she had discerned from four previous meetings that this young man's anxiety to be punctual was a manifestation of his OCD.

The session was less fruitful than their previous one, leaving Julia wondering if her person-centred approach was suited to someone suffering from OCD. Something else to discuss with her supervisor the following week, she reflected, as well as the challenges posed by Mark Smeaton. Locking the door behind her client, she was surprised to find herself disappointed that there was no sign of Derek across the street after his earlier promise to 'keep an eye'. Telling herself that the rough sleeper would have moved on for good reason, she returned to her office.

Reaching into her bag for her mid-morning snack, her hand closed on an envelope. Withdrawing it, she found it was the envelope the postman had given her earlier from the Council. She slid her thumb under the flap and extracted the letter.

The letter wasn't from the Council Tax Department regarding her mother's house as she had expected. Instead it was from Social Services. The print swam before her eyes as she read it through a second time, though the message was clear enough.

Social Services had been informed anonymously that an infant had been abandoned in a shed at Julia's home. Social Services requested Julia contact them to discuss the matter further at her earliest convenience.

20

Julia stared at the letter. Who had contacted Social Services? As far as she knew, no-one but she and Grace had known about Emmeline being left in the shed. Had Grace confided in someone? It was tempting to ring Social Services immediately, but she decided to wait until she had spoken to Grace. She rang Frances's number.

The phone was picked up instantly. 'Hello?' Frances sounded unusually guarded.

'Hello, Frances. It's Julia. Is Grace around?'

'Oh. Julia.'

The woman's tone was definitely subdued. Could it have been Frances who had contacted Social Services? Julia shivered, recalling the other woman's suggestion that the two of them needed to 'make a plan' about Emmeline's care, and her hints that Grace was unwell in the same way her mother had been. She found herself editing out Frances's talk of demon possession.

The pause lengthened. Julia stood up and began to pace the office. 'Could I speak to Grace, please?'

'She asked not to be interrupted before twelve thirty.'

Julia looked up at the Artex ceiling. There was a cobweb hanging from the pendant light. She rose on to her toes to dislodge it with the letter from Social Services. 'I see.' She thought rapidly. Perhaps it would be better to have the conversation with Grace face to face. She hadn't told Ray when she would be home, so he wouldn't be expecting her at any particular time. 'Perhaps I could visit after work. My last client leaves at four, so I could come over then.'

'That should be convenient,' Frances said in the same colourless tone.

'OK.' Julia hesitated. 'Is everything all right, Frances?'

'No. No, it's not. Suzanne didn't come home last night. I thought you might be her phoning.' The words came out in a rush. 'Do you think I should ring the police or hospital?'

'The police or hospital?' Julia drew to a stop by the window and peeked through the slats of the blind along the street. Traffic was crawling along as usual, and the sunshine had brought out more pedestrians than she had seen during the last few days of rain. She remembered that she had spotted Suzanne earlier. She hadn't seen her face, but there had been no mistaking the loose strawberry blonde hair and the leopard faux fur coat.

'Yes. I'll need to report her as missing, won't I?' Frances's voice wavered.

'Actually, I saw her first thing this morning,' said Julia, 'across the road from my office on High Street. I wondered if she worked round here?'

There was a fractional pause. 'No. She works at a nursery near home. I rang, but she didn't turn up for her shift this morning. That's very out of character.' Frances spoke slowly, processing the information. 'Are you sure it was her?'

'Certain.' Julia hesitated. 'You mentioned you thought Suzanne has a boyfriend. Maybe she stayed—'

'No!' Frances's voice was so sharp that Julia nearly dropped her mobile. 'We brought Suzanne up to have strong morals. She's only been seeing this boyfriend for a couple of weeks. I'm sure she wouldn't...' Her voice trailed off, before she continued in her usual more strident tone. 'What a relief that you've seen her! I'll have something to say to that young lady when she turns up, not letting me know, and missing work! I hope she's not having a late teenage rebellion!'

Julia rolled her eyes as she moved away from the window. Suzanne was an adult, for goodness' sake. 'I'm sure she'll turn up soon.'

'Yes. No doubt you're right.' Frances's brisk tone gave Julia the distinct impression that the other woman wished she hadn't confided in her. 'We'll see you after four then. Bye.' She hung up.

Julia stared down at the blank screen of her mobile. Frances was clearly anxious about Suzanne not having been in touch. However much Julia considered this was irrational given that Suzanne was an adult, it wasn't her place to say so. At least Frances hadn't said anything further about Grace worrying she was being followed.

Julia frowned in concentration as she folded the letter from Social Services and replaced it in its envelope, dropping it into her bag along with her phone. From the little she had had to do with the woman, nothing had dislodged her initial impression that Frances was domineering. But Julia had no reason to doubt the genuineness of the woman's concern about Suzanne, Grace and Emmeline. On balance she didn't think it was likely that Frances would have contacted Social Services. Whilst she couldn't be certain, Julia considered it was more probable that Frances would have been content to look after Emmeline at home rather than involve the statutory authorities.

In need of fresh air, Julia decided to pick up a sandwich. She put on her coat and unlocked the door, almost cannoning into her sister-in-law.

'Clare. Hi.'

'Are you going out? I was just passing and thought I would call in to see you.'

'Oh?' Julia wondered if her sister-in-law had a specific reason for seeing her – it was rare for anyone to be 'just passing' along this end of High Street, and it was a fifteen minute walk from the office where Clare worked as a legal secretary. Taking in the other woman's glowing cheeks and bright almond eyes, it struck her that Clare appeared more animated than she had in a long time. Their heated phone conversation three evenings ago seemed to have been forgotten. Julia made a mental note to phone James later, to see how he was following his angry departure from the office the day before. Yet another difficult family situation to navigate.

'I'll only take a minute,' pressed Clare.

'It's fine. I was just going for a sandwich.' Julia glanced at the white dial of her slim gold wristwatch. 'They have a few tables at the bakery if you've got time for a quick lunch. What time do you need to be back at work?'

'I'm taking the afternoon off. I'll come with you.'

Julia locked the office and the two women made their way up the street. The bakery was busy, but there was a free table in the corner of the small café to the rear.

'We need to order at the counter,' said Julia. 'If you bag the table, I'll order. They don't do green tea. Would you like normal or a coffee?'

Clare gave a little smile. 'I'm off coffee at the minute. Hot water will be fine, thanks.'

'OK. Sandwich? The cheese salad and prawn mayo are both good.'

Clare screwed up her button nose. 'Not prawn. Cheese salad on wholemeal would be great.'

'Right.' Julia joined the queue behind a stout elderly woman who was struggling to decide whether her husband would want mustard or salad with his ham sandwich. Apparently the chemist was taking longer than usual to make up his prescription.

'You could wait till he gets here,' suggested the plump middle-aged assistant, as two more people lined up behind Julia.

'Queue again? No, thank you! I'll get both, but he'd better like them. How much?'

The assistant told her. The woman fumbled around in a battered beige clasp purse for the exact change, grumbling that the price had increased. There was something vaguely familiar about her. When she turned from the counter, Julia saw that it was the woman who had complained to her and Greg about the cost of incontinence pads at the supermarket. The woman didn't notice Julia, intent on dragging her shopping trolley towards the front table in the café. Her cherry red anorak was already hanging over the back of a wooden chair.

Julia exchanged a sympathetic smile with the assistant before placing her order. Thinking of Greg, she hoped again that he had been well clear of the cottage before Pete and Ray arrived. Although she knew Ray would never judge her, she would still feel obliged to explain Greg's presence to him, and she dreaded to think of Pete's reaction if he found Greg there. In hindsight it had been a bad decision to allow him to stay the previous evening; it had given him an opening she should have avoided.

The old woman's trolley almost blocked the access to the rear tables. As Julia stepped carefully past it, she decided not to confide in her sister-in-law about Greg's recent reappearance in her life. A few months ago she would have done so without a second thought, but a gulf had opened between the two women. Julia realised that this wasn't only because of Clare divorcing James. There was something about her soon-to-be ex-sister-in-law's smile which gave Julia a frisson of unease as she took a seat opposite. She registered a sudden misgiving about the reason Clare had sought her out.

'I've got some news.' Clare leant forward across the round mahogany table.

'Oh?' Julia reached for two green paper napkins from the grey enamel cutlery holder. Passing one to Clare, she began to unfold the other.

'Yes. Can't you guess?' Clare was beaming. She looked happier than she had done for years, from the time when Julia had first known her. That had been soon after she and James had got together.

'Have you met someone?' Julia remembered their conversation the other night. 'The man you mentioned at work?' She succeeded in maintaining a neutral tone, recalling that the man was married.

'Better than that.' Clare glanced up at the waitress who had brought over their drinks. 'Thanks.' Lacing her slender fingers around her white cup, Clare went on. 'I thought you might guess from my order.'

Julia's mouth fell open as she took in the significance of Clare refusing coffee and prawns. 'Clare! You're not...?'

Clare nodded. 'Yes! I'm pregnant! Isn't it amazing?'

'It's wonderful news,' said Julia simply. 'I'm very happy for you.' And she was, she realised, even though she sensed the familiar pang at her own childlessness. She managed a smile. 'When's the baby due?'

Clare sat back and placed her hand over her stomach. It was as tiny as ever beneath a close-fitting burnt orange puff sleeve top. 'Not till May. I'm only eight weeks.' She took a sip of hot water and set the cup back down on the saucer. 'I wanted you to be one of the first to know.' There was a watchfulness in her eyes, a tightness in her smile.

A memory of Greg buying a toy for a cat they had looked after for friends one summer surfaced in Julia's mind. Greg had spent hours teasing the cat with the blue furry mouse suspended from a rod and string. Greg had never let the cat grab it, and Julia had thought it cruel to torment the animal.

'Thank you,' she said warily.

'I knew you would be pleased for me. I thought I should warn you that I told James too.' Clare shook out her napkin as the waitress returned with their sandwiches.

Julia's heart skipped a beat. She thanked the waitress automatically before asking, 'How did he take it?'

Clare ran a manicured hand through her newly cropped blonde hair. 'As you would expect. Not well.' She picked up a triangular wholemeal sandwich. 'These look good. I'm starving!'

'When did you tell him?'

Clare finished chewing before she replied. 'Yesterday afternoon. He turned up at the house, and I can tell you he wasn't in a good state. He was drunk.' Clare's face hardened. 'I'd appreciate it if you could warn him that I'm going to ask my solicitor to take out an injunction against him if he comes round again.'

Julia paused in the action of raising her second sandwich to her mouth. 'Aren't injunctions usually taken out in cases of violence or real threat? Surely James didn't...?'

Clare took another bite before answering. 'I did feel threatened. I was probably unwise to let him in. But it was an opportunity to tell him about my baby. I was hoping we could be civilised about it. No chance! He gave me a mouthful of abuse.' She gazed across at Julia coolly. 'I checked with our family solicitor and she said that verbal abuse could be enough for me to get an injunction.'

'OK. I'll have a word with him.' Julia was no longer hungry. She set down the last half of her sandwich on the plate and pushed it away.

Clare laughed hollowly. 'His double standards are amazing: when we were going through the IVF, he had that affair with his student' – her lip curled – 'and now we're separated, he dares criticise me!'

'Probably the shock of your news,' ventured Julia. She wiped her mouth with her napkin. 'Not that that gives him an excuse,' she added hastily, seeing Clare's mouth tighten.

'Quite.' Clare's tone was clipped. 'James is in my past now. I've moved on.' She laid her hand over her stomach, and again Julia experienced the dull ache of sadness. 'This little one is my future.'

Julia hesitated before she steered towards the question which lay between them like a boulder. 'So… the baby's father, is he going to move in with you?'

'No.' Clare sipped her hot water. A wisp of steam rose from the white cup.

Julia took a gulp of tea. 'You mentioned a married solicitor…?'

Clare gave a little smile. '*He's* not the father! I thought he might be a possibility when I saw you at "Giuseppe's". That was before I realised I was already pregnant. Just a one night stand with an old friend. How lucky was that?'

'Right.' Julia's voice was barely audible above the rattle of pots being cleared from the next table.

'We agreed it would be no strings attached,' continued Clare. 'I felt more comfortable knowing him than trying to find some random man.'

'I see.' Julia set down her cup. 'I think I'd better get back to the office,' she said, standing and sliding into her coat. Her fingers trembled as she tried to button it. She gave up, uncharacteristically swearing under her breath. Clare was looking up at her. Julia suspected that her puzzled expression was as fake as the corny plastic loaf and muffins on the window sill behind her.

'You are pleased for me, aren't you?'

'Of course,' said Julia quickly. 'It's just… I guess I didn't expect you to go about it like this.'

Clare arched her eyebrows. 'Isn't that a bit judgemental, Julia?'

'Maybe,' admitted Julia. 'I'm sorry if it seems like that. And I do hope it all goes well for you, Clare. Truly.'

Clare reached behind her for her silk scarf with its seasonal pattern of autumn leaves. She wound it slowly round her neck, then rose and put on her bottle green coat. 'Thanks,' she said. 'Of course, this gives me an extra reason to pursue James financially.' Her eyes bored into Julia's.

'What do you mean?'

Clare moved round the table and put her mouth close to Julia's ear. 'I've not finished with your family yet, Julia.'

Julia stepped back so that she was almost pinned against the side wall. 'I don't understand,' she said faintly.

Clare's malicious smile sent shivers down Julia's spine. 'I mean that your brother will be ruined by the time my solicitor's finished with him. I'm going to do my damnedest to see if I can get in on this inheritance too. For me and my baby.' She touched her stomach briefly, her eyes never leaving Julia's face. Then she turned on her heel and stalked out of the café.

Julia gaped after her, wondering when her sister-in-law and friend had turned into this cold-hearted stranger.

21

The sun was dipping below the horizon when Julia pulled up on Frances's drive at twenty past four. Julia locked the Mondeo and leant against the driver's door. She breathed in the crisp autumn air and gazed at the sunset. The salmon-tinged sky and the colourful leaves swirling around her feet lifted her spirits for the first time since her fraught lunch. She had been wired all afternoon, struggling to give her full attention to her two clients and unable to switch off from the conversation with Clare.

She turned reluctantly as the door clicked open behind her.

'There you are!' called Frances. 'I was watching out for you.'

Julia followed her inside. She bent to unzip her boots, then jerked her head upstairs as Grace shouted, 'Leave me and my baby alone!' A door slammed.

'Oh dear.' Frances placed a forefinger on her mouth and shook her head at Julia. 'What are we going to do? She sounds quite hysterical.'

Suzanne appeared at the top of the stairs. She was wearing the same outfit as the previous evening. She paused when she saw Julia in the hall.

'Oh. It's you.'

'Now, Suzanne. That's no way to greet Julia, is it?'

Julia detected a nervous note in Frances's laugh.

Suzanne shrugged. 'Whatever.'

She sashayed downstairs, her attitude reinforcing Julia's impression of her as a sulky teenager rather than a grown woman. Frances chewed her lower lip as she contemplated her daughter. The uncertain gesture prompted Julia to wonder what had passed between them since Suzanne returned home from her night out.

The young woman flicked a glance at Julia as she descended the final step. 'Are you here to talk some sense into Grace? She's totally paranoid, if you ask me.' She tossed back her strawberry blonde hair. 'All I did was lift Emmeline out of her cot for a cuddle.'

Frances looked at Julia. Julia noticed that her eyes were swollen behind her glasses. 'Grace has had Emmeline up there all day. She wouldn't even let me bring her downstairs to mind her whilst she got on with her research. *Most* unusual for her to reject any help when she's studying.'

Julia wasn't going to give Frances the satisfaction of agreeing with her. 'Grace was concerned she was being followed yesterday,' she pointed out. 'That might explain why she is being so protective today.'

'But surely you don't believe her, now that you've had the opportunity to think it over? Whoever would want to follow Grace and Emmeline?'

'I don't know,' said Julia. 'However unlikely it might seem, the possibility can't be discounted. Unfortunately, you do hear cases of babies being snatched.'

Frances shook her head. 'It's just too fantastic,' she insisted. 'Not in our respectable neighbourhood.'

Julia bit back a smile. 'I'm not sure child snatchers are so discriminatory,' she said dryly.

Frances flashed her a resentful glance. 'I've never heard of anything like that happening round here,' she said stiffly. 'Have you, Suzanne?'

'No.' Suzanne straightened up after squeezing her feet into her high-heeled black ruched boots.

'You must agree it isn't good for the child to be cooped up there with Grace all day,' Frances continued, pointing towards the stairs. 'Grace wouldn't even take her for a walk. We all know how important it is for children to get fresh air when possible, don't we, even if we haven't experienced the joys of motherhood for ourselves?' She smiled condescendingly at Julia, who found herself lost for a reply in face of the woman's tactlessness.

'It isn't healthy,' chimed in Suzanne. 'We make sure the children at nursery get outside whatever the weather.'

The two women looked at Julia, awaiting her response.

'I understand that,' she said. 'But suppose Grace is right, and someone was following her and Emmeline yesterday. That would make it perfectly reasonable for her to stay at home today, wouldn't it?'

Frances raised her eyebrows at her daughter then turned back to Julia. 'I was concerned you might not see our point of view.' She sighed. 'Suzanne offered to accompany them, but Grace would have none of it. Surely it's ridiculous to think that anyone would try to snatch Emmeline – if that is this supposed person's intention – if both girls were out with her?'

'It does seem unlikely,' conceded Julia, 'but Grace was clearly worried after yesterday. Besides, I don't think one day's missed walk is going to harm Emmeline unduly.'

Frances pounced. 'That's just the problem, don't you see? We have no idea how long Grace is going to insist on keeping Emmeline inside. She said earlier she had no intention of taking her out until she is certain it's safe. Who knows when that will be? What if she takes this view for weeks?'

'I'm sure she won't do that. Maybe if I speak to her—' Julia took a step forward but Frances blocked her route to the stairs.

'Then of course there's what happened when she was staying with you to think about, isn't there?' She blinked earnestly behind her large-framed glasses.

'I have to say I'm very concerned,' Suzanne broke in before Julia could reply. She looked at her mother meaningfully. 'You know what I think, Mum.'

'I do, darling.' Frances puffed out her cheeks and turned to Julia. 'There's no easy way of saying this. I'm afraid that Suzanne believes that Grace might not be fit to look after Emmeline in her present state.'

'What makes you say that?' Julia asked sharply, although she had been expecting this since her conversation with Frances the previous evening.

Suzanne rolled her eyes. 'Grace told Mum about Emmeline being abandoned in the shed,' she said, 'and that Grace had no idea how she got there. That doesn't sound like adequate parenting, does it?'

Julia felt a sudden chill despite the uncomfortable warmth of Frances's hall. As she stood there under the sphinx-like gaze of the two women, it occurred to her that maybe she had misjudged the situation. What other explanation was there than that Grace had left Emmeline in the shed? Julia recalled Pete's warning that she must make sure she wasn't prioritising Grace's well-being at the expense of Emmeline's. Suzanne and Frances were simply echoing his view.

'It could have been hours before you found Emmeline,' pressed Suzanne. 'She would have been cold and hungry.

If you had called the police and they had found her in the shed, they would have made an immediate referral to Social Services.'

Julia broke the eye contact. At that moment she wished that Grace hadn't confided in her stepmother. She felt her cheeks redden. 'I don't know what to think,' she admitted. 'There might be some other explanation.'

'Such as?' There was no mistaking Suzanne's hostility. 'If we heard anything like this at nursery, we'd have to report it as a safeguarding matter.'

Julia looked at her. She thought of the letter from Social Services and unconsciously placed a hand over her bag.

'I do understand your concerns,' she said. 'But wouldn't you usually have a conversation with the parent or carer first, find out their side of the story, before contacting Social Services?'

Suzanne gazed at her stonily. 'The child's welfare must always be the main concern.'

'Of course it must!' exclaimed Frances. 'Suzanne is absolutely devoted to the children at nursery. And they love her too. You'll make a wonderful mother one day, won't you, with all your experience?' She beamed proudly at her daughter.

Not so devoted that she didn't skive today, thought Julia. Suzanne was still staring at her. Julia's skin prickled at the small smile which was playing around the young woman's lips. Was Julia imagining it, or was there a sly triumph in the smile – perhaps it was Suzanne who was responsible for tipping off Social Services? She was tempted to challenge them, but decided against it. She didn't want to put ideas into their heads. If neither was responsible for the letter, a second allegation to Social Services would surely be viewed very seriously.

Julia's mind raced as she pondered what might happen to Emmeline if Grace were found to be unfit to care for her – would Frances be able to claim that she should have custody of Emmeline as grandmother? Julia had to acknowledge that Suzanne was correct in asserting that Emmeline's welfare must be paramount. She realised suddenly that what she wanted more than anything was for Grace and Emmeline to return home with her. There was something disquieting about the haste with which Frances and Suzanne had dismissed Grace's claim that she and Emmeline had been followed the previous afternoon. The two women also seemed far too eager to view Grace as being responsible for shutting Emmeline away in the shed, however difficult it was to think of an alternative explanation.

She spoke firmly, refusing to be intimidated by their criticism of Grace. 'I'll go up and talk to Grace now.'

'Good luck with that!' Suzanne fastened the toggles of her faux fur leopard coat. 'See you later, Mum.'

'You'll be back tonight?' There was no mistaking the pleading note in Frances's voice. Julia glanced between mother and daughter. She sensed that the balance of power had shifted between them since yesterday.

'Probably,' replied Suzanne airily. 'I'll drop you a text if not. I've got my phone today.'

'All right,' said Frances. 'Enjoy yourself.'

'Don't worry, I will.' Suzanne tossed back her hair in the open doorway, her crimson lips widening in a smirk. She closed the door behind her. The click of her heels receded down the drive.

Julia knew she should go straight up to see Grace, but curiosity got the better of her.

'So Suzanne got home after we spoke earlier?'

'Yes,' said Frances. She flashed her teeth in a poor imitation of her horsey smile. 'I needn't have worried. She spent the night at a friend's. The silly girl had left her mobile at home so she couldn't phone me.'

Frances's reference to 'silly girl' struck Julia as more fitting to a much younger person than Suzanne. In their different ways, both Grace and Suzanne seemed immature, and Julia suspected that they had suffered under Frances's overbearing personality. She resisted the temptation to express surprise that Suzanne's 'friend' didn't have a phone. From Suzanne's attitude, Julia suspected that the 'friend' was the boyfriend alluded to the previous evening. Frances's next words proved her right.

'I'm pleased she's met someone, of course, but I can't pretend to be happy with her staying out. It's not how my late husband and I brought her up.' She twisted her hands together. 'But when she told me the young man had already invited her to move in with him, I felt I had no choice than to encourage her to take things more slowly, even if she does stay over from time to time. I would hate to drive her away from home by being too critical.' She shook her head. 'It is very distressing. First Grace and the scandal of an illegitimate child, and now Suzanne taking up with some young man I know nothing about.' Her lip wobbled and she sniffed loudly. 'I don't know what their father would have said. I really don't.'

Julia felt an unexpected pang of sympathy for the other woman even though she recoiled from the pejorative use of the word 'illegitimate' in relation to Emmeline. 'I'm sure it will work out,' she said.

Frances extracted a tissue from the pocket of her pleated grey skirt and took off her glasses. 'I do hope so.' She wiped her eyes. 'All I ever wanted was to be a good mother, you see. Having a family was the most important thing for me.'

'I'm sorry,' said Julia.

Frances sniffed and peered at Julia short-sightedly. 'I don't suppose you would understand that, as a career woman.'

Any sympathy Julia felt evaporated like steam in freezing air. 'I enjoy my job,' she said, when she recovered her voice, 'but it's just one aspect of my life. Family is very important to me too, even if I don't have children of my own.' She took a deep breath. Suddenly the impulse to puncture the other woman's assumptions overwhelmed her. 'I regret not being a mother. I'm telling you this because you may meet other childless women who have similar regrets.'

For the first time since Julia had known her, Frances was lost for words. Julia suspected she was unaccustomed to people contradicting her. Eventually the woman raised her hands. 'Please. I didn't mean any offence. It was just...' Her lip trembled. 'Family has been so central to my life,' she continued. 'I've felt lost since my husband died, and now with Suzanne spreading her wings...' She blew her nose. 'I'm so sorry. I really want what's best for Emmeline. You do understand, don't you?'

Surprising herself, Julia placed a hand on the woman's arm. 'I think so,' she said gently. 'And you're right, Emmeline must be the priority. Now if you'll excuse me, I'll go up to see Grace and Emmeline.'

Frances gave a watery smile and stood aside to allow Julia to make her way upstairs. Grace's door was ajar. Julia tapped lightly before pushing it open. Recalling that she had heard the door slam shut behind Suzanne, Julia suspected Grace had been eavesdropping. Grace confirmed her suspicions.

'You do believe me, don't you, about being followed yesterday? And that I didn't put Emmeline in the shed?' The words tumbled out. There was a hectic flush in her cheeks and a feverish expression in her eyes which Julia didn't like.

Julia was saved from giving an immediate reply by Emmeline. The baby was sitting in the middle of the blue carpet, surrounded by soft toys and board books. Her face broke into a dimpled smile as she stretched her arms towards her great-aunt. A surge of joy filled Julia, who grinned back, stooping to pick the baby up. She tossed Emmeline in the air and caught her. The little girl chortled in delight.

'Aunt Julia? Please say you believe me! I heard what you were all saying. You don't think Suzanne would report me to Social Services, do you?'

Julia decided that now wasn't the time to share the contents of the letter from Social Services with her niece. The last thing Grace needed at the moment was more stress. 'I heard you shout at Suzanne when I arrived,' she countered. 'Telling her to keep away from you and Emmeline.'

Grace sank down on to her bed and put her head in her hands. 'She said I wasn't a fit mother, that I didn't know how to look after Emmeline properly. She offered to take Emmeline out for a walk. I didn't want her to go out after we were followed yesterday.'

Julia frowned as she sat down with Emmeline on the floor. She picked up the child's teddy and embarked on a game of peekaboo. Suzanne had said in the hall that she had offered to accompany Grace and Emmeline, not take the baby out on her own. Obscurely, Julia felt that it was important to clarify the point. 'You mean Suzanne was suggesting taking Emmeline out without you?'

Grace glanced up. 'Yes. I didn't like the idea. She made it sound like she was doing me a favour, so I could get on with my research, but I said there was no way I was letting Emmeline go out without me. I suggested she could come with us another day. After yesterday I wanted to stay in.' She glanced towards the window. Dusk had swallowed up the vibrant sunset. 'I can be sure we're safe inside. I've been looking out to check that no-one is around.'

'And you haven't seen anyone?'

Grace shook her head. 'No. Maybe it was just some random nutter yesterday and I was unlucky.'

'That's possible,' Julia agreed. Grace's attitude struck her as reasonable. If her niece was to be believed, then Suzanne had misrepresented their conversation. Or had she misunderstood? Julia felt a qualm of unease as she contemplated Suzanne's rush to condemn Grace's parenting skills.

Distracted, Julia had forgotten to hide the teddy bear again and Emmeline gave a squawk of protest. Julia quickly concealed the toy behind her back.

'I gather Suzanne didn't come home last night?'

'Frances was beside herself! Suzanne has never stayed out before, always followed her mother's rules. She's always lived at home, didn't go to uni or anything. I suggested that she was probably just with a friend. Suzanne could have phoned, but I guess she was worried that Frances might hit the roof if she told her she was staying over with this man.' Grace managed a half-smile. 'I've never known her miss work, so I'm guessing she's fallen head over heels for him, whoever he is.'

Julia could see from Emmeline's glazed expression that she was tiring of peekaboo. She drew the baby on to her lap and turned the pages of a multi-sensory board book.

'So he's Suzanne's first serious boyfriend then?' Julia moved Emmeline's tiny forefinger along a finger trail in the book.

'Yes.' Grace tugged the bobble from her plait and combed her fingers through the strawberry blonde hair she shared with her sister. 'It was a bit weird when she took Emmeline out of her cot and suggested taking her for a walk. She said something about having a baby with this man. Then she made some jibe about how much better it would be for Emmeline to have her father in her life. I didn't like how she looked at Emmeline...' She shook back her hair and shivered suddenly.

Julia's hand froze over Emmeline's on a fluffy yellow chicken. 'What do you mean, Grace?'

Grace went across to the window to draw the duck egg blue curtains against the darkness. She turned back towards Julia, her smooth forehead furrowed in anxiety. 'She looked... hungry,' she said at last. 'Hungry, and horribly jealous when she looked at me. That's when I told her to leave.'

22

'It's the best thing that's happened all day, seeing you.' Julia stood on tiptoe to kiss Ray's lined cheek. She sniffed appreciatively. 'And you've been cooking. That's so kind of you. Shouldn't you be resting after your journey?'

The old man smiled and turned back towards the kitchen. Julia was struck again by how he had aged whilst caring for his late daughter. He seemed more stooped than when she had seen him at Linda's funeral, and his shuffle was even more pronounced. She followed him into the kitchen, where he lifted the lid off a large saucepan bubbling on the hob. 'I've spent most of the afternoon reading the paper. I found a few carrots and an onion, enough to make soup. Nothing taxing.' He stirred the broth and turned back to Julia. 'It looks like you're the one who could do with a rest.'

She was touched by the concern in his blue eyes, which had lost none of their sharpness despite his eighty-six years. 'It's not been an easy day,' she admitted. She sank down on to one of the dining chairs. 'Did Pete pick you up OK?' she asked cautiously, wondering sadly if Pete had given Ray any indication of their current difficulties.

Ray took a wooden chopping board across to the sink and ran water over it before he replied. 'Yes. He was waiting on the platform for me,' he said, his back to her.

'It was very kind of him to meet me. You've not seen or heard from him since?'

There was a studied neutrality in his tone which put Julia on her guard. 'No,' she said. 'He didn't come back to the office, and I went over to see Grace after I finished work. I guessed he was still at the hospital with his mother.'

'I see.' Ray scrubbed the chopping board with the dish brush. 'I was hoping you might have spoken to him. I think there might have been a… misunderstanding when we got here.'

'A misunderstanding?'

'Mm.' Ray scoured the board vigorously.

Julia's heart sank. 'You don't mean Greg was still here when you arrived?'

Ray propped up the board in the drainer basket. 'I'm afraid so.' He turned to her, resting his tall frame against the sink, his expression serious. 'He was just leaving. I'm sorry to say Pete didn't react well.'

Julia massaged her temple. 'What did Greg say?'

'He said that he had had a good night with you.' Ray scanned her face. 'You can imagine how Pete took that. From his expression he'd have punched the man if I hadn't been here. As we both know, Pete doesn't have a violent bone in his body. With his mother sick, he's at the end of his tether. He left immediately, so he didn't see that Greg had obviously spent the night on the sofa bed in the sitting room.' He hesitated. 'It struck me as rather late for him to go, half past eleven. Does he not keep regular working hours?'

'No. He's a freelance computer technician.' Julia closed her eyes. 'That is so typical of Greg! He'll have waited in deliberately.' She got up and went across to the window to draw the blind against the windy night.

'Pete mentioned that he'd bumped into Greg here earlier in the week as well,' observed Ray. 'You can understand how he jumped to the wrong conclusion.'

Julia sighed as she took a wholemeal loaf from the bread bin. She cut two thick slices which she placed on a plate and took over to the table. She resumed her seat. 'I should never have let him in.'

'I'm sure you had your reasons.' Ray took a jar of tarragon from the wooden spice rack and shook some into the soup.

Julia found it easier to talk to his back. 'I didn't think it through,' she said. 'Greg turned up unexpectedly that first evening. I bumped into him at the supermarket last Friday. We chatted, and it broke the ice. When he arrived last night, he said that his partner had thrown him out and he had nowhere to go. I was tired, and it was such awful weather. It just seemed easier to let him stay. But I know it would have been better if I hadn't. For him to imply to Pete that we...' She buried her head in her hands.

Ray gave the soup another stir. 'Greg was undoubtedly mischief-making. Appropriately enough when you think about the date yesterday.'

Julia frowned. 'The thirtieth of October?'

'The thirtieth of October has a long history as Mischief Night,' explained Ray. 'In some parts of Canada and America it goes by other names, Gate Night or Devil's Night. That gives you an idea of its nature. I understand it's not so common here in England.'

'I've not heard of it,' admitted Julia. 'Hallowe'en has become more popular here over the last few years. There wasn't much going on when I was a child. Now there are parties and lots of children go trick or treating. I saw a few around on my way home, and we'll probably get some visiting us. But I've not heard of anyone celebrating on the thirtieth. You said 'Gate Night' was one of the names for last night. Why's that?'

Ray eyed her seriously. 'The idea behind it is that the gates of hell open the night before Hallowe'en.'

'That's horrible.' Julia shuddered. 'I mean, I don't believe in hell, but it still sounds frightening. I've never been keen on Hallowe'en. I know it's silly, but the costumes make me shiver, even though it's fun for the kids.'

Ray looked more stern than she had ever seen him. 'It's a dark season. One when it's especially important that we pray for protection. You might not believe in hell, Julia, but you must be aware of good and evil forces around us, light and darkness.' He turned back to his broth.

Ray's words brought Frances to mind, and her suggestion that Grace might be demon-possessed. The language was too outlandish, too archaic, for Julia's rational outlook. But there was something in Ray's solemn words which rang true, although she couldn't have explained why.

She picked up a red highlighter which Grace had left behind on the table and began to doodle on a corner of Ray's newspaper, pondering his words about light and darkness. She certainly felt that she had witnessed the darker side of human nature lately. Greg had undoubtedly been mischief-making as Ray said. Clare's vengeful attitude, James's anger, Suzanne's hostility, even Grace's erratic behaviour, each were disturbing in their own way.

Julia shuddered and laid her pen down. Her idle drawing of red lines and squiggles put her in mind of fire. Ray had talked about hell, which could have prompted the image. Or maybe she had sketched it remembering the fire Linda had started when Grace was a baby, fresh in her mind from Friday when she had found the cottage ablaze with light and Grace terrified that Emmeline had been stolen. Ray didn't know about that incident yet, and Julia wasn't sure if she wanted to disturb him by telling him about it on his first night.

The priest was still preoccupied with Greg's visit. As he turned off the hob and Julia took two bowls from the cupboard alongside, he asked, 'Did you say Greg's partner has thrown him out? They have a child, don't they?'

'Yes.' Julia swallowed, thinking not only of Greg's son but also of Clare's pregnancy. Her visit to Grace had taken her mind temporarily off Clare's revelation. Now she found herself telling Ray about it.

The elderly priest didn't comment as he ladled out the steaming soup and set the bowls on the table. Julia half-rose to fetch spoons but he stilled her with an outstretched hand and fetched them himself whilst she finished her account. Taking the seat opposite Julia, he bowed his head in the silent grace he always offered before eating. Unexpectedly, Julia found herself ducking her head too, in an unspoken 'Thank you' to the God she barely believed in for Ray's visit. His wisdom and calmness were a welcome antidote to the problems which beset her.

'Now before we talk further, let's eat.' Ray broke off a piece of bread and dipped it in his soup.

She obediently picked up her spoon. The carrot soup was thick and nutritious. Eating in the restful presence of the elderly priest with the familiar sound of the grandmother clock ticking in the hall, Julia felt the tensions of the day begin to ebb away.

When they had scraped their bowls clean and Julia had complimented Ray on the soup, he asked, 'So James told Clare about your substantial inheritance from Linda?'

'Yes. He wasn't happy about it, especially when Clare seems so determined to pursue him for every penny she can get.' Julia tapped her spoon against the rim of her terracotta bowl. 'I should speak to him tonight. I've not heard from him since he stormed out, and that was before he found out about Clare's pregnancy.'

'I'm sure he'll appreciate a call. You said he's been drinking heavily lately?'

Julia nodded. 'Yes. And he's been suspended.'

'Poor man.' Ray looked thoughtful. 'I do hope you are able to speak to him tonight, Julia. I'm afraid it sounds as though he is using the alcohol as an escape from depression and regret. That will have crossed your mind as a counsellor, I'm sure?'

'Yes,' said Julia. She felt a pang of guilt that she hadn't made more effort to get in touch with James earlier, sidetracked as she had been by Greg's unexpected visit the previous evening and the letter from Social Services today. 'I'll try to phone after we've eaten.'

'Good. Now, how are Grace and Emmeline faring with Frances?' There was a slight quaver in his voice which wasn't lost on Julia.

'Not very well,' she admitted. 'Ray, are you sure you want to hear all this tonight? Wouldn't you prefer to wait until tomorrow?'

'Certainly not!' He tilted his head proudly. Julia caught a momentary glimpse of the Wing Commander Brooke with whom her mother had fallen in love in 1943.

Julia launched into the story of Emmeline's disappearance and described how she and Grace had discovered the baby in the shed. Ray's mouth settled into a grim line as she recounted the incident. Then she outlined Grace's conviction that she and Emmeline had been followed on their walk the previous day, and how disbelieving Frances and Suzanne had been. She told him that Frances and Suzanne were raising doubts about Grace's capacity to look after her daughter. Finally, she explained how Grace and Suzanne had given different versions of their argument about taking Emmeline out that afternoon, mentioning Grace's disquiet about Suzanne's attitude towards Emmeline.

'I wouldn't want to be unfair towards Suzanne, and I realise Grace is very stressed, so she might be over-imaginative,' said Julia, as she drew her account to an end. 'But it is possible that she and Emmeline were followed yesterday, and Suzanne might have her own motives for suggesting Grace isn't fit to be looking after Emmeline. I've invited them to come back here tomorrow.'

'That's good.' Ray's face had grown increasingly grave as Julia spoke. 'Emmeline could be in danger. She and Grace are definitely better here with us. How did Frances take your suggestion that Grace and Emmeline should move back here?'

'Surprisingly well. She seems shell-shocked by Suzanne taking up with a new boyfriend, and didn't argue with me. I'm sure she wouldn't want the stigma of Social Services being called in to deal with her stepdaughter and baby, if Suzanne has contacted them, or plans to. She's going to bring Grace and Emmeline over first thing tomorrow.'

'It sounds as though Suzanne is jealous of Grace and Emmeline,' said Ray gravely. 'There's no love lost between the two of them, from what you've seen?'

'None at all. I already suspected that from what Grace has told me. In fact, she once said that their relationship contributed to her fascination with her research into the relationship between Mary Tudor and her half-sister Elizabeth.'

'Indeed.' Ray steepled his long tapering fingers and rested his chin on them. 'As you say, it sounds as though Grace and Emmeline would be safer here.'

Julia hesitated. 'But what about Emmeline being left in the shed?'

Ray frowned, accentuating the creases in his high forehead. 'I'm not sure.' He angled his body towards the back door. 'Is there any possibility someone could have got in through the back door when Grace was upstairs?'

Julia gaped. 'And taken Emmeline out? Whoever would do such a thing? Besides, the gate is always bolted. Except...' She put a hand to her mouth.

'Except?' prompted Ray.

'Except Greg found the gate open on Monday. I didn't understand how it had happened,' said Julia slowly. She remembered what Grace had told her. 'Grace said the phone was ringing when she came back from her walk with Emmeline. It was Suzanne, calling to tell her about this new boyfriend. Grace said that when she came back into the kitchen after she hung up, the key for the back door was missing. I haven't come across it since. I've been using the spare in the drawer.'

'So if the gate was open last Friday and the back door was unlocked—'

'It's possible someone did come in. Someone who took the key and moved the buggy out to the shed. But who would do that?'

'Someone with a grudge against Grace,' said Ray soberly. 'The same person who followed her and Emmeline yesterday.'

Julia shuddered. 'But who...?'

Ray shook his head. 'That we don't know. But I do think Grace and Emmeline are safer here, where we can watch over them. From what you say, Frances and

Suzanne don't believe Grace was followed yesterday. At least if we allow for the possibility that someone has malicious intentions, we can take precautions.'

'I suppose so.' Julia thought for a moment. 'There wouldn't be any point contacting the police with our suspicions at this stage, would there?'

'Not yet. We would need more evidence,' said Ray. 'You look stricken, my dear. I don't mean to frighten you. I'm sure you've seen the worst of human nature as well as the best in your work, as I have.'

Julia nodded. 'I was just thinking before we ate that that's true in my personal life as well at the moment.' She toyed with her spoon in the empty bowl. 'It's a shock to contemplate something like this happening at home though.' She looked around the familiar kitchen and shivered. Her gaze came to rest on the back door. 'I'll have to get the lock changed.'

Ray nodded. 'It's only a possibility that someone intends harm to Grace, but we should be on our guard.' He contemplated his steepled fingers, his expression troubled. 'We talked of Suzanne being jealous of her sister,' he observed. 'She isn't the only jealous person in all this. James is jealous of your inheritance. So too is Clare.'

'Yes.' Julia fiddled with her watch strap. 'But I doubt she can make a claim against it in the divorce proceedings, whatever she threatens, since Linda divided her property between Grace and me.'

'I'm sure that's right. There's no possibility that James could successfully challenge Linda's will even if he wanted to. He wasn't dependent on her in any way.' He glanced down, but not before Julia had seen the shadow pass across his face as it always did when he mentioned the daughter he had known for such a short time.

'So why did Clare mention it to me?' mused Julia.

Ray brushed some breadcrumbs off his beige pullover and rose to his feet. He winced. 'I can't sit for as long as I used to. My old bones stiffen up.' He smiled briefly. 'I suspect Clare simply wanted to worry you, resenting that you are going to benefit. Maybe she thinks you might help James out financially, and intends to bring the inheritance to her solicitor's attention.'

'That's ridiculous!' said Julia. 'I am intending to help James, but surely that should be between the two of us. It's nothing to do with Clare.'

Ray took their bowls over to the sink. 'It isn't, but Clare is clearly vengeful towards James. And not only that.' He ran water into the dishes, his back to her. 'Suppose Greg has bumped into either James or Clare recently and has learnt about your inheritance?'

Julia frowned. 'What difference would that make? He didn't say anything, although…' Her eyes widened as she thought back over her conversation with Greg the previous evening, how he had asked whether she or James would inherit their mother's desk, and how she had been taken aback by his questions about family secrets.

'Although?' prompted Ray.

'I think he might have known about it,' conceded Julia. 'It makes sense of some of the things he was saying last night. It crossed my mind that he was goading me, seeing if I would confide in him. He mentioned bumping into Clare too.'

'Ah.' Ray's expression was gentle as he turned to look at her. 'Then it's possible Greg knew that you were going to benefit from a substantial amount of money when he reappeared in your life this week?'

There was a brief silence as Julia thought through the implications of what Ray was saying. Outside, a cat yowled. Julia jumped at the sound, though Ray was unperturbed.

'It was only by chance that we met at the supermarket,' she said at last. 'But I guess that cleared the air between us, gave him an opening to come round here and try…' Her cheeks flushed beneath Ray's steady gaze. 'Nothing happened,' she said quickly. 'There was a moment—'

Ray raised his hand. 'It would be surprising if there hadn't been,' he said. 'You've been under a great deal of strain this last week. The powerful feelings you had for Greg for so long don't simply disappear.' He sat back down at the table.

'You're very understanding,' said Julia. She got up and strode over to the kettle. 'I should never have got into that position. He could so easily have made a complete fool of me, got his hands on some of the money…' She ran water furiously into the kettle, splashing over the edge of the sink.

'But he didn't,' said Ray softly when she had turned off the tap. 'You didn't give him the opportunity.'

Julia flicked the kettle on and took two mugs from the mug tree. 'I shouldn't have let him in. Not when Pete…' She bit her lip and swung round to face Ray. 'I think Pete and I have split up,' she said miserably. 'I've been so wrapped up with all my family problems that I've not offered him any support with his mother, and he's had enough. Now there's no chance he'll want me back after what Greg said to him today, is there?'

Ray smiled at her with such tenderness that she thought she might cry. 'I think you need to talk to Pete, don't you? He's a good man, Julia. Naturally he is very upset about his mother, and he is dealing with that in his own way. I suspect that if you speak to him at the right time, he will understand. Remember, you saw Greg off. The way he left you so abruptly, so cruelly, last summer' – an uncharacteristic sternness spread across his lined face – 'that scarred you, Julia. Maybe sending him away yourself has helped heal some of that damage?'

Julia nodded mutely, unable to speak. Ray's insight and understanding were almost more than she could bear after the emotional turmoil of the last few days. She took a packet of teabags from the cupboard and waved them at him. He nodded before resuming.

'You and Pete have had a great deal to cope with during your short relationship, as much as some couples experience during a long marriage.' He paused and looked down thoughtfully at his hands, the liver spots clearly visible under the ceiling light. 'Now, forgive me for being an interfering old man' – he smiled over at her as she poured water over the teabags – 'but I've seen you give an awful lot of your time and attention to Grace and Emmeline, and indeed to me, over these last few months. You were wonderful with Linda too.' His voice caught, and the sadness flickered over his angular features again. 'Now you have worries about James. On top of all this, you have your counselling practice.'

He paused as Julia set down a mug of tea for him and nodded his thanks. 'But you need to make time for yourself and Pete as well, Julia.'

'I know,' said Julia. She blew on her tea and smiled at the old man. 'Thank you,' she said simply.

The doorbell pealed. Ray grimaced as he stood and picked up his mug. 'I expect you have some trick or treaters to attend to. Now if you will excuse me, my dear, I'll settle down for the night. I found your airing cupboard this afternoon and changed the bedding. I have everything

I need.' He rested his hand briefly on her shoulder as he passed her. 'Good night.'

23

Julia woke with a start. She had been dreaming, recent fragments of conversations spooling through her mind, along with images of scurrying masked figures.

She sat up in bed, hugging the duvet to her. You didn't need to be an expert in dream analysis to work out that the masked figures had their origins in the trick or treaters in their spooky costumes who had called the previous night.

The shrill ring of the phone shattered the quietness of the house. Julia leapt out of bed and ran downstairs barefoot, the parquet floor of the hall cold beneath her feet. The grandmother clock chimed six.

She was still standing there, phone in hand, when Ray emerged from the sitting-room. He flicked on the light, rousing Julia from her trance. She replaced the phone on its base.

'Is everything all right?'

'No.' She shook her head, leaning against the walnut bookcase for support. Her teeth were chattering. 'It was the hospital. James is there. He…' She hesitated, struggling to repeat the terrible words delivered by the nurse with gentle efficiency. 'He made a suicide attempt last night. Tablets and alcohol. He was picked up near the cathedral. He's had his stomach pumped.'

She gazed at Ray, trying to process the news. He was wearing blue flannel pyjamas, his white hair sticking up like a parrot's crest. A comical sight under other circumstances, but Julia was far from laughing.

'It's my fault,' she said. 'I should have paid attention to what he said when he stormed out of the office. I tried to phone him last night, after you'd gone to bed. He didn't pick up. I should have gone over to Mother's cottage to check he was OK. But I was too tired.' She pressed her fingers to her temple.

'No, Julia.' Ray's voice was kind but firm. He moved gingerly towards her, his elderly limbs stiff from lying so long. He gazed down at her earnestly. 'It is most certainly not your fault. You are not responsible for James's actions. You must not blame yourself.' He paused, letting the words sink in.

She looked up into his blue eyes, so strikingly undimmed by age, so clear and certain. She nodded hesitantly.

'Good,' he said. 'Besides, if you had gone to the cottage, he wouldn't have been there, would he? You said he was found near the cathedral.'

'Yes. Even so—'

'There is nothing you could have done. Let me make you some tea.'

'But I should go straightaway! I'll go and get dressed.'

'James is in safe hands. You need some strong tea before you go anywhere. Maybe a slice of buttered toast?' Ray raised his hand when she opened her mouth to protest. 'Now, let's not argue. Let someone look after *you* for a change.'

She managed a wobbly smile before making her way slowly upstairs. She changed into jeans and a caramel ribbed jumper and ran a comb through her hair. Her face in the bathroom mirror was pale and strained, and the crows' feet at the corners of her brown eyes looked more pronounced. There was no time for make-up beyond a dash of beige lipstick. She hastened downstairs for Ray's tea and toast.

The simple breakfast was restorative. By the time she drove across the north side of the city twenty minutes later, Julia felt less shaky. The rain had returned with a vengeance. Huge drops splattered the windscreen. Even with the wipers on at full speed, she hunched forwards, straining to see in the half-light of the autumn morning. She gripped the steering-wheel and switched off the 'Today' programme on Radio 4, the better to concentrate. Once she had to swerve past the large bough of a tree which had blown down overnight. *Cut down in its prime.* She shivered, thinking that had so nearly been true of James.

At the hospital, she found the receptionist's office empty. Blinking in the brightly lit entrance, Julia consulted the plan on the wall to locate James's ward. She set off down a long hospital corridor, passing doctors and nurses and a few patients in dressing-gowns. She always found the hospital corridors disorientating, and in her anxiety she somehow missed the access to the lower level where James was. A friendly porter pointed her in the right direction. By the double doors to the ward she squirted sanitiser over her hands. As a counsellor, she had worked with two clients who had made suicide attempts. Another client had lost her teenage daughter, a girl with a history of self-harming. Rubbing in the gel so thoroughly that it stung, Julia was aware that she was delaying going in to see James. All her professional training and experience were no preparation for this visit to her brother who had tried to take his own life.

The nurses' station was busy as staff who had been on duty overnight handed over to their daytime colleagues. The nurse who had phoned Julia told her that James was in the bay across from the station and was sleeping. The kindly young woman reassured Julia that although his throat would have been irritated during the stomach pump procedure, there should be no lasting physical damage. She explained that a mental health nurse would see him later in the day.

Julia took a seat in the high-backed cobalt chair alongside James's bed and studied him. His face was grey beneath his matted blond fringe, his cheeks rough with stubble. His green polyester pyjamas were identical to those worn by the elderly man opposite, evidently hospital attire. It was impossible to imagine James owned such nondescript nightwear. But nor could she ever have conceived that her half-brother, attractive and confident to the point of being cocksure, would ever have fallen prey to such self-neglect or to such a desperate act.

With a jolt, Julia realised James put her in mind of Derek. Not for the first time, she wondered what had led Derek to life on the streets. Watching her dishevelled brother as he dozed, it sickened her to think how quickly a well-ordered life could be destroyed. She was overwhelmed by such a deep current of sympathy for the man she had held in her arms as a baby that she found herself choking back tears.

James coughed suddenly and jerked awake. Julia watched as he blinked a few times, taking in his surroundings. She leant forward and took his hand.

'Hi.' He managed a weak smile.

'Hi.' She smiled back. 'How are you feeling?'

He massaged his neck and grimaced. 'Sore throat.'

Julia stood and poured some water from the plastic jug on the bedside locker. She handed him the beaker and he took a few sips, screwing up his face when he swallowed.

'Do you know why you're here? Do you remember what happened?' she asked gently. She pulled the orange curtains round the bed to give them some privacy.

He handed the cup back and she set it down on the locker. 'I remember most of it.' He fingered the blue cotton blanket and gave her a bitter half-smile. 'I couldn't even manage to get this right, could I?'

'Don't say that!' Julia swallowed. 'You should have phoned. If I'd known how bad...'

He pushed at his tangled fringe. 'I didn't think you'd want to know,' he muttered. 'I tried to say something the other day, although I wasn't sure I'd go through with it then.'

Julia looked down at her hands clasped tightly in her lap, their knuckles white. 'I'm sorry,' she said quietly. 'I am so sorry, James.'

They were both quiet for a long moment.

James shuffled higher up the pillows. 'I thought you'd had enough of me and my problems. You made it clear you thought I'd brought everything on myself.' He turned his head away. Rivulets of rain ran down the windows through which other hospital buildings loomed out of the mist.

Julia stopped herself from making a swift denial, recalling their exchange. 'I didn't mean it,' she said. 'I'm sorry if that's what you thought. I was angry too. You've had a run of bad luck, James. Your infertility, Clare's overwhelming desire for a child...' She trailed off, thinking it was probably news of Clare's pregnancy which had pushed her brother over the edge.

He plucked at the blanket again with bitten fingernails crusted with dirt. 'About that,' he said, 'I spoke to Clare last night. She said she'd told you about her pregnancy. I called on her on Wednesday afternoon. I didn't react well. Did she tell you?' When she nodded, he went on, 'I rang her last night to apologise. She didn't want to hear it. She said any further contact should be via our solicitors, threatened me with an injunction. Can you believe it? After all our years together.'

'It's hard to take in.' Julia thought her words insufficient, but he nodded.

'We were so happy, weren't we, until the IVF took over?' He rubbed his forehead and looked at her, his eyes pleading for confirmation that his memory of a happy marriage wasn't a delusion.

'You were very happy,' Julia agreed. She remembered how solid their relationship had seemed. James had had several girlfriends before Clare. It had been obvious from the beginning that she had been different. Where he had been cagey about other partners, he had introduced Clare to Julia and his mother within weeks of meeting her. Neither Emily nor Julia had been surprised when they announced their engagement within a few months.

'I'm so sorry, James.' Julia reached for his hand. 'I know how difficult it is to accept.'

He squeezed her hand. 'I'm sorry too,' he muttered. He had always found apologies difficult. 'I've been thinking a lot lately, and I realise I didn't offer you the support I should over Greg.' He swallowed. 'I was too caught up with Clare and the IVF, and I… I miss Mum.' A tear leaked out of his eye. He turned his head to brush it away. Julia didn't remember seeing him cry since he had fallen off his bike and broken his arm when he was a small boy.

'Of course you miss her,' she said softly. 'So do I.'

They were silent for another moment. Julia realised it was the first time they had spoken openly of their shared grief for Emily. She was glad that their mother wasn't here to see her blue-eyed boy in such despair, even as it occurred to her that James might not have sunk so low had Emily still been alive.

'I didn't realise how bitter Clare was till last night,' James said. 'She's out to get whatever she can from me financially. She's even talking about me making a claim towards Linda's inheritance to see if she can benefit.'

'Yes.' Julia recalled Clare's threat as she brushed past her on the way out of the café the previous day: *'Your brother will be ruined by the time my solicitor's finished with him.'* She shuddered, wondering if Clare would even care that James had tried to take his own life.

James glanced at her uncertainly. 'Have you seen Greg?' he asked. 'Clare said she'd bumped into him somewhere. She said he'd seemed very interested to hear about the inheritance. Even though I was in a bad way yesterday, I figured it would be typical of Greg with his poor financial track record to get in touch with you if he could scent the possibility of some money. I gather things aren't going well with his new woman.'

'Yes, I've seen him,' said Julia grimly. 'But I'm pleased to say that I sent him packing.'

Her tone elicited a ghost of a smile from James. It quickly disappeared as he continued, 'She said she'd leave no stone unturned in pursuing me financially. She was laughing when she hung up. That laugh! It was vindictive, cruel. It made me think that I'd never known her after all, never realised what she was capable of. I found that unbearable.' He swallowed and pulled his face. Julia passed him the beaker again. He took a few sips before giving it back.

His face crumpled. 'It was the final straw, Jules. I'd been drinking since I saw you in the morning. I'd wandered round the city all afternoon, made my way up to the cathedral. I went inside to pray, I suppose. You remember how I had organ lessons there when I was at school? I hadn't been in for years.' He rubbed the stubble on his cheeks. 'It didn't help, to be honest. I thought about that boy, all his potential, his hopes and dreams...' He looked away, but not before she had seen the regret in his face.

'You don't need to tell me this now,' she said gently.

He shook his head impatiently. 'No, I need to get it out, purge myself of it. Does that make sense?'

Julia nodded, thinking of all the clients who had opened their hearts to her over the years. Never would she have expected to be listening to her self-possessed brother in a similar way.

Encouraged, James continued. 'A steward asked me to leave when they were locking up. I sat on a bench in Castle Square drinking the whiskey I had with me. A group of students went by, in Hallowe'en costumes. Two of the girls recognised me. I could see them nudging their friends, pointing me out. One of them shouted, 'All right, Dr. Butler? How drunk are you tonight?' Then they carried on their way, cackling like witches.' He buried his head in his hands.

'How horrible.' Julia bowed her head, regretting how her immersion in Grace's problems had meant that she had failed to give her brother the support he needed at a time of acute mental strain. As Ray had pointed out,

James's anger and drunkenness had been masking depression.

Determined now to give James her full attention, she prompted, 'So it was after you saw these students that you called Clare?'

He nodded. 'The cathedral clock had just chimed nine. After that it's all a bit of a blur.' He shivered. 'I remember wandering around Castle Square. I was so drunk I think I passed out for a while. I'd found some paracetamol in Mum's cottage last week.' He shuffled about under the blanket and chewed his lip. 'I put them in my pocket, telling myself I was just taking them with me for my hangover.' His voice dropped to a whisper. 'But I'd been thinking about... ending it all for a couple of days.' His eyes were haunted. She clasped his hand tightly, not interrupting, sensing how important it was for him to unburden himself of his tangled emotions. His voice wavered as he continued.

'I loved Clare. My infertility was no excuse for my affair. I know that, though somehow I used it to justify myself at the time. Then there was Mum's death. It's been an awful year.' He passed his hand wearily over his unshaven face. 'When Clare hung up on me' – he paused and swallowed – 'I knew that was it. No going back. The life I had built with her was over. The hope that she might take me back had kept me going during my sabbatical. But that call last night was the end.' He shook his head in a mixture of disbelief and pain which wrung Julia's heart. 'So I dragged myself over to the cathedral door and sat down and took those pills with the rest of the whiskey.'

'Oh, James,' she said softly, 'you poor thing.' She said nothing else, holding his hand as he wept.

Eventually James leant back exhausted against his pillows. They sat quietly for a while listening to the sounds of the ward: the beeping machinery, the footsteps of nurses and patients, the tapping of a Zimmer frame, the jangling of dishes on a breakfast trolley. Presently an auxiliary nurse poked his head through the curtains and offered breakfast. Because of the irritation in his throat from the stomach pump, James declined, but accepted a cup of tea.

After he had drunk the tea, Julia gave him a hug and urged him to rest. She needed to phone her four clients of the day to reschedule their appointments. She glanced at her watch. It was after eight. Frances would be driving Grace and Emmeline back to the cottage now. She would have liked to have been there to meet them in other circumstances. But since the phone call from the hospital, and especially whilst James had been talking, she was reproaching herself for not listening to him more carefully since his return from sabbatical. Now she promised him that she would return later and wait for the mental health nurse with him.

He smiled at her gratefully. 'Thanks,' he said. 'I need to thank that bloke who found me too, if I can find him.'

'Would you recognise him?'

James nodded. 'I think I would.' He gave a lopsided smile. 'He wasn't the most likely looking hero. He was slapping me and yelling to someone to call an ambulance. His face was lit up by the moon. He might have been wearing a Hallowe'en mask. Or maybe there was something badly wrong with his face.' He grimaced. 'It was grotesque. I could only see one eye.'

Julia became very still in her chair. 'Do you remember anything else about him?'

James screwed up his eyes, trying to remember. 'A beard,' he said eventually. 'And a bad cough. Phlegmy, you know.'

'Yes. I know.' Julia shook her head in wonderment. *Derek. It had to be.* As James closed his eyes, Julia promised herself that she would seek out the rough sleeper and thank him. She wondered vaguely if he would accept some kind of help to get him off the streets. Again she heard Linda's words from that January night when she had given the rough sleeper money outside 'Giuseppe's': *'I always think, "There but for the grace of God, don't you?"'* Looking at her sleeping brother, so nearly lost to her, Julia whispered, 'I do, Linda. I do.'

24

The hospital café was quiet. Julia carried her wooden tray over to a corner table by the window and took out her mobile. She spoke to three clients and left a message for the fourth, apologising for cancelling their appointments at such short notice and confirming she would see them the following week. Fortunately, she had established good relationships with all of them. She contemplated ringing home to see if Frances had arrived with Grace and Emmeline, but decided to give them more time to settle in. Last of all she rang the office, thinking that Pete might already be there. When he didn't pick up, she tried his mobile. It went straight to answerphone, so she left a stilted message saying that she wouldn't be in due to a family emergency.

Julia guessed that Pete would suspect the 'family emergency' concerned Grace, but she couldn't bring herself to tell him about James's attempted suicide in a message. That would have to wait until she saw him, whenever that might be. She rested her forehead in her hands, drained from the conversation with James, and saddened to think about the problems in her relationship with Pete.

Gazing out of the window, Julia saw that the rain had abated to a drizzle. The spacious restaurant was on the third floor of the hospital and would usually afford a good view of Lincoln. But this morning a blanket of mist shrouded the cityscape and she turned her attention back to the room. Her hand froze on the handle of the stainless steel teapot. Pete and his mother Brenda were queuing at the drinks counter behind a middle-aged woman. As Julia watched, Brenda turned and shuffled towards the table closest to the counter whilst Pete waited for their drinks. The old woman unzipped her green anorak and folded it over the back of a plastic chair. Even from the other side of the restaurant, Julia noticed with a pang that Brenda had lost weight since she had last seen her. Her movements too were much slower.

Pete turned with the tray. Julia ducked her head, her heart beating fast. He might not see her if he took the seat opposite his mother, which had its back to her. She was unprepared for this encounter, and far from certain that she could manage any kind of small talk with Brenda. She took a few quick sips of her green tea before risking a glance across the room. Brenda chose that moment to look around. Her face lit up when she spotted Julia, and she beckoned the younger woman over.

Pete swung round to see who had attracted his mother's attention. He jumped to his feet when he saw Julia. Warmth spread through her as she saw the mingled shock and concern in his expression. Whatever had happened, Pete still cared. She kept her eyes pinned on his face as he bounded across the room.

Both spoke at once. Pete asked, 'Are you OK? Is Ray all right?' and Julia said, 'Does your mum have another appointment today? How is she?' They smiled awkwardly at one another.

'I'm OK, and Ray's fine. Thank you for picking him up yesterday.' Julia saw his jaw clench and rushed on,

'Nothing happened between me and Greg, whatever he told you.' She laid a hand on his arm. 'Please believe me.'

His blue eyes searched her brown ones. Then his face cleared. 'OK,' he said quietly. He glanced back towards his mother, who was watching them with undisguised curiosity. 'Will you bring your tea over? It will take Mum's mind off the chemo.'

'Of course.' Julia allowed Pete to carry her tray and followed him across the restaurant.

'Hello, Julia. It's lovely to see you.' Brenda smiled warmly.

'You too, Brenda.' Julia sat down in the seat between them. Close up, she could see how the old woman's face had shrunk since their last meeting. 'I am so sorry about your illness.'

'Thanks, duck.' Brenda sipped her cappuccino. 'I expect Pete has told you that I'm going to be a guinea pig today?'

'I told Jules that you're here for chemo, but not that it's a clinical trial,' interjected Pete.

'Ah.' Brenda looked between them. 'Well, it's worth giving anything a try, isn't it?' she asked gamely.

'It is. I think you're very brave,' said Julia.

Brenda wrinkled her nose. 'It's what you younger folk call a no-brainer. I've had a good innings at seventy-nine, but that doesn't mean I don't want longer. There are still things I want to do, you know.'

'Oh?' Julia poured a second cup of green tea.

'Yes. I might have to give up my dream of my own TV cookery show, or being there when the Imps finally win the FA Cup. No need for that!' Brenda leant over and poked her son in the ribs. Pete was rolling his eyes at the idea of Lincoln City ever achieving the coveted footballing prize. 'I probably won't make it to Australia to see Alice Springs.'

'Alice Springs?' asked Julia.

Brenda nodded. 'I've wanted to go ever since I was a teenager. Have you read 'A Town Like Alice'?'

'No. But it was one of my mother's favourite books. Wasn't there a TV series back in the 80s?'

'That's right. Such a romantic story.' A dreamy expression spread over Brenda's creased face. 'That actor who played Joe in the TV series, he was something, he was.' She pursed her lips in a silent whistle.

Julia spluttered over her tea. Pete shook his head. 'Mum! What are you like?'

Brenda coughed suddenly and fished a tissue from the pocket of her tweed skirt. She wiped some fluid from the corner of her mouth, then took a few deep breaths. Pete looked down into his black coffee. Julia's heart constricted.

'Anyway,' Brenda went on, as if nothing had happened, 'I like a happy ending. Don't you?' she asked Julia.

'Well, yes.' *Not that I've had so many,* thought Julia. She instantly chided herself for self-pity, thinking of the depths into which James had sunk.

'Good. Bill and I were married for thirty-eight wonderful years. We met at Skegness one summer. Maybe Pete's told you?'

Julia nodded, wondering where the conversation was leading. She glanced at Pete, who was stirring his black coffee with great concentration.

'People used to ask us what our secret was.' Brenda drank more tea. 'We told them about our golden rule. Never go to bed on a quarrel.' She eyed them both. 'Maybe something you two could do with learning.'

'Mum!' protested Pete.

'"Mum" nothing,' retorted his mother. 'You can't pretend it was only worry about me that's made you so miserable this past week.'

She eyed the two flushed faces in front of her and smiled before downing her tea. 'I know I'm an interfering old woman. But at this stage of life I reckon I've earned that right.' She turned to Julia. 'Pete's going to take me for my chemo now. I'm going to be wired up for most of the morning. Can you meet him back here in half an hour?'

Julia looked over at Pete, who was examining his teaspoon as if it were a valuable archaeological find. She would go and see James and then come back. From her enquiries before she'd come up to the restaurant, she knew that the mental health nurse wasn't expected until early afternoon. 'Yes,' she said. 'That is, if you would like to, Pete.'

It was the first time in their months together that Julia had been uncertain of him. Brenda stood, gripping the table for support. This visible sign of the older woman's weakness added to Julia's sense that she had failed Pete since his mother's diagnosis. She laced her hands tightly around her cup, holding her breath as she waited for Pete's reply.

'I'll be here at ten.' Pete pressed her shoulder lightly as he got to his feet. She exhaled.

'That's sorted then.' Brenda grinned at them. 'Maybe I'll get my happy ending and see one of my dreams come true.'

Pete's flush deepened to crimson. 'Mum!' he remonstrated. 'Come on, we're going to be late.' He picked up her bag and bundled her into her coat.

Brenda smiled all the more at her son's chivvying. 'All right, not the time or the place. I get it.' She looked down at Julia. 'Come and see me soon, duck, won't you?'

'Of course.'

With one last smile, Brenda allowed her son to lead her towards the restaurant exit. They paused by the swing doors when she submitted to another paroxysm of coughing. Julia saw Pete's shoulders tense inside his black leather jacket and resisted an impulse to go with them, to try to offer the support she had failed to give so far. But to do so would be intrusive; she and Pete needed to talk first, as Brenda had discerned. She twisted her cup in her hands, wishing yet again that she had paid more attention to Pete in these last few weeks. Pete and James: she'd let them both down. She'd been in a fog, she realised, as she stood and slipped back into her coat, casting a further glance through the windows into the murky morning.

Back on James's ward, Julia discovered that he was still asleep. She resumed her seat beside him. It was calming to listen to the even rhythm of his breathing. Intuitively she knew that he was resting more peacefully than he had done for a long time. She hoped that after reaching the terrible nadir of last night, his unburdening to her would provide the catharsis he needed. Whilst she was well aware that his mental and emotional recovery would take a long time, Julia was cautiously confident that he had turned a corner.

She made her way back up to the café at ten as arranged. Pete hadn't arrived. She bought another green tea and took it across to the corner table which she had occupied earlier. She fiddled with her phone, as anxious as a teenager on a first date. From the way he scanned the restaurant when he came in, she suspected that he too was nervous. His gaze settled on her, and he signalled to ask if she would like another drink. She shook her head. She folded her hands in her lap when he came over so that he wouldn't see them shaking.

'Was your mum OK when you left her?' she asked before he had sat down, wanting to avoid an awkward silence.

He nodded. 'Yeah. Chatting away to the nurses. You know what she's like.' His smile was strained.

'I meant it when I said she was brave joining a clinical trial.'

'That's Mum. Always positive.' He stared down into his mug of black coffee. 'It's her only chance.'

'You never know...'

'I've seen the X-rays. It doesn't look good.' Pete spoke with uncharacteristic brusqueness. He jiggled his knee under the table, rattling the teaspoons in their saucers.

Julia took some quick sips of her green tea, scalding her mouth. 'I am so sorry for what you're going through, Pete.' She looked at him earnestly. 'Most of all, I'm sorry that I wasn't there for you when your mum got the diagnosis.'

'You've had a lot going on.'

'That's no excuse.' Her voice was small.

He passed his hand across his eyes. 'I shouldn't have shut you out,' he said quietly. 'Mum was right. I've been miserable as hell ever since I walked out of the office that afternoon after saying I couldn't manage our relationship. I wanted to tell you that when I came round the other night. Then I met that scumbag...'

'He won't be back,' she said. 'I'm sure of that. I should never have let him stay on Wednesday.' She saw Pete's eyes darken and blurted out, 'He slept on the sofa bed downstairs. I was tired, and I wasn't expecting him, but that's not an excuse.'

'OK. But why did he turn up in the first place? His partner wouldn't be happy if she knew, would she?'

Julia closed her eyes, not sure where to start. 'They've been rowing,' she said. 'But there's a lot more to it.' She looked out of the rain-spattered window. The thickening mist was nearly a fog now, obscuring the buildings below the hospital. She still hadn't told Pete about the inheritance from Linda. Her conversations with Ray and James had left her in no doubt that Greg's main motivation in seeking her out had been to profit from the money.

'I've got time whilst Mum's hooked up to the drugs,' Pete offered. 'But you haven't told me what you're doing here yet.'

'It's an ugly tale,' she said. 'I truly don't want to burden you with more of my family problems when you've got your mother to look after.'

His blue eyes softened. 'It'll take my mind off what's happening to her.'

'OK.' She took a deep breath. 'There's no easy way of putting it. James tried to take his own life last night. He should be fine,' she said quickly, in response to the horror which spread across Pete's face. 'He's had his stomach pumped, and the mental health nurse will be round later.' Her voice wobbled and she blinked back sudden tears. 'Sorry,' she said, groping in her bag for a tissue. 'Reaction, I guess.'

Pete reached across the table and stroked the inside of her wrist whilst she composed herself. He didn't withdraw his hand as she filled him in on the unexpected inheritance from Linda and described Clare's vengeful attitude towards James. His grip tightened when she mentioned Greg's attempt to convince her he regretted leaving her for

Lisa. She ploughed on, scarcely drawing breath, determined to tell him everything. She concluded by describing how badly James had reacted to Clare's news of her pregnancy, and how their conversation the previous night had triggered James's suicide attempt.

Pete was silent for a few moments when she finished. 'Poor guy,' he said eventually. 'To be so... alone.'

'I know. I wished I'd listened to him more carefully the other day.' Julia gulped. 'I realised earlier that I've always struggled because of his affair happening so soon after Greg left me. I blamed him for messing up his marriage, but I couldn't see beyond that. It was unfair of me.'

'You're only human, Jules. Don't beat yourself up.'

She smiled. 'Thanks.' She shivered, thinking for the thousandth time that morning how close she had come to losing her brother. She looked down at the table, pushing some granules of sugar with the forefinger of her free hand. 'You were right,' she said in a low voice. 'I was so caught up with Grace and Emmeline that I didn't pay enough attention to what was happening with you or James.'

Pete's expression clouded at the mention of Grace. 'Are they settled with Frances?'

Julia grimaced. 'I'm afraid not.' She told him about Grace's belief that she and Emmeline had been followed, the letter from Social Services, and Suzanne's hostility towards her sister. Pete looked sceptical when she described how she and Ray thought it possible that someone had entered the cottage and taken Emmeline out to the shed in her buggy.

'It's possible,' he conceded doubtfully. 'But you can't discount her mother's psychiatric history, Jules. Grace may have inherited the condition.'

'I know,' said Julia. 'Although I was convinced by her account that she and Emmeline had been followed.'

'All right.' Pete folded his hands behind his head and leant back in his chair. He stared out of the window. 'Suppose someone is out to make Grace look like an unfit mother. Who has the motive? Unless—' He swung back to face Julia, struck by a sudden thought. 'What about her ex? What if he's found out about Emmeline?'

'That would make sense,' said Julia slowly. 'It's time I asked Grace more about him, isn't it?'

'Definitely.' Pete nodded emphatically. 'He might be furious if he has somehow found out about Emmeline.'

'Yes.' Julia pushed a strand of hair behind her ear. 'Grace saw him at uni last week. From what she said, he was very pushy. I'm glad they're coming home today. Frances and Suzanne are both so quick to doubt Grace. Especially Suzanne. But...' She paused, gazing across the table into Pete's blue eyes. They were so clear, so kind. 'Let's not talk about them any more now. I really want to try,' she said, her voice trembling, 'I *promise* I will try to make sure we have time if you want...'

'Yes,' Pete interrupted her. 'Definitely. Mum's illness completely floored me. I wasn't thinking straight the other day.' He fiddled with the gold stud in his ear. 'But hearing about James... We've got something special, you and I, haven't we, Jules?'

'We have,' she said quietly. 'And I don't want to lose it. I don't want to lose you, Pete Hinds.'

25

It was mid-afternoon by the time Julia left the hospital. She'd spent a further half hour with James after the mental health nurse had seen him. The copper-haired young woman had combined sensitivity with efficiency. James had answered her questions briefly and agreed to attend counselling once he had been discharged. When she learnt he lived alone, the mental health nurse advised that he should remain in hospital over the weekend. James accepted her advice without question. This was a relief to Julia. She had considered offering to stay with him at their mother's cottage for a couple of nights, but was worried about leaving Ray, Grace and Emmeline at home if Grace and Emmeline were in danger.

Driving home cautiously through the steady drizzle and schools' traffic, Julia mulled over the situation. The fog had begun to lift, leaving behinds swathes of mist. It would soon be dark. The mist reflected Julia's own confusion as she pondered how she could best support James as well as Grace and Emmeline. She felt pulled in all directions, but was comforted that she and Pete had cleared the air. He had promised to phone that evening. Their reconciliation was the one bright spot in the gloomy day. Whatever competing demands Julia faced within her family, she was resolute in her determination to support him during Brenda's illness.

Vehicles were queuing at the roundabout close to the cathedral. Glancing at its towering hulk as she waited for a gap in the traffic, Julia was chilled once more by the thought of James lying in its shadow after taking his overdose. She turned up the heater, wondering again at the coincidence that his rescuer had been Derek. She was becoming increasingly fond of the rough sleeper. He was turning into something of a protector, watching out for her at the office and now playing a crucial role in saving James's life.

Twenty minutes later, she pulled up outside the cottage and switched off the engine. She leant back against the headrest as a wave of tiredness washed over her. It had been a demanding day, with the early shocking phone call from the hospital and the subsequent intense conversations with James and Pete. The prospect of a further potentially difficult discussion with Grace over Emmeline's paternity was less than inviting. All she wanted to do was to soak in a hot bath and sink into an armchair with a novel. But the more she had considered Pete's suggestion that if anyone harboured malicious intentions towards Grace it was likely to be her ex-boyfriend, the more convinced she was.

She climbed out of the car and locked it behind her, the drizzle cold on her face. The four chimes of the cathedral clock were muffled by the mist. Above the street the castle wall was no more than a patchy outline. Involuntarily Julia hunched her shoulders inside her trench coat as she waited for two vehicles to pass before making her way to the pavement. She took a large stride over a puddle which covered a drain blocked with sodden leaves, then stopped dead by her front gate.

Sitting atop the low brick wall which separated her compact front garden from the pavement was a row of four carved pumpkins. Triangular eyes stared at her above grinning jagged mouths in the light cast by the Victorian street lamp.

Julia shuddered. She was sure they hadn't been there for Hallowe'en last night, and didn't recall seeing them in the morning, although it was possible that she had missed them in her haste to get to the hospital. She bent to peer into the gaping eyes of the one nearest her. Inside was a mess of congealed wax. Examining the others, she saw that these too contained burnt out candles. Presumably some children had lined them up as a prank, or maybe some passer-by had tidied them up along the street and deposited them randomly on her wall. Telling herself that these were the most likely explanations, Julia resisted an impulse to knock the sinister jack-o'-lanterns on to the pavement. She didn't want the ghoulish things anywhere near her house and family.

She hurried up the path, the leaves slippery as ever after another wet day. The front door opened as she reached the porch, revealing Ray's tall figure.

'You're back,' he said.

Detecting relief in his tone, Julia stiffened. 'Is everything all right?'

He stood back to let her in, rubbing his temple. 'I hope so. Grace took Emmeline out rather suddenly twenty minutes ago. Her sister had texted, asking to meet her at the castle.'

Julia frowned, shutting the door against the dank afternoon and the jack-o'-lanterns. 'Grace took Emmeline to meet Suzanne at the castle? At this time? It closes early in winter.'

'I suggested she could wait until tomorrow. But she said she needed to meet Suzanne today. She was very determined.' Ray's voice was quavery. Somehow he seemed even more stooped than he had when Julia had rushed out in the early morning.

Without taking off her coat, she placed a hand under the old man's arm and steered him into the kitchen. She guided him to a chair before putting the kettle on.

'I should have tried harder to stop them going. She had been on edge since she got back with Emmeline.' Anxiety was etched in the deep lines of Ray's face.

'How do you mean?' Julia dropped a teabag into a mug.

'She unpacked in her room whilst I watched Emmeline in the jungle gym.' He smiled briefly, recalling the joy of playing with his great-granddaughter. 'When Grace came downstairs, she was constantly looking out of the sitting-room window and she checked the doors were locked more than once. She couldn't settle to her research, not even when Emmeline had a nap after lunch. That struck me as unusual.'

'It is.' Julia poured boiled water on the teabag, swishing it around the mug with a teaspoon. 'So Grace was still concerned that she was being watched, even though they'd moved back here?'

Ray nodded. 'I suggested that was unlikely and asked her how anyone could know she had left her stepmother's. She had no answer.' He rested his chin on steepled fingers.

Julia deposited the teabag on a saucer. 'That *is* strange,' she agreed.

Ray sighed deeply. 'I'm afraid it's made me wonder if it is possible that she has inherited her mother's illness after all. I've always rejected the thought before, but she seemed so anxious and irrational.'

Julia's stomach clenched as the old man pressed his veined hands to his forehead. She splashed some milk into the tea and contemplated this fresh turn of events as she replaced the carton in the fridge. She tried to push away the niggling thought that the sinister jack-o'-lanterns had some connection with Grace's return, telling herself that fatigue had made her over-imaginative.

'I've wondered about the possibility that Grace has post-partum psychosis too.' Julia placed the steaming mug in front of the old man and passed him the sugar bowl, which was hidden behind a pile of Grace's books. Even in her concern, Julia noted wryly that it hadn't taken long for Grace to reclaim the table. 'But on balance I did believe her when she told me that she and Emmeline had been followed. You said yourself that someone could have got in here and taken the buggy out to the shed last Friday. That fitted in with the bolt being drawn back on the gate and the missing key.'

Ray spooned two sugars into his tea. 'I hope and pray you're right. I just wish they'd come home.'

Julia glanced towards the window. Darkness was falling rapidly on the miserable day. She buttoned up her coat.

'I'll walk up to the castle. I expect I'll meet Grace and Emmeline on their way home.' She tried to sound upbeat, and was rewarded when Ray's expression cleared momentarily.

'Good. I was thinking of going along myself when you arrived. Grace said something else about why she should go immediately…' The old man frowned into his tea. 'That it was time to get things sorted out once and for all. That was it.'

'Mm.' Julia's skin prickled with apprehension. She was careful not to let her anxiety show in her expression. The priest was trembling so much that he needed both hands to raise his mug to his lips. At that moment he looked every one of his eighty-six years.

She hastened back out into the murky evening. The car parks were emptying and the street was clogged with traffic. Exhaust fumes mingled cloyingly with the smell of decaying leaves and damp. Looking up towards the castle wall, she saw it had disappeared entirely in the mist. She cut through the car park and the alley leading to Bailgate. The welcoming lights of the independent shops and appetising aromas from the restaurants would usually have cheered her. Now they offered scant comfort as she rushed past the hotel and into Castle Square, her unease growing with every step she took without sight of Grace and Emmeline.

The cathedral materialised through the fourteenth century Exchequergate Arch to her left. She stopped for breath and glanced towards the magnificent church, unable to repress a shudder at the thought that last night her brother had nearly died in its precincts. Less than twenty-four hours later, she was worried about other family members at Lincoln's other great historic monument, its Norman castle.

She turned right to head towards the East Gate entrance, threading her way past a raucous group of women. One of them was carrying a purple balloon emblazoned '30 today'. Above their shrieks of laughter, she heard familiar plaintive music which grew louder as she approached the ancient gateway. Despite her haste, Julia paused just inside the gate entrance as the final notes of 'Annie's Song' died away. Derek was hunched there, sheltering from the rain. He lowered his recorder when she stopped in front of him. The burns on his face were scarcely discernible in the gloom as he looked up at her.

'Afternoon, duck.'

'Derek, I'm looking for someone,' she said breathlessly. There would be time later to thank him for helping to save James's life. 'A young woman with a baby in an old-fashioned pram. Have you seen them?'

Derek reached up and pressed his trilby down on to his head. 'Came in about half an hour ago. Just after the cathedral clock chimed the three quarters.'

'Did you see them leave?'

'No. I was watching out for them, as it happens. The young lady looked rushed, panicky.' He gave one of his wheezy coughs. 'Mind you, they could've left the other way.'

Julia sighed. She hadn't thought of that. There was another entrance to the castle on the west side. It was possible that Grace and Emmeline were already safely back home and she had come on a wild goose chase. She'd left her mobile in her bag at the cottage, so she couldn't call them. Reasoning that since she was here, she might as well look for them anyway, she thanked Derek and turned away. She surveyed the shadowy path through the grounds. Nobody was in sight as far as she could see.

'I've seen them folk around.' Derek's call arrested her mid-stride. 'Them I told you to look out for. I reckon they were the ones sprayed your window. They were outside your office early yesterday and ran off when I came along. I saw them again just before you took your woman in. I tried to point them out to you, but you didn't see.'

His words penetrated Julia's desire to press on quickly. She remembered Derek waving to her across the street when her client had arrived the previous morning. She had thought that he hadn't seen her wave back, so she had raised her hand to him again. Now she realised that he hadn't been acknowledging her; he had been trying to attract her attention. She spun round on her heel.

'Who, Derek? Who did you see on High Street that you've seen here today?'

Derek tilted his head towards her, caught by the urgency in her tone. 'A girl with bright hair,' he said. 'It was her coat that made her stand out. Animal print. She's with the same young man as yesterday. They'd disappeared by the time I'd gathered my things together and set off up the street after them.'

Suzanne. It had to be; the strawberry blonde hair and the leopard faux fur coat matched Derek's description. But not only had Suzanne, accompanied by a young man, summoned Grace and Emmeline to meet them on this dank autumn evening; from what Derek said, the pair were also responsible for the graffiti at the office.

Julia slapped the heel of her hand to her head, replaying that scene yesterday morning when she had spotted Suzanne disappearing round the street corner opposite her office. Suzanne had skipped work after a night out with her new boyfriend – the boyfriend with whom she had told Grace she would like to have a baby.

With a shudder, Julia recalled how Grace had described Suzanne's expression as 'hungry' when she looked at Emmeline, and 'horribly jealous' when she looked at Grace.

Julia remembered something else too as she reran the scene from yesterday in her mind's eye: she had seen the man following Suzanne round the corner. A man in a black jacket, presumably Suzanne's boyfriend. A man who had a reason for wanting to spray paint Julia's office window with the slogan 'KIDS NEED DADS'.

Her mouth was dry as she looked down at Derek. 'You said there was a young man with this woman?'

Derek's description was succinct. 'Glasses. Dark hair and moustache. Black leather jacket. I'd seen him at your office before. One of your clients, maybe?'

Frozen to the spot, Julia stared down unseeingly at the rough sleeper. An icy hand gripped her. Swirling up from the depths of her subconscious, like the mist encircling them, swam the face of her former client Mark Smeaton. His parting words after their first session drowned out whatever else Derek was now saying: *'I know where to find her.'*

26

Mark Smeaton was Emmeline's father and Grace's ex-boyfriend. Dizzy, Julia rested a hand on the gatehouse wall for support. Everything made sense. Why hadn't she guessed earlier? Her intuition at their first meeting had been right. The man was dangerous – a stalker, obsessed with Grace, who had discovered that she had borne his child and hadn't told him. It must have been Suzanne who had told him about Emmeline.

Scenes from the past ten days reassembled in Julia's mind with new clarity as she gripped the gatehouse wall. There had been her two fraught counselling sessions with Smeaton and the sinister encounter with him on the car park. Grace had been disturbed to see her ex at the university and mentioned how pushy he had been. Julia remembered glimpsing someone apparently tying their shoelace across the road from the cottage that morning. She was certain now that it had been Smeaton. He had followed Grace home, presumably after hanging around the university knowing that at some point he would see her there.

Running into the castle grounds, Julia remembered how disgusted she had been by his scornful reference to the sister of the woman he had declared was 'The One': *'I guess I used her, the other girl.'* He had used Suzanne to find out about Grace after Grace had spurned him at the university the previous week. Both Frances and Grace had commented how rapidly Suzanne's new relationship had developed. But Suzanne had already known Mark Smeaton. Grace's sister was so besotted that she had gone along with his plan to lure Grace and Emmeline to meet them on this dismal November evening. It had niggled Julia that Suzanne had phoned Grace just at the moment when Grace had arrived home with Emmeline last Friday, knowing that it was rare for the sisters to be in contact. Now she guessed that Suzanne and Smeaton had been watching the house. Suzanne had phoned to distract Grace, and Smeaton had seized the chance to take the back door key.

The castle, impressive in sunshine, loomed bleak and forbidding in the rain and mist. It had a chilling history. After being besieged twice in medieval times, a jail had been established on its site in the late eighteenth century. The prison had been renowned for using the separate system where prisoners were kept isolated from one another. Julia paused in front of the shop and studied the walls above her, hoping to see or hear something which would lead her to Grace and Emmeline. She could just make out the dim outline of Lucy Tower before it disappeared again under the low-lying cloud.

She strained her ears as Derek shuffled up alongside her. Very faintly she could hear a baby's cry from the direction of Lucy Tower. The grisly recollection that the tower had been a burial ground for prisoners executed at the castle added to her sense of dread as she broke into a run. Derek limped along behind her. At the base of the uneven stone staircase, Emmeline's old-fashioned perambulator stood empty.

An indignant male voice stopped Julia in her tracks. 'Hey! You can't go up there! It's too late. And you need a ticket!'

Julia spun round. A stocky young man had emerged from the shop. She could just make out the castle logo on his purple fleece. 'I'm looking for someone. A woman with a baby. I think I can hear them up there.'

'Then it's time they left. I'll go and get them down. You two can wait here.' The man cast a disparaging glance at Derek.

A scream pierced the still air.

'Grace!' Ignoring the protests of the young man, Julia raced up the stone steps.

'Well, look who's here.' Mark Smeaton's sardonic voice greeted her as she stumbled on to the bumpy ground at the top. She saved herself from falling by lurching towards the wall, the mossy stone cold and damp beneath her hand. 'Glad you could make it. How's the counselling going?'

Julia couldn't see his expression across the sunken burial ground which separated them, but there was no mistaking his derisive tone.

'There was I thinking person-centred counselling was all about self-awareness and awareness of others. You didn't have a clue about me, did you, and my connection with your family? Was it the derelict who told you? Unlikely backup, I'd have thought,' Smeaton jeered as Derek, wheezing, emerged beside Julia.

Julia's heart banged against her ribs as she took in the scene. Her former client was standing against the opposite wall. Emmeline was whimpering in his arms. To their left, Grace was bent double, clutching her stomach. Bile rose in Julia's throat as she guessed that Mark had struck her niece, prompting her scream. On Mark's right stood

Suzanne, hands folded across the chest of her faux fur leopard coat, head tilted towards him.

'Shall we go, Mark?' Suzanne asked.

'Yeah. I think we're done here. Time for me to get to know this young lady at last.' He jiggled Emmeline up and down. Her whimpers rose to wails.

Julia stepped towards them down the grassy slope, not caring about falling as her ankle boots slid around in the mud. There was a strong smell of decaying vegetation. In a corner of her brain she realised she was stepping on the unmarked graves of the poor souls who had been executed in the castle. But that macabre thought was nothing compared to the horror that Mark and Suzanne were attempting to take Emmeline.

From the corner of her eye, Julia could see that Derek hadn't moved from the top of the steps, coughing from the effort of the climb. She was confident that he would do his best to block Mark and Suzanne if they tried to take Emmeline. The steward was alongside him and had pulled out his phone. Julia hoped he was calling the police.

Grace reared up. 'You can't go! Not with Emmeline!' Still winded, her voice cracked.

Suzanne gave a titter of satisfaction. 'Oh yes we can, Grace. Mark is Emmeline's father. We'll look after her well, won't we, Mark?' She gazed at Mark adoringly. Julia shivered inside her trench coat.

'Definitely. I've got so much time to make up for.' He sneered down at Julia. 'Kids need their dads.'

'It was you, wasn't it?' Julia paused on her way up from the burial ground. 'You who spray painted my office window. Did *you* help?' She shot a glance at Suzanne. The young woman stared back with an insolent smile.

Mark sniggered as Julia resumed her ascent. 'Took you long enough to work it out, didn't it? Everything's going to change now. Emmeline's coming with us. She's not safe with her mother.'

'Of course she's safe with me!' spluttered Grace. She took a step towards him. He wrapped his arms more tightly around Emmeline. The baby moaned and arched her back.

'That's not what Social Services think.' His voice was smug. 'Not after they found out about the danger she's been exposed to. Abandoning your daughter – *our* daughter – in the shed. Very careless.'

'*You* did that! I'll tell them it was you. You'll never be able to keep Emmeline!' Grace's voice rose hysterically. She turned on Suzanne. 'How could you help him in this?'

Suzanne shrugged, simpering.

'Where's your proof? And tell me this: who will they believe when they know about your mother's psychiatric history?' Mark laughed mirthlessly. Suzanne joined in with a cruel snort.

'But Emmeline needs me! I'm her mother.' Grace's voice choked on a sob.

Smeaton turned his head from Grace to Suzanne and back again. 'I suppose we could work it out another way,' he mused.

'Maybe we could,' said Grace eagerly. 'Please, Mark, please don't take her!'

'There is an obvious solution.' He edged round the wall towards her. 'You could come too. You know I never wanted us to break up, Gracie.'

'Mark!' The smile had disappeared from Suzanne's face as she ran up behind him, making a grab at his arm. He shook her off impatiently.

'What about it, Gracie?' His voice was low. 'We could be together. A proper family.'

'No.' Grace shook her head fervently. 'We're over, Mark. You know that.' She stepped backwards as he continued to advance. Just below them, scrambling up the top of the bank, Julia could see her niece's eyes were wide with fear.

'You don't want her, Mark! It's over; you heard what she said!' Suzanne tugged at her boyfriend's leather jacket. 'It's me you want. We're going to be a family – me, you and Emmeline! You know how good I am with babies. We can have more of our own too.'

Mark Smeaton turned. 'You silly cow.' He spoke slowly, his words dripping contempt. 'You're not the one I want. You never were.'

'But—'

'But nothing. Don't you get it? I used you. What a pushover! Desperate for a man, jealous of your sister. So very easy in every way.' He gave her a hard push.

Suzanne toppled down the slope, narrowly missing colliding with Julia. The young woman crumpled into a sobbing heap in the sunken graveyard.

'Oy! That's enough!' Derek's voice from the steps sounded hoarser than ever in the mist.

Mark ignored him. He was standing directly in front of Grace now, practically pinning her against the wall. Emmeline whined softly. With a final step, Julia reached Grace's left on the narrow path. Derek had begun to advance slowly around the perimeter from the other side.

Smeaton seemed oblivious to everyone except Grace, even though Emmeline was still flailing around in his arms. Julia was close enough to see the darkness in his eyes as he stared intently at his ex-girlfriend. There was no doubting his obsession now. Beneath his scrutiny, Grace was shaking. Julia's breath caught in her throat.

'It's you I want, Gracie. Always has been. Always will be. You know that, don't you?' His voice was husky with longing.

'You don't understand, Mark. We can't be together.' Although Grace's girlish voice was high-pitched and tremulous, her heart-shaped chin was raised in the determined gesture Julia knew well.

'Yes, we can.' He pushed his face towards her. Instinctively Grace turned her head away. 'What's stopping us? You broke up with that other bloke you were involved with, didn't you?'

There was a long pause.

'Mark, I don't want you. I don't love you.' Grace enunciated the words clearly. Julia admired her determination, even as she feared for the safety of Emmeline, the daughter of this ill-matched union. Grace looked down desperately at her baby, then back at her ex-boyfriend. 'You can see Emmeline,' she said. 'We can make arrangements. I'm sorry I didn't tell you about her before.' She pushed her braid back over her shoulder. 'But I'm sure you can see it's better if she comes home with me now. Out of the cold and damp.'

Another silence. Julia could hear Derek's rasping breath as he moved closer to stand on the other side of Grace. Julia didn't look towards him, unable to take her eyes off Mark Smeaton as they waited for his response.

He shook his head slowly and sorrowfully, lifting Emmeline so that she was resting against his right shoulder, encircled by his right arm. Leaning forward, he ran the stubby fingers of his left hand down the side of Grace's white face. Then he tugged her plait gently. Julia sensed Grace stiffen at his touch.

'That's not how this works, Gracie.' His voice was low, soothing, as though he were speaking to a small child. 'Such lovely hair. I used to love winding it round my fingers. Do you remember?' He traced the coils in her plait.

Grace closed her eyes, trembling uncontrollably. 'I remember,' she said. Tears ran down her cheeks.

'Do you know what they used to do to women who were unfaithful?' He suddenly yanked her head back hard against the wall. She yelped with pain. Julia moved a step closer. She didn't dare venture further when he held out a warning hand without taking his eyes from Grace's face.

Grace shook her head mutely.

'They used to cut their hair short. The sign of the adulteress. Everyone would know. A mark of shame.' He lifted the braid again, then let it fall and plunged his right hand into his pocket.

Grace gave a sharp intake of breath. Julia gasped too as she saw the flash of metal in his hand. He turned the Swiss army knife over slowly, considering. Emmeline was still writhing against his shoulder.

'Think about it, Gracie. You and Emmeline come home with me. We'll call it a fresh start. We'll forget all the nonsense of the last few months, and everything that's happened today. I'll have to cut off your hair though.' He thrust his face into hers. 'Because you cheated on me, you see. You shouldn't have done that, Gracie. That was wrong, very wrong. You know that, don't you?'

'But you'd been with Suzanne,' whispered Grace. 'What's the difference?'

Wrong answer, thought Julia. *You can't reason with a madman.* Her heart was hammering harder than ever as she watched Smeaton's knuckles clench on the knife.

He leant in even closer, his forehead brushing Grace's. 'Don't argue with me, Gracie. Don't you understand you should have kept yourself for me?'

Grace's eyes darted from the knife to the wriggling baby. Julia imagined she could hear Grace's mind whirring, trying to find some words which might defuse the desperate situation. 'I'm sorry, Mark,' she said meekly. 'You're right. I'll come with you and Emmeline now.'

He examined her face for a long moment. Julia held her breath.

Finally, he nodded. 'Good girl. I knew you'd see sense.'

Across the burial ground Julia heard footsteps. She strained her eyes through the misty gloom and thought she could make out three shadowy figures at the top of the steps. She prayed that they were the police, alerted by the steward.

Mark seemed not to have heard them. He bent forward over the squirming infant and pressed his lips against Grace's. Her body went limp against the wall as she resigned herself to his kiss. Julia felt sick.

That was when Derek saw his chance. He moved sideways and made a grab at Mark's left wrist. Taken by surprise, Mark's hold of Emmeline loosened as he turned towards his assailant. Grace seized the baby. Julia squashed herself against the wall to allow Grace to run past her on the narrow path, carrying her precious child to safety.

Then there was a terrible groan and Derek was tumbling down the slope. He ploughed into Suzanne, who was still crouching at the bottom. She screeched on impact. With no concern that she might fall, Julia slid down the bank towards them. She could hear Smeaton pounding along the path after Grace and Emmeline, but didn't watch, knowing he would be cut off by the police.

Julia's overwhelming concern now was the rough sleeper whose brave action had averted disaster.

Someone shone a torch down into the desolate burial ground where Derek lay, his hand clutched to his side. Julia knelt down beside him. In the glare of the torchlight she could see his eyes were losing focus. A dark stain was seeping across his filthy coat, spreading below his outstretched fingers.

There were shouts above her and a string of curses from Mark Smeaton. Julia didn't watch him being arrested. All her attention was focused on the rough sleeper.

'Ambulance!' she called desperately. She tapped Derek on the cheek, oblivious now to the rank stench of his body odour and stale cigarettes. None of that mattered any more. 'Stay with me, Derek, please!'

Julia cradled the man in her arms as his breaths became more laboured. Footsteps drew alongside her, but she didn't turn. Derek was struggling to say something. She put her ear close to his mouth.

'Thanks for your kindness, duck,' he whispered.

She stroked his face, his poor, burnt face, touching the disfiguring scars gently with her fingers, washing them with her tears. 'Oh, Derek,' she sobbed, 'it's you who have been kind to me, to us.'

Sensing his life ebbing away, she had an unexpected vision that his breaths were mingling with the mist swirling around them in the burial ground of forgotten souls. Later, she would recall a mysterious and agonising beauty in the moments she held him, a strange peace which settled on them both.

Then he gasped out hoarsely, 'God bless, duck.' And was gone.

27

'What an amazing bloke.' Pete whistled through his teeth. 'To think he was the one who saved James too. Coincidence or what?'

'Ray would say it was more than that.' Julia wound spaghetti around her fork. It was Saturday evening, the day after the dramatic events at the castle, and she'd brought Pete to 'Giuseppe's'. She'd dithered over the choice, because of its poignant associations with both Derek and Linda, but then decided that there was nowhere more appropriate.

'He said Derek was like my guardian angel,' went on Julia. 'Ray quoted the Bible too, where Jesus talks about a man laying down his life for his friends. However odd it sounds, I'd begun to count him a friend.' Her voice wobbled. She set her fork down, taking a tissue from the pocket of the slim-fitting pink and grey wool dress which showed off her slender curves.

'I'm sorry,' she said, when she had composed herself. 'I hardly knew him, really. But he's been around for me, watching out for me these last few weeks.'

'It doesn't matter how much we know people sometimes though, does it?' Pete took a couple of gulps of his chianti. 'You get a sense of them, don't you?'

He was looking at her intently. 'Like Mark Smeaton, you mean?' Julia suppressed a shudder. 'He gave me the creeps at his first session. I was worried I was being judgemental and non-professional, so I ignored my misgivings.'

'That's not who I was thinking of.' Pete bent his shaved head over his vegetarian pizza. He deftly sliced it into six equal pieces with the pizza cutter.

'Oh?' She looked at him questioningly.

But when he looked up, Pete didn't clarify whom he had in mind. Instead he asked, 'Since you mention Smeaton, would you do the same again? Let someone come back for another session after you'd had doubts about them?'

Julia wrinkled her nose. 'I might, to be honest. "Unconditional positive regard", as Carl Rogers called it, is so fundamental to my counselling practice that whenever I recognise I'm responding negatively to someone, I battle it. There's always the possibility that I'm the one with the problem, not the other person.'

'Hm.' Pete munched a slice of pizza. 'What place does intuition have then? In the case of Smeaton, your gut instinct was dead right, wasn't it? Sorry,' he added hastily, seeing Julia flinch at the word 'dead'.

'It's all right.' She chewed some bacon thoughtfully, savouring the cream and garlic sauce. 'I guess I have to weigh my intuition alongside my reasoning, try to work out why I'm reacting negatively to someone. That can be very difficult when I'm in a session with a client. Sometimes it's too much to process all at once.'

'I can understand that. You do realise this shows that we must get a receptionist, Jules? I'm going to be out of the office with Mum a lot over the next few weeks whilst she carries on with her chemo.'

Pete ducked his head again, but not before Julia had seen the shadow flit over his face.

'You're right,' she agreed.

'Wow. I don't think I've heard you say that before.' Pete's blue eyes crinkled and Julia laughed. Then she sobered.

'You've been right about other things too. I should have found out more about Grace's ex earlier. I didn't push her about him, because I was concerned not to add to her stress whilst she was grieving for her mother.' She speared a mushroom. 'How ironical is that? Maybe if I'd asked her about her ex, yesterday would never have happened. Derek might still be alive.' She dashed a tear from her eye.

'Hey, you can't blame yourself. You couldn't know that you were dealing with a psychopath.'

'I suppose not,' conceded Julia. 'It's so frightening, isn't it? To think Grace was involved with that man.'

'Too right. How is she today?'

'Not bad. Very shaken, as you would expect. But she feels that a weight has been lifted now everyone knows that she wasn't responsible for putting Emmeline in the shed.'

'Did Smeaton follow Grace when she was out with Emmeline that night and take her key? Has he told the police?'

Julia's mouth hardened. 'Yes. They told him it would go better for him at the trial if he makes a clean breast of it. From what they told Grace, it sounds as though he was boasting about it.' She shivered, suddenly cold despite the usual warmth of the restaurant. 'He followed Grace home from uni that morning when Frances came to visit. That Friday evening he hung around with Suzanne, waiting for his chance. When Grace got home, Suzanne rang the house number. Grace ran in to take the call. Smeaton sneaked in and stole the back door key. When Grace went up for her shower, he came in and took Emmeline out to the shed. Then he sent the letter to Social Services.'

Pete shook his head. 'Scary stuff. Then he followed them the other afternoon when Grace and Emmeline had moved to Frances's?'

'Yes.' Julia's hand was shaking so much that she lay her fork on her plate. 'It could have all been so much worse. That's what frightens me, looking back. Emmeline and Grace could have both come to serious harm.' She shuddered. 'It's awful to think that one day we'll have to tell Em about him. How will we do that? Tell her that her father killed someone?' She reached for her wine glass.

Pete screwed up his face in sympathy. 'There's no easy answer to that one.'

'I know.' Julia's brown eyes were troubled as she looked at him. 'I've never sensed evil like I did yesterday.'

'Evil? Wouldn't you usually say "disturbed"?' Pete asked quizzically.

Julia frowned into her wine. 'Usually I would, but somehow "disturbed" doesn't seem to go far enough. I've talked to Ray about it. We had a conversation the other day about Mischief Night and Hallowe'en. Ray mentioned the co-existence of light and darkness.'

'I'd go with Ray. But I'm a believer.' Pete grinned at her. 'Don't tell me you're moving away from your rational agnosticism.'

She tipped her glass. Ruby sparks danced in the tea light which sat on the white tablecloth between them. 'I'm not sure. It's certainly made me think. I had this sense yesterday that there was another dimension at Lucy Tower. You know it's a spooky place at the best of times, and the atmosphere didn't help. The rain, the mist, darkness falling. Ray has this theory about how places carry echoes of what went before, that when a place has so many negative associations, they lend themselves to terrible things happening.' She took a gulp of wine and set her glass down. Her hands had steadied and she loaded more carbonara on to her fork.

'Go on,' Pete urged.

'That's it, really. Only I couldn't help thinking that Derek was similar to those other people who died there, the executed prisoners thrown into unmarked graves. Unknown, forgotten, un-mourned.' She set her cutlery down and kneaded her forehead with her fingertips. 'So alone,' she whispered.

Pete wiped his hand on his napkin and reached across the table. He took her slim hand in his muscular one and held tight. 'Derek wasn't alone,' he said softly. 'He was with you at the end.'

She ducked her head, the wings of her freshly cut and highlighted brunette bob falling forwards over her cheeks. 'I suppose so.'

Pete changed the subject. 'I had a chat with James at the hospital before I took Mum home yesterday,' he said. He knows now that you're on his side. Although he didn't say anything directly, I could tell that means a lot to him.'

'That's good.' She managed a smile.

'It is. And this pizza looks good too.' He released her hand with a grin and picked up another slice.

They ate in companionable silence for a few minutes.

'That was gorgeous,' said Julia, lining up her cutlery on her empty plate.

'Seriously delicious.' Pete licked some crumbs from his fingers and looked around the busy restaurant, a cosy refuge from the wet November evening. 'You said it was Linda who introduced you to this place?'

'Yes. That reminds me. I've been thinking about her legacy, especially the farmhouse.'

Pete tensed in his bentwood chair for a reason Julia couldn't fathom. 'Oh?'

'It's a wonderful property, isn't it?'

'A beautiful house,' Pete intoned, his voice devoid of enthusiasm. He folded his hands behind his head and leant back, gazing up at the low Artex ceiling. Shadows flickered across it.

'What is it?' asked Julia.

'Nothing.'

Giuseppe glided over, immaculate as ever in evening wear.

Pete pre-empted him. 'No dessert for me, thanks.'

Giuseppe's smile faltered. He flicked Julia a quick glance. 'For you, signora?'

'I might,' she said, her eyes on Pete.

The waiter handed her the black leather-bound menu, picked up their plates, and withdrew.

'Right,' said Julia, as soon as Giuseppe was out of earshot. 'What's wrong?'

Pete drummed his fingers on the table. 'Nothing,' he repeated, then squirmed under her steady gaze. 'OK,' he said. 'Is this the part where you tell me how great it would be to move to Norfolk?'

'It's a possibility, isn't it? As we both agree, it's a lovely house. It would be a fresh start after all that's happened. What have you got against the idea?'

'So that's all it is at the moment, just an idea?'

Julia's brow furrowed. 'Yes. I certainly think it's worth considering. That's why I'm asking you about it.'

'Oh.' His shoulders relaxed and he flushed slightly. 'Sorry. I thought it might be one of your unilateral decisions, like taking in Grace and Emmeline. What does she think about it?'

‘I haven’t asked Grace yet. She needs some space after everything that’s happened. I don’t want to unsettle her by telling her I’m thinking of moving. I thought that if she and Emmeline are settled here, they could stay in my cottage. It will suit Grace for uni, and they will have the cottage to themselves once Ray moves into his retirement housing. Grace has friends here. Frances too.’

Pete hunched over the table, flicking a pizza crumb. ‘Sounds like a good arrangement for them.’

‘I think so.’ Julia took a sip of wine. ‘I want to stay a while to give them some stability, so I’m not thinking of going imminently. Linda’s house will need some improvements, maybe alterations.’

‘What kind of alterations?’ Pete raised his head.

‘For a start the outbuildings could be converted, so the business premises could be separate from the house. What do you think?’

Pete did a double take. ‘What do *I* think?’ He took in her glowing cheeks. ‘I can see you’re very enthusiastic, or is that the wine? It sounds like you’ve made up your mind. I’m happy for you.’

Julia frowned at his unsmiling face. ‘You don’t look it! What’s the problem?’

Pete’s jaw tightened. ‘What did you expect me to say? That I’m delighted you’re moving a three-hour drive away?’

‘Oh!’ Julia fingered the scooped neckline of her woollen dress, heat spreading upwards from her chest. ‘I’m so sorry, Pete. I realise you want to be with your mum now. You need to be with her whilst she’s going through her treatment. I totally understand that. That’s another reason why I’m not thinking of an immediate move. I should have explained.’ When he didn’t respond, she babbled on, 'I should have waited, shouldn't I, and not mentioned it yet? I'm sorry for being so insensitive.'

Julia buried her head in the dessert menu. The words were jumbled in front of her eyes.

'Wait.' Pete swallowed. 'You're not talking about moving to Norfolk on your own?'

'No! I was thinking – I was assuming, and of course I shouldn't have – that you might like to come too.' She looked at him under her eyelashes as Giuseppe reappeared.

'Tira misu, please,' she said. 'Are you sure you won't join me in dessert, Pete?'

There was a long pause. Pete passed his hand over his head. Giuseppe waited patiently, pen poised over his black leather notepad.

'Um, actually I will. Make that two tira misus. That would be great. Fantastic.' Pete didn't take his eyes off Julia as he gave the order.

Giuseppe sidled away.

Pete was still staring at Julia. 'Let me get this right. You're asking me to move to Norfolk with you, to set up business at Linda's farmhouse, to live with you?'

'Is it such a bad idea?' Her voice was small. 'I mean, I know it's a big commitment, and—'

'But Jules, this is your inheritance. I'd be getting a substantial benefit. Are you sure that's what you really want?'

'Oh, Pete,' she whispered. 'I can't think of anything better.'

'Then neither can I.' He paused, fiddling with his earring.

Julia waited, sensing he had more to say.

'What I said earlier,' he began finally, 'about getting a sense of people...'

'Yes?'

'It can be good as well as bad, can't it?'

'Well, yes.' Julia felt as though she were burning up. She'd forgotten how warm 'Giuseppe's' was, and regretted the wool dress, itchy now against her skin. She fanned herself with her hand.

'That's what I feel about you, Jules. About us. That we're good together.' There was an intensity in his voice which Julia had never heard before. Her heart flipped.

'Me too,' she answered breathlessly.

'So I'm asking, Julia Butler, will you marry me?'

Julia's voice stuck in her throat. She looked back at him, her brown eyes luminous. 'Yes,' she whispered. 'Of course I will.'

Pete's face broke into a grin. He called Giuseppe back over. 'A bottle of your finest champagne, please.'

'Ah! Something to celebrate?' Giuseppe glanced benignly from Pete to Julia.

'Absolutely,' they replied in unison.

Gazing into one other's eyes, they clasped hands across the table. In that moment they were both certain that nothing would ever come between them. Julia remembered Linda's words when they had eaten in the restaurant in January: *'It's one of those magical places where you think everything will turn out well, whatever's wrong, you know?'*

'I do, Linda,' whispered Julia. 'I do.'

About the Author

Gillian Poucher was born in Bolton. After studying history at undergraduate level, she worked as a solicitor before training as a church minister. She was ordained into the United Reformed Church in 2006 and completed her Ph.D. in Biblical Studies in 2013.

Gillian lives in Lincolnshire with her husband and daughter. *A Question of Loyalty* is her second novel and is a sequel to *After the Funeral*, published by RedDoor in 2019.

To contact the author, please send an email to:

gillianpoucherauthor@gmail.com

You can also connect with her on

Facebook: *@GillianPoucherAuthor*
Twitter: *@GillianPoucher*
Instagram: *@gillianpoucher_author*

Or visit the author's website for more information:

www.gillianpoucherauthor.co.uk

After the Funeral

READ THE PREQUEL TO *A QUESTION OF LOYALTY*

You don't know me but I know you...

When a stranger approaches Julia Butler at her mother's funeral and hints at a disturbing family secret, her life is turned upside down.

Who is this woman and how does she know so much about Julia's life?

Grief-stricken, Julia finds her well-ordered life unravelling and her relationships in turmoil. As the mystery around the stranger deepens, she must not only make peace with those around her, but with the ghosts from her past to find hope for the future.

After the Funeral explores the complex relationships between three generations of women with sensitivity and compassion.

After the Funeral by Gillian Poucher
ISBN: 978-1910453766
Published by RedDoor Press

Similar Books from the Publisher

When I Lost Me
Claire Lagerwall
ISBN 978-1-78815-927-2

We all have secrets. Some we keep to protect others. Some we keep to protect ourselves. As Catherine and Rebecca find their stories intertwining, hidden truths will be uncovered that will change their lives forever.

Sapphire Beach
Maressa Mortimer
ISBN 978-1-78815-559-5

Martha has left everything she knows behind. Her marriage, in which she experienced domestic violence, is over. As she seeks solace in her new job as a holiday rep, the afflictions of her past still haunt her. Can she find healing and peace in her new life in Crete?

Books available from all good bookshops and the publisher's website:
www.onwardsandupwards.org